A DINNER TO DIE FOR

A DINNER TO DIE FOR

SUSAN DUNLAP

ST. MARTIN'S PRESS   NEW YORK

Library of Congress Cataloging in Publication Data

Dunlap, Susan.
   A dinner to die for.

   I. Title.
PS3554.U46972D5   1987   813'.54   87-16382
ISBN 0-312-01019-2

First Edition

10 9 8 7 6 5 4 3 2 1

For Bernadette and
Douglas Croy

With special thanks to Inspector Stan Muller of the Berkeley Homicide Detail and Officer Karan Alveraz of the Albany Police Department for their help and patience in answering my questions.

A DINNER TO
DIE FOR

CHAPTER 1

Berkeley's Gourmet Ghetto: One Bite Too Many? p.54.

I stared at the glossy in-flight magazine as the 747 headed west toward the Sierras and then on into Oakland International Airport. Beside me the window looked out on darkness. The lights of Reno were off to the right, the captain had just announced, but I couldn't make myself look down.

On the flight *to* Florida I had insisted on an aisle seat. Now, a month later, I was better. I had ridden in a car without covertly bracing my feet against the floorboards; I had progressed from merely turning my head toward the side window when we crossed the Florida drawbridges, to staring into the distance, stiffly pretending there was no water below, to taking quick glances at it. Toward the end of the month, my throat had ceased to tighten as much, my stomach hadn't jumped as much, or maybe by then I was bracing my neck and stomach so automatically that they seemed normal that way. From the bare rise of the drawbridges the water beneath no longer looked as if it were gushing up to swallow me.

But the bridges had been only thirty feet above the water. They had just been practice for today. Soon, I promised myself, I would look down—when we started to descend toward Oakland; I *would* look down.

But not yet. I still had a few more minutes' respite between the charade of healthiness I had performed for my parents all month and the tough facade I'd need when the plane landed. It wouldn't do for a homicide detective to admit to panic, particularly not a woman detective.

Clutching my remaining moments, I turned to page 54 of the magazine. It was a collage of Berkeley history and gastronomy: photos of Mario Savio leading the Free Speech Movement of the sixties; National Guardsmen pointing rifles at the People's Park marchers of the early seventies; the vine-covered gate of Chez Panisse, Berkeley's most famous restaurant; a couple eating tapas by the fire in Augusta's; and Mitch Biekma in the eccentric front yard of Paradise, the newest of the gourmet restaurants in town. It was hard to tell from the picture whether Mitch Biekma, the spiked-haired owner of Paradise, was looking down at his front garden or at the text of the article superimposed over it. Whichever, it seemed to amuse him.

The loudspeaker cackled. My breath caught. The speaker clicked off—no word of descent yet. The air flooded out from the overhead nozzle; it was too warm. Why couldn't they regulate these planes? The man next to me shifted in his sleep, sending out waves of sickly sweet after-shave. Tensely, I stared at the photo of Biekma, following his glance to the printed text:

The city of Berkeley, California, sits next to San Francisco Bay, almost as far west as you can get, or, some would say, as far left. Berkeley has a long and flamboyant history of radical politics. The Free Speech Movement on the University of California campus there gave birth to the student protests that would change the next two decades. Berkeley is a nuclear-free zone, and a sanctuary city. But when it came to pollution, this bastion of peace turned really militant, blocking off streets, installing the most expensive metered parking in the area, and mandating nonsmoking sections in every restaurant. That militancy peaked to crusade proportions in city council elections, bitter campaigns between the infantry of the radical slate and the flying columns arrayed against it. Even elections for the board of the Berkeley Co-op food stores have been major skirmishes.

But there's a flip side to those Spartan warriors, an epicurean side. In recent years Berkeleyans have been abandoning the organic lettuce and alfalfa sprouts of their co-ops for the gourmet greens in Park and Shop, a chain which has been called the wonderland of supermarkets. Stalwarts who once walked picket lines now queue up for reservations at gourmet restaurants. What they spend on one dinner would support a striker's family for a week. Has Berkeley gone the way of the yuppie?

I smacked the magazine down on my knee, startling the after-shave–coated man to my left. His head twitched, his shoulders jumped, but his eyes remained closed. Who was this—I looked back at page 54—this Lee Lewis, and where did he or she get off with this smug tone about my city?

I almost smiled. I hadn't realized how much I missed Berkeley. After a month convalescing at my parents'—a month of hearing their friends brag of chairmen-of-the-board sons and mother-of-four daughters, of seeing pictures of babies that all looked alike; a month of tearful entreaties to find a job that wouldn't endanger my life, to find a husband who would take care of me, to move to a real house—I longed for the Berkeley that cherished the freedom of nonconformity, the Berkeley that honored those who postponed real jobs with health insurance and dental plans in order to write poetry, design leaded-glass windows, or collect unsalable but edible food from the groceries to feed the hungry. And I longed for the innocence of my life before I had been forced to realize it could end at any moment.

That life had died when the helicopter crashed. *I* could have died. But I hadn't, and I wasn't about to take the chance of waiting again. I'd given notice on my flat. Now I didn't know where I would be living. (I would be house-sitting somewhere in town for the next month.) I didn't even know what the status was between Seth Howard and me. Before the crash we had been buddies, buddies with the suggestion of something more dancing ever out of reach. Afterwards, we'd tacitly acknowledged things were different. Different how, we hadn't discussed. I didn't know if Howard knew. I wasn't sure I did.

"In preparation for landing we ask that you bring your seat backs to an upright position, and put your tray tables up," a stewardess announced. "Please extinguish cigarettes at this time. It will be necessary to collect all glasses and cups now." The plane sucked back as it began the first slowing of descent. Engines roared in protest. My stomach jumped. Slowly, I turned my head to face the black square of the window. But the 747 window faded; it was the rain-streaked window of the helicopter cockpit I saw, with the copter reeling a thousand yards above the bay waters. I pressed my eyes shut. There was no need to look down yet. The captain hadn't said we were landing. He hadn't mentioned Oakland, officially. I didn't have to look down.

Pushing away the memory of that cockpit, of the cold bay wind that streaked through the open doors, I breathed in the safe jumbo-jet air and stared down at the magazine.

From the stridently heralded Spartan ideals of the sixties, the rise of the Gourmet Ghetto was an abrupt about-face into the lap—or the palate—of conspicuous consumption. Within a few-block area surrounding Shattuck Avenue in north Berkeley, the eager gourmet can find a variety of pâtés, truffles, cheese from French Raclette to Spanish Manchego, fresh arugula and wood blewit mushrooms, just-caught coho salmon, whole-bean decaffeinated Sumatra coffee or Darjeeling Extra Fancy Selimbong tea.

But, in fact, the Gourmet Ghetto is not merely a long-suppressed burst into epicurean materialism; the California Cuisine, which is the mainstay of the Ghetto, could have been born few other places. It needed the sophistication the university graduates brought to it. It needed their fond memories of sun-dried tomatoes in Salerno, mâche lettuce in Nice. And it needed the old leftist ethic of Berkeley, the willingness to forego big bucks and retirement plans in order to create exquisite experience. Disdaining any but the freshest ingredients—baby carrots grown in friends' gardens, goat cheese from goats with bloodlines worthy of a Hohenzollern—these largely self-taught chefs (many with some European training) have transformed the heaviness of continental cuisine by such innovations as the use of pureed vegetables instead of flour to thicken sauces. In the time-honored Berkeley tradition, they've experimented, viewing ingredients from wholly new angles, using them in untried ways, mixing fruits with meats and making little-known items like radicchio and rocket into household (or gourmet kitchen) words.

From the corner of Shattuck and Vine one need walk no more than three blocks to nearly thirty restaurants, gourmet shops, or boutiques—more than some entire states could boast.

Are those Berkeleyans who vied to discover the newest "in" cafe grateful for the availability of fresh mangoes, champagne sausages, and Pont l'Évêque cheese within one block? The answer is no. Transcending epicurism, Berkeleyans have come to realize man lives not by brioche alone. There is a higher need. That need is parking.

Rising rents have squeezed out hardware stores and shoe repair shops; neighbors are forced to drive across town for nongourmet necessities. And they return to find a BMW from Pleasant Hill or Walnut Creek parked in front of their houses while the drivers settle in for dinner at Paradise.

But in Berkeley tradition, the city council has come

through for these curb-robbed underdogs. In doing so, it has produced yet another first: the Gourmet Ghetto Ordinance. The ordinance limits the number of restaurants and boutiques in the area to twenty-seven. Now the Nouvelle Croissant cannot open till the Old Bun goes under. Where will it end—this all-out war—creature comfort pitted against creature comfort? "A chicken in every pot and two cars in every garage" are no longer compatible in Berkeley.

Cont. on p. 86

But I didn't continue. I had had enough. The plane jolted back; the engine roar increased. Was it always this loud? I stuffed the magazine into the seat pocket, knocking the sleeper's knee. He jerked awake, launching a gaggingly sweet tidal wave. My tight stomach jumped, setting off its own wave of bile. I grabbed the armrests. On duty I had seen corpses with faces shattered by bullets, or smashed past recognition; I'd seen bodies so decomposed they were hardly recognizable as human. I'd controlled the urge to throw up then. I damn well wasn't going to do it now.

"Good timing, huh?" he said, leaning in front of me to stare out the window. "Just about ready to hit the ground. That must be—what—Concord, Walnut Creek down there?"

I exhaled against the smell, and nodded.

"That's the airport! And Oakland. Look, you can see the streetlights."

I didn't look. I squeezed my eyes shut. But the specter of the helicopter cockpit engulfed me: the briny smell of the air; the maelstrom whipping my hair; the sharp edge of the seat belt cutting my stomach as the copter flopped from side to side. I grabbed for the controls. It was too late. I couldn't get the nose up; the ship plummeted toward the icy bay water.

My eyes sprang open. Swallowing hard, I stared at the tray-table latch in front of me, imprinting it on my mind to block out the moment when the copter hit. The engines shrieked and the floor of the plane seemed to slide forward as the seat recoiled. In a minute we'd be on the ground. There was no time to baby myself now. The helicopter crash was in the past; over; done. I had *now* to deal with. I *had* to look down. Haltingly, I turned my head. Hands clutching the armrests, I moved my gaze inch by inch down the scarred plastic of the window, from the black of the sky, down to the muted streetlights of the tree-covered hills, lower to Oakland and the blur of white lights. Holding my breath, I stared at them till they cleared into individual dots, white mixed with lines of yellow, specks of green and red.

The plane vibrated mightily. Metal rattled. I forced my gaze down. Brighter lines of white—the runways. Black—the bay. My stomach lurched, bile shot into my throat, my fingers ached from the pressure on the armrests. The engine's roar cut silent. My eyes closed. I tried to force them open. They didn't move. The plane bounced. It was down. The impact slammed me forward against the seat belt. I heard a gasp. It had to be my own. The plane had landed. Safely.

"Please remain seated till the aircraft has come to a stop," the stewardess begged in vain.

Sweat sheeted my back, dripped from my armpits, coated my face. I inhaled into lungs still locked in fear. Slowly my eyes opened. The man in the aisle seat jumped up, and popped open the overhead luggage rack. The man next to me undid his seat belt and slid into the aisle seat. And then the overhead lights were on, everyone was up, everyone was talking to everyone else, squeezing into the aisles.

I slumped forward, my head throbbing with humiliation. I had had my chance and I had blown it.

There would be other chances; I wasn't going to live my life as a coward. But, for now, all I could do was carry a sponge and pail for the sweat, and make damn sure no one on the force found out.

CHAPTER 2

On the cab ride from the airport I grumbled to myself about Howard's not meeting me. "Out on a sting," his message at the airline counter had said. How important was this sting? My question made me realize how long I'd been away. The implicit demand that he postpone collaring the perpetrators is one no cop should make. Least of all to Howard.

Howard is the department's great sting artist. He loves them. He sets them up like a quarterback drawing the defensive backs in closer and closer with each running play, each short drop pass, watching with glee as each play pulls the defensive perps in tighter, till, barely able to contain his glee, he steps back in the pocket, pumps and then pulls the ball back in, watches the defensive perps blitzing in toward him, scrambles left and lets go with the bomb. He's the Joe Montana of Vice and Substance Abuse.

I sat back in the cab, watching the foggy June streets of Berkeley pass. Spring and fall are supposed to be our best seasons. Winter is cold and rainy, summer cold and foggy. This year June must have joined summer.

The cab turned off University Avenue and began climbing into the north Berkeley hills toward the address Connie Pereira had given me. As she had said in her letter, I would be living out of my element, house-sitting for an investment banker friend of hers. It wasn't till the cab pulled up that I realized what kind of friends she had. The house was a palace. In the driveway my Volkswagen that Connie had delivered looked like a toy.

I spent the first half hour just wandering from room to room to room. The living room alone could have held the

8

ten-by-forty converted porch I had lived in for two years, and still have had half its space free to hold the baby grand piano, the two Herendon sofas on either side of the stone fireplace, and the "conversation pod" at the far end of the room. The dining room looked like a set from "Masterpiece Theatre." And the kitchen! There would be no more rinsing out coffee cups in what had been the basement utility sink. Now my decision was whether to pour from the Mr. Coffee, use the Melitta, or find out how to work the espresso machine; whether to pour the coffee into the silver pot and carry it down to the family room, or back to the bay window in the dining room that overlooked San Francisco (or would have if the fog hadn't been so thick), or drink it in the kitchen while pondering the Cuisinart, four ovens—standard, wall, and microwaves, regular and mini—and the freezer that held enough food to stake a Gourmet Ghetto restaurant for a night. But I'm not the best person to judge—I don't cook. There are things that the average person takes for granted that I've never cared to learn—the meaning of sauté, for instance. Junk food is fine by me. But even I realized the stuff in the freezer was gourmet. This was definitely out of my element.

Then there was the breakfast nook, the lanai, the sauna, the hot tub–Jacuzzi, and the four bedrooms. Briefly, I considered sleeping in the guest room. No, if I was going to take my life by the horns now, I might as well do it in the master bedroom, where I would need to pad just ten or twelve feet, across carpet thick enough to lose my ankles in, to the Jacuzzi-equipped tub for two.

Looking at the bed in there—king-sized, of course; anything smaller would have looked ridiculous—I felt the weight of the day's tension land on my back, as if it had been released from a sack above me. It was only six P.M., still light, even through the fog. I extricated a nightshirt from one of my suitcases and crawled into the bed—and found myself shaking.

I pulled the covers closer around my chin, and thought of

Howard—Howard who, after a month's separation, hadn't met me at the airport. I wasn't angry. I was too drained for anger. Was I disappointed? Maybe. No, not so much disappointed as relieved.

I wasn't ready to deal with Howard. And I didn't want him to see me yet, not shaky like this. Still, through the increasing fogginess of my mind I couldn't help wondering what kind of sting he was running. Was it so vital for him to be there? Or was he having qualms about me, too? Or was . . . but the warmth of the down comforter reassured me, blurred the thoughts till they evaporated into sleep.

It took three rings for me to realize the phone was ringing, another to find the light, and a fifth and sixth to ferret out the receiver. (It was in a mahogany box on the bottom bedside shelf.) Dropping the lid on the carpet, I pulled out the phone.

"Sorry to wake you at one A.M.," the dispatcher said, "but I got the word that you were back. You okay?"

I swallowed, trying to get the sleep-congealed juices moving in my mouth. "I'm fine. All my bruises are healed, and if I still have any black and blue marks, they're hidden under my superb tan," I said with a lot more bravado than I felt. "What have you got for me?"

"DOA at Paradise—not the place where the corpse is heading—the restaurant," he said. "One of *the* gourmet restaurants. Not exactly your kind of place, huh, Smith? It's at—"

"I know where it is, Dillingham. I've been to dinner there."

Dillingham whistled. "They serve gourmet donuts?"

I slipped my feet over the side of the bed. "They have three entrees per night. What I had was good, real good, but there were lots of things on my plate—odd greens and tiny vegetables—I haven't seen before or since. It was kind of like eating on Saturn, at sixty dollars a head." I didn't need to add that I had been there only once, for a very special occasion. Dillingham knew me well enough to assume that.

Overcoming the urge to prolong this conversation—this interlude in which I could still consider the murder just a crime, unconnected with a real person, and his or her real friends and relatives—I said, "Do you have any particulars—name, cause of death, time?"

"Check with Doyle. He's in his office."

Before I could comment, the phone clicked as Dillingham tried to transfer my call, always a chancy operation. But at one-oh-nine in the morning, the chances were better. I barely had time to clear my throat before Inspector Doyle came on the line. "Smith?"

"Yes?"

"You're up." He meant next on the rotation. "I've got the doctor's release. He says you're fine. That right?"

"One hundred percent."

"Sometimes those doctors don't see everything, you know," he said with a hesitancy I hadn't heard in his voice before.

"Thanks for your concern, Inspector, but I'm fine." Fine except for that ridiculous fear of descending, and I wasn't about to admit to that.

"You sure? It was a bad crash."

"Yes," I snapped, "fine."

"Okay then," he said, all business now. "You've seen Mitchell Biekma, haven't you?"

"The owner of Paradise? Everyone in the Bay Area's seen him on the news. Half the country's heard him on 'Good Morning Whatever.' I read an article about him and Paradise and the Gourmet Ghetto on the plane. His picture was on the first page. He looked amused."

"Well, he won't again. Body's still in the restaurant. Grayson's out there supervising the scene. He's got a couple of patrols bringing some of the witnesses in. I'll handle things here. You check out the scene." He sounded tired, not just one A.M. sleepy; his was the weariness of one who

11

had long abandoned hope of refreshing sleep. He would be up all night tonight, but he wouldn't catch up on his sleep over the weekend; he'd just sink down a notch toward lassitude. Many cops retire before they reach Inspector Doyle's age. There are no desk jobs in Homicide Detail; being an inspector just means carrying your share *and* supervising. Why Doyle stayed on was a question batted around the squad room. It was one that none of us were about to ask. "Smith," he said, pausing as if to reconsider.

"Yes?"

"Mitchell Biekma got a lot of publicity in the last year. He'll get even more now. Every newspaper's got his picture in their morgue, all the TV news crews have film on him and his garden. They'll jump at the chance to pull it out and rerun it. This case is going to be a bonanza for them. You hear what I'm saying? Everyone in Berkeley, no, not just Berkeley, everyone in the Bay Area is going to have his eyes on you. It's a situation we can look very good in, Smith, or very bad. If Eggs and Jackson weren't snowed under. . . . You sure you're up to this?"

Was I? I had assumed I would ease back to work through a few days of paperwork; I hadn't planned on starting with a murder. Maybe I wasn't ready; maybe I did need some time.

"Smith?"

The inspector hadn't wanted a woman in Homicide; but when I had handled a few murders he had changed his opinion. I wasn't about to give him reason to change back. "I can handle it, Inspector! How much help can you get me?" There had been a time when beat officers did all the legwork for any case on their beat, be it shoplifting or murder. That was before the reorganization, before the staff cuts. Now homicide detectives did their own legwork, and getting a patrol officer assigned to assist was like winning the lottery. "How about Pereira and Murakawa? Or Parker?" I suggested without much hope.

"I'm ahead of you, Smith. You can have Pereira in the

morning. Murakawa's already there and Parker's on his way."

That, more than anything he had said, underlined the importance of this case. And his hesitations about giving it to me. "What about the particulars?"

"Not much yet. The wife called an ambulance. But Biekma was DOA. Body's still at the restaurant. Grayson will fill you in on the rest."

I hung up, took a shower (spigots on two walls) that was closer to a baptism, pulled out a pair of too-wrinkled, too-thin-for-this-weather brown cotton pants from a suitcase (my Berkeley clothes were still stored at Howard's), and put on the beige turtleneck and tweed jacket I'd worn on the plane. I penciled eyeliner under my gray-green eyes, ran a comb through my hair, plucked two errant long brown hairs off my sweater, and headed out.

The fog was thick enough for the wipers. I sat, letting the Volkswagen engine warm, staring at the wet windshield, fog-streaked like the helicopter's, and seeing Mitch Biekma as he had been pictured in the airplane magazine— tall, with that spiked strawberry-blond hair and that amused grin. My stomach churned. I swallowed hard, but that didn't help. There was a line of sweat at my forehead.

Damn! How long was this absurd fear going to control me?

I turned on the ignition and backed the Bug out of the driveway, slamming on the brakes inches from a dark car across the street. "Two blocks to Cedar and then down," I muttered as I shifted into first and headed more slowly toward Cedar. Cedar was steep, but empty at this time of night. It took less than five minutes to drive down from the Berkeley Hills to the flatlands and Paradise. But I was sweating through my Florida tan when I got there.

Outside of Paradise red pulser lights from the patrol cars and the ambulance turned the two-story white stucco building fiery red, and shone on the metal flowers that filled the front yard. The flowers weren't the soft, pretty types like roses or delphiniums, but spiky tropical birds of paradise, with long stems and flowers that resembled birds frozen in the fury of flight, with orange wings poised at their apex ready to thrust downward, and blue tail feathers lifted skyward, sharp enough to sever a hand.

The bronze garden had been one of Mitchell Biekma's early entrees in his preopening smorgasbord of publicity events. The opening of another gourmet restaurant in the Gourmet Ghetto was as newsworthy as another morning of fog. But the metal garden was something else. Biekma had commissioned the most controversial metal sculptor in the East Bay to create it. And controversy was what he got.

Before the last spiky bird of paradise had been "planted," neighbors had complained to the city council. Several had threatened to dump trash in their own front yards "in an effort to have a unifying theme on the block." In response, Biekma had raced to the city council chambers, pictures of garden in hand, and invited the council members, the neighbors, and every reporter in hearing range to be his guests on opening night.

Before that controversy had died down, twelve members of the North Berkeley Art Association had arrived, surveyed these ultimate perennials, and delivered twelve varying critiques. "Genius" and "junkyard" were the two most frequently heard evaluations, though the ones chosen to headline the story were "Front Yard of Paradise, or Foyer of Hell?"

By the time Paradise opened, color photos of the bronze birds of paradise had blossomed in all the Sunday supplements. Reporters had interviewed the sculptor, the neighbors, and, it seemed, anyone who had ever held a soldering iron or a garden hoe. But mostly they had interviewed Mitchell Biekma. With his tall, thin body, his long, mobile ruddy face and spikes of strawberry-blond hair, Biekma resembled one of blooms in his garden. By the time he made the television news, he had taken command of the situation. It was he, not the reporters, who had laughingly rattled off the less flattering descriptions of the garden and announced that the baby carrots and tiny cucumbers he featured in his salads had been called the embryonic vegetables. Then his mouth had twisted halfway up his cheeks, giving him the same puckish expression he had had in the airplane magazine picture. Seemingly overnight, Mitchell Biekma had become a Berkeley hero—a restaurateur who could poke fun at gourmet pretensions while serving meals the pretentious would queue up for.

For Mitchell Biekma, and for Paradise, the garden had served its purpose. For us at the Berkeley Police it was an attractive nuisance. Drivers screeched to a halt in both lanes of Martin Luther King Jr. Way, causing a flurry of minor accidents and one rear-ender serious enough to put a woman in traction.

But now a patrol officer guided traffic around the four patrol cars, one unmarked car, and the ID tech's van double-parked in front of the building. Through the open car windows the staccato crackle of the radios poked into the night. Two patrol officers held the crowd back. On both sides of the yard the red pulser lights flashed on groups of onlookers with down jackets wrapped over jeans or night-clothes, turning their drawn faces crimson as they stood shivering in the thick fog. Startled at each attack of light, some had the wary but transfixed look of those who might, indeed, be in the front yard of hell. Others hung back, dividing their attention between a TV reporter describing the scene on camera and the restaurant door through which Mitchell Biekma's body would be carried. They vacillated, unwilling to miss the drama, and equally unwilling to be spotted gawking at it when they turned on the morning news.

Hurrying past before the reporter spotted me, I headed up the path to Paradise. A bitter spice aroma floated out through the open door.

The front door—a Plasticine box surrounding a free-form

grate meshed with coils of orange and blue lights—was open. For a moment it looked like any restaurant after closing time.

I nodded at Sergeant Grayson, the crime scene supervisor. He was a short, barrel-chested man with thick black hair, thick black eyebrows, and a thick mustache that hung down far enough to hide any curl of his lip. He pointed to the other side of the partition that separated the foyer from the front section of the dining room. The sickening stench of vomit and feces struck me. Taking a long last breath of night air, I remembered Mitch Biekma as I had seen him on TV, laughing with reporters, urging them with unbridled glee to taste his special lemon cucumbers or his red and gold nasturtium salad. More than one reporter had been caught up in that enthusiasm. Mitchell Biekma had been an appealing man; he had made Paradise a place you wanted to like.

I swallowed hard, and walked around the partition to Biekma's body. There was no remnant of Biekma's fervor now. His eyes were wide with horror. Vomit, thick with unchewed onions and baby carrots, clung to his cheeks and chin. It had sprayed over his shirt and hands, and down the front of his blue corduroy pants.

Then the stench of bile, garlic, and horseradish really hit me. My stomach lurched. Swallowing harder, I turned back to the open front door and took a long, deep breath. It was a moment before I looked back at Biekma's body. The spiky strawberry-blond hair that had been part of his Tom Sawyerish appeal now hung limp and matted. His ruddy complexion had paled in death; in contrast, his hair appeared garish red. His hands were clenched but they held nothing. The only things I had missed on my first look were the dark stain right above his belt, and the sturdy gold chain that peeked from inside his neckline. I bent down and pulled it free. On the end was a key, a very ordinary brass key that could have been to a very ordinary door. I glanced up questioningly at Grayson.

"To the wine cellar." He pointed to the door beside the desk. "That's the only key. No one but Biekma got near the wine."

"I'll need it. Have the tech look at Biekma's neck first. Any idea why there's only one key?"

He shrugged. "Some restaurants have a problem with the staff drinking up the profits."

"They'd have to choose the best, and drink fast to make a dent in Biekma's profits."

"Guess Biekma wasn't taking any chances. One of the waiters said Biekma kept it round his neck in the shower. Probably slept with it on."

"He sounds overly suspicious to me," I said, looking back down at Biekma's vomit-stained body, "but then you could argue he had good reason to be. What did the medics try with him?"

"No point in doing anything. He was good and dead when they got here. Biekma ate half a bowl of soup. After that, he didn't have time to do much more than upchuck and die."

CHAPTER 3

Biekma's building had originally been a typical Berkeley house. To transform the ground floor for Paradise, Biekma had turned the living room, dining room, and den into one large L-shaped dining room that ran from front to back, with a door to the kitchen midway on the north side near the foot of the L. Across from the front door a heavily carpeted stairway led to another Plasticine door. Patrons, undeterred by hour-long waits, would seat themselves on these steps, glasses of white zinfandel in hand, as they congratulated themselves on snagging a reservation. The railing was a Plasticine coil filled with the type of tiny white lights usually associated with tabletop Christmas trees. At the lower end it angled down to form the front of the desk where reservations were acknowledged and credit cards processed.

Next to the desk was the door to the wine cellar. Grayson had unlocked it and turned on the light. I walked down the short flight of stairs to a room that could more accurately have been described as a closet. Basements are rare in the Bay Area, and it was clear that this room had not been part of the original house. One wall was covered with a wine rack, the other with a unit that resembled a refrigerator. I pulled open the door and glanced inside at ten rows of wine. About a third of the slots were empty. Closing the door, I surveyed the open rack. It was slightly fuller. On the wall beside it hung a clipboard. Beneath the clipboard was a wooden box containing a soldering iron, a couple of roots and bulbs, and garden implements—all apparently for Mitch's gardens, metal and natural. Everything in the room would have to be catalogued, then we'd lock it up. There had to be well over a thousand dollars in wine here. I didn't want any questions later.

I climbed back up to the dining room. The dishes had been cleared and the linen stripped, baring scraped and stained pine tables that would have looked more at home in the Salvation Army dining hall. A two-foot-high Mexican vase stood by the kitchen wall; the drooping shasta daisies and pampas grass, and the almost plastic-looking birds of paradise mixed in with them, were half again that high. The arrangement must have been striking when Paradise opened at six P.M., but now, after long, hot hours in the glare of too-bright lights, it looked like a spray of flowers left on a grave overnight.

Grayson stood next to Biekma's body, his jaws pressed hard together behind the shield of his mustache, his arms crossed over his thick chest.

"Any leads?" I asked.

He shrugged.

"Witnesses?"

"Yes and no." There was an edge to Grayson's voice. His mustache twitched. Grayson had been one of the candidates for the Homicide slot that I got. According to rumor, he had claimed sexual bias. But he hadn't said that to me. In fact, in the four years I'd been with the department, I doubted we had exchanged two sentences. But his resentment now screamed through his stance. "You just got back from sick leave, right, Smith?"

"Yesterday."

"You up to handling a murder?"

"As up as anyone ever is." My stomach still churned; my legs felt shaky. I locked my knees and leveled my gaze at him. "What does 'yes and no' mean?"

His black mustache twitched, then subsided, signaling a swallowed retort. When he did speak his voice was controlled. "The kitchen was full when Biekma got the soup. The cook, the under chef, the wife—she was acting as salad chef—the dishwasher: they were all busy cleaning up. They all heard Biekma come in, they all saw him scoop out a bowl of soup from the pot, go back to the pantry, and take out a jar of horseradish. He was turning away from it, horseradish jar in one hand, soup dish in the other—this according to the dishwasher—when there's this crazy knocking on the back door. Matthew Timothy Dana by name, one of Berkeley's resident crazies. Seems Biekma's wife was in the habit of feeding Dana, but Biekma was no bleeding heart. When Dana opens the door, Biekma starts carrying on about Paradise not being St. Anthony's dining hall, not being in business to feed every ne'er-do-well in town, and so on."

"Biekma was standing there, clutching his soup and his horseradish, and telling Dana he couldn't feed him? Definitely, no bleeding heart."

"According to the dishwasher, Biekma screamed at the

crazy. He worked himself up till he turned purple. The wife tried to calm him down, pointed out it was twelve-thirty in the morning, they had enough food for the staff and him too, that Dana was poor and hungry. Then she said the magic words, which were: 'We have to feed him. How would this look if word got in the paper?' "

"So Biekma had his soup right next to Matthew Dana. Biekma's back was to the kitchen, right?" I didn't wait for Grayson's nod. "Biekma's body had to block the view for some of the witnesses. How much would it have taken for Dana to slip some arsenic or whatever into the soup? If he was as crazy as you say, Biekma's tantrum could have set him off."

Grayson glanced toward the kitchen, then let a beat pass before he said, in a "gotcha" tone, "Dana was wearing a cloak." He let another beat pass. "No zipper. No buttons. The kind that slips over the head. And the handholes were sewn closed."

"Sewn closed! How was he planning to eat, lick the food off the plate?" I shook my head. "Only in Berkeley!"

Grayson shrugged, tacitly saying that was my problem.

Ignoring that in the face of the greater problem, I said, "So we've got a kitchen full of people who see Biekma scoop his soup out of the pot. And we've got one person who's close enough to poison that bowl of soup, and his hands are imprisoned behind his cloak."

"Uh-huh." Grayson's smile was one of triumph.

Trying not to get caught up in Grayson's competitiveness, I said, "Then what?"

"Like I said, Biekma worked himself into a state. Cooks said his face was red, he looked like he was going to burst. So worked up he couldn't breathe. Couldn't get his words out. Meanwhile, the wife's trying to calm him down."

"Where was she?"

"At the warm table by the dining room door, fifteen feet away."

"Go on."

"So Biekma sort of chokes on his words. Then he gives up, pours the whole container of horseradish in his soup and stomps out."

"Pours? You don't *pour* horseradish, you spoon it out of the bottle."

Grayson shrugged. "That's how it works for you and me, Smith, when we get our horseradish at Safeway. But say Safeway to these people and they start screaming libel. They don't buy things like horseradish and catsup, they buy ingredients, and even those they don't get from groceries. The cook was carrying on about their own special farmer who raises their chickens, and the one who grows the lettuce—not the same farmer, either. God forbid their meat man should try his hand at vegetables. When I asked her about their horseradish, she got all indignant and said they don't *keep* condiments *around*—like I was saying their shelves were covered with mold."

"But they did have the horseradish around."

"Not *they*, Biekma. It was Biekma's private reserve," Grayson said with a twitch of the mustache. "Seems he made it specially, which is no special thing here, and reserved it for himself alone. He even sterilized the jar each time before he put the horseradish in."

"That sounds pretty special."

"They all said he used it to clear his sinuses when he had a cold. According to the dishwasher, he was just getting over a cold."

"So *he* kept it around."

"Only since last night. Made it fresh every two days."

I nodded. "And his special horseradish is thin enough to pour."

"Right. From the look of the cook, using thick horseradish is like . . ." He threw up his hands.

"Like spreading cheese food product on your crackers?"

"Yeah." He started to smile, but caught himself.

A crime scene supervisor who has it in for you can mean waiting days for reports, or spending hours chasing him down to confront him. I wanted Grayson on my side. I smiled and said, "So Biekma poured the horseradish on his soup. Did he get anything else to eat?"

"No."

"Just the soup? Not much of a meal after a long night."

"It was an hors d'oeuvre, Smith. Guy had a habit of getting something to nibble on while he went over the receipts. Then, when the rest of them were done cleaning up, he got a couple bottles of wine and they all had dinner together." Before I could comment, he added, "He was a big guy, Smith, and wiry, the type that burns a lot of fuel."

"Okay. So then he stomped out of the kitchen?"

"The wife gave the crazy some soup. The crazy took his plate out to the backyard. Dana smells like he's been scooped out of the bay. I guess even Biekma's wife, the peacemaker, didn't want him inside." Grayson's mustache twitched as he almost smiled. "So you don't have to ask, Smith, I'll tell you how Dana got the food outside. He was holding his bowl, palms up, through his cloak."

Interviewing Dana sounded like the death knell for a stomach like mine, but I wasn't about to let on in front of Grayson. "So he went out to the yard. Alone, I assume?"

"Unless there were raccoons out there."

"What about Biekma?"

"He picked up his soup bowl, took it to the reservations desk, ate enough to feel sick, and ran a few steps and died. So, Smith, in a nutshell what you've got is that they were all there in the kitchen, they all saw Biekma get his food, and no one saw how he could have been poisoned."

"What about the cooks? How close were they?" I asked without much hope.

"Never near enough. Nor the dishwasher. The only ones near the bowl were Biekma and Dana—"

"And Dana's hands were sewn inside his cape."

"Right."

"What about the soup? What was in it?"

"Leeks, baby carrots, greens, eggplant, onions, and dill."

22

I sighed. "Is that all?"

"Looks like it. His bowl's still half-full. ID tech's got it—exhibit one."

"No wine?"

"No glass."

"Well something in here killed him. Make sure the ID tech gets samples of every substance in the place—kitchen, bathrooms, garden supplies."

Grayson's mustache twitched downward. "I know how to run a scene, Smith."

"I'm sure you do." I smiled. "Oh, and don't forget the horseradish jar," I said, aware I had just trampled on all that rapport I had hoped to cultivate. I only had to look at Grayson's rigid stance to know he wasn't going to *give* me anything now. Any other data I would have to ask for piece by piece.

I walked back to Biekma's body and stared down. In the minutes Grayson and I had talked, the vomit had solidified on Biekma's shirt and pants. It looked darker. I knew it was too soon in this warm room for rigor mortis, but Biekma's body looked like it had hardened under the vomit, as if it had become part of a scene in a wax museum.

I gave my head a shake to clear the image; then, holding my breath, I bent down over the body, printing in my memory Biekma's mobile face. His forehead was creased in anguish. His mouth was open wide as if he had tried to holler for help—but what had come out was not sound but vomit, like the final scene of a nightmare. "Grayson, what's this?" I asked, pointing above Biekma's belt to the dark brown oval, partially camouflaged by a spray of vomit. "Blood?"

"Looks like it."

"Blood?" I snapped, not bothering to hide my anger. "Grayson, I thought you said he was poisoned?"

"He was." Even the mustache didn't cover his satisfied smile.

I took a breath and said slowly, "Then why the blood?"

When he didn't answer immediately, I bent down within inches of the stain. But there was no raw edge of skin. The poison hadn't eaten through his stomach lining. In the middle of the blood was a perforation hole.

"Stabbed," Grayson pronounced.

"Poisoned *and* stabbed?"

"Right."

I stood up, taking a last look at Biekma. "Are you telling me Biekma was stabbed in the dining room of his restaurant, next to a kitchen full of people, and no one noticed?"

"No, Smith, that's not what I'm saying. Biekma didn't die here. This is just where they brought his body."

I stopped trying to picture what might have happened. "Grayson, I don't have all night. What went on here?"

Grayson waited till I turned to look at him. "From the look of that vomit, he was poisoned all right. He grabbed his throat or maybe his stomach. Maybe he tried to scream. Then he dropped the bowl and ran outside, into that junk garden in the front. Into one of those birds of paradise. The bird of paradise, it gutted him."

CHAPTER 4

"You want to see the bird of paradise that speared Biekma?" Sergeant Grayson asked.

I eyed him, trying to decide whether his offer could have been as innocent as it sounded, or if he was angling to set me up. But Grayson was well schooled in bluffing; his dark eyes hadn't narrowed, his full cheeks hadn't risen a millimeter in an anticipatory smile. "Not now," I said. "All we need is for those reporters to spot us eyeing that, and realize Biekma was speared by his own garden. Can't you see the headlines—'Biekma Beaked'? No, we'll check it out after they leave."

Grayson shrugged, as if to say it wasn't the way he'd run an investigation. Having made his point, he folded his arms and leaned back against the partition that separated the foyer from the front part of the dining room, where Mitchell Biekma's body lay.

By the front window Raksen, the ID tech, stood tapping a finger against his camera. He looked like a miniature schnauzer, dark-eyed, wiry-haired, frenetically eager to get going.

Photographing the dead was not everyone's choice of what to do at two in the morning. But Raksen loved his work. According to the book, the tech photographs the body from intersecting directions, so that by checking the two prints an observer can discern where the body is in relation to doors, windows, furniture, etc. No tech I knew of took just two photos; no one was that confident, or foolhardy. No one else took the number that Raksen did, either. His goal was one print so definitive that it would answer any question any expert could conceive, any challenge any lawyer could attempt. In his effort to get that masterpiece, Raksen used more film than a portrait photographer photographing an ugly child. He was always in hot water with the auditor. The captain had given up preaching moderation. And though the definitive shot still eluded Raksen, his work had clinched a case more than once.

I had seen him balancing precariously on wobbly chairs or hanging over rickety railings, to get the right angle. I'd seen him checking and rechecking each measurement, dusting for a print with the loving care of an archaeologist uncovering the Ten Commandments, pondering urine samples like a wine connoisseur.

"Poison?" Raksen savored the word. Grayson had briefed him. Without pause for a clean breath, he bent down close to the body.

"Any guesses?" I asked. Raksen wasn't an expert, but it

would be days or weeks before we got a report from one. No autopsy, no matter how vital, could be expected in less than twenty-four hours. Three days was more likely. Lab tests took an average of three weeks. And no matter how important the deceased, how much pressure you got from the press, from the inspector, or from the city council, lab cultures grew at their own rate. The best you could hope for was an educated guess from the coroner, and he, a twenty-year survivor at the job, was too wise to stick his neck out.

"Amount of the vomit and the evidence of convulsions are consistent with poisoning, but, of course, not conclusive."

I nodded. Unintentionally, Raksen mimicked the coroner, word and intonation. Raksen had applied to medical school three times.

"On the other hand, the metal spear pierced the skin, and may have caused severe internal damage," Raksen continued, managing to avoid committing himself in classic coroner fashion.

I sighed. "This could give us a lot of trouble in court."

"Right," Grayson said, "unless we want to put the metal stalk behind bars."

"Any idea where the poison came from?" I asked.

"In a restaurant?" Raksen laughed, his thin, schnauzer-like body shaking. "Listen, they tell you the bathroom's the most dangerous room in the house. But the kitchen! If you knew what could be there, you'd never eat again. Just for starters, there are mushrooms. Mushrooms grow wild all over the Berkeley Hills. A place like Paradise, into exotic food. The chance to introduce a exotic fungus . . ." He opened his hands in delight. I should have remembered that Raksen's enthusiasm extended to the lethal possibilities on every table. I'd sat next to him at one Christmas party when he'd discussed the carcinogenic potential of every ingredient in the fruitcake I was about to eat.

"Wasn't eating mushrooms," Grayson muttered.

"Well, the amount of vomit would suggest an irritant. Maybe cashew-nut oil. It'll cause vomiting and diarrhea. Or mustard-seed oil—a single drop can cause blindness."

"He was eating carrot soup from the pot," I said. "If the poison was in that, there must have been a shovelful—"

"Or very potent," Raksen said.

"And it must have been added after the last customer ate. None of the customers complained," Grayson said.

"Wait! Dana's bowl of soup. You said Mrs. Biekma gave it to him *after* Biekma left. Did Dana react?"

"He didn't eat it. He dropped the bowl."

To Raksen I said, "To get back to the horseradish, it was Biekma's own recipe."

"From a ceramic jar he brought back from France," Grayson added. "Looks like something you could pick up at Pay Less, but the word is it's an original, signed by the artist."

"Grayson," I snapped, "you didn't tell me that before."

"You didn't ask. Sorry."

"This jar, was it rare?"

"One of a kind. Wait till you see it, you'll understand why the artist didn't bother to make two."

"Well, that's the first break we've had. At least no one's likely to have been substituting jars." I made a note to have someone check up on that jar. The artist could have had a back room full of disasters, each to be sold to a rich American as unique.

"About the horseradish," Raksen prompted.

"Made with a dash of chili he had imported from Thailand," Grayson announced. "They tell me that chili is so hot the Texans grab for water."

He hadn't told me that either. "Grayson, this isn't Twenty Questions. I expect you to *tell* me what's gone on here. Is that clear?"

"Yes, ma'am," he snapped.

Raksen paled. "People think poison is poison," he said quickly. I had never seen anyone connected with the police department as unnerved by conflict as Raksen. "I'll tell you," he went on, rushing his words as if Grayson or I would plunge viciously into any pause, "there are as many kinds of poisons as there are people. There are corrosives, metallics, hydrocarbons, alcohols. There are stimulants and depressants. You've got your poisons that take hours and you've got ones that cancel you so fast you're lucky to know you're on your way out."

When neither of us responded, he said, "You think the poison was in the horseradish, don't you?"

"It's all he added to the soup. But make sure you test any of his Thai chili peppers that are left. Could be something in them, couldn't it?" I asked.

"I'll check everything. Are you through with the body?"

I thought a moment, hesitant as always to let the body be moved. But there was nothing more it would tell me there. "Go ahead. The sooner it gets to the coroner the better."

"Right." Raksen lifted his camera.

Grayson stood unmoving, his face taut. I would have liked to ignore him and get on with my own survey of the premises before I started on my share of the witnesses. Even with patrol officers doing the initial interviews and sharing the task of reviewing them with Inspector Doyle, it was going to be a long night. But practicality told me not to leave Grayson like this.

"One more thing," I said to the two of them, as members of the investigating team, "there's another odd point in this case. Biekma gets his soup and carries on with the guy at the door, then he pours in the rest of the horse-radish, stomps in here to the desk, and stands there and gobbles down enough to feel sick, right?" I looked at Grayson.

Stiffly, Grayson nodded.

"And then Biekma runs outside. Why would he run out-side? Why not the bathroom or the kitchen?"

"Bathroom could have been *occupé*," Raskin said.

"But he could have thrown up in the kitchen. It just meant shoving someone aside."

"Maybe he didn't want anyone seeing him throwing up," Raksen said.

"Maybe," I said. "But it didn't sound like he had time for modesty. If the poison worked as fast as everything indicates, Biekma just had time to react. You'd think he would have run for the nearest sink, to the place where someone would help him."

"Maybe, Smith"—Grayson crossed his arms and sighed—"he wasn't the type to want help."

"May-be," I said, mimicking his condescending tone. I could understand refusing help, but not when you were as sick as Biekma had been. "Even so, what would make Mitch Biekma run out front of all places? He owned this restaurant. The last thing he'd do would be to throw up in the front yard where someone might see him." I looked from Grayson to Raksen, waiting for a theory, but Raksen's interest was not in something as incorporeal as the psyche. And if Grayson had a theory, he was not about to offer it.

"Well," I said, "maybe the person who found him can tell us something. Who is that?"

Grayson shook his head, but there was a twitch at the corner of his mustache. "Earth Man."

"Earth Man!" Earth Man was one of the well-known Telegraph Avenue eccentrics. "We're really batting zero. Earth Man and the guy at the back door, Dana, too." I shook my head.

"One in the same," Grayson said.

"The same? Dammit, Grayson, you mean Earth Man is Dana, the guy at the back door? The guy with his handholes sewn shut, he's the one who found Biekma's body?"

"Yeah, closest thing to Biekma not being found at all." He nodded slowly. The edges of the mustache moved more firmly upward. "They say, Smith, that you're good with these people," he said, laying out the challenge.

Ignoring that, I demanded, "What else are you holding back?"

"*Nada*, detective."

"Grayson, the role of the scene supervisor is to assist the detective. If you can't plan to cooperate in *my* investigation, I'll get someone else to supervise the scene," I said, keeping my voice carefully even. I didn't need this hassle, not tonight. "What's your decision, Grayson? Can I assume you'll do your job?"

His expression didn't change; his half-closed eyelid didn't lift, the sideways tilt of his head didn't alter, only a slight twitch of his mustache showed his anger and the effort he was making to mask it. He nodded.

"The reports on the scene—yours, Raksen's, the patrol officers'—see that they're on my desk at eight tomorrow morning. And Grayson," I said, pulling the pettiest of rank, "I'll need yours typed."

Grayson's mouth opened, then slammed shut.

I was willing to bet he wasn't a touch typist. And budget cuts had so reduced the clerical staff that it was unlikely he had enough clout to get them to help, not without my okay. It might be petty, but what was petty power for if not situations like this? "About Dana, is he at the station?"

"No. When we started to cart him off, he kicked up a fuss. He kept screaming he didn't want to leave here."

"How come?"

But Grayson just shrugged.

I could have asked what someone like Earth Man was doing at Paradise to begin with. He was hardly a candidate for its sought-after dinners. But I balked at giving Grayson the satisfaction. The patrol officer who'd had the undesirable job of dealing with him so far could tell me. "Where do you have him?"

"Squad car around the corner."

"Bring him in."

CHAPTER 5

Agitated as I had been when I'd arrived at Paradise, I might have expected to be completely unsettled by the set-to with Grayson. Instead, I found my stomach had settled down. I would have liked to think that I was comforted by the routine of investigation, by doing something I knew I did well, but I had to admit that my squalid bureaucratic victory over Grayson had heartened me.

I could, of course, have interrogated Earth Man immediately. But I decided to look over the scene first.

Briefly, I checked the upper floor, the three rooms the Biekmas lived in. I didn't expect to find much there, and Evans, who was conducting the in-depth search, hadn't come up with anything incriminating either. But he was only on the front room. In the back room Murakawa was doing the initial interrogation of one of the suspects.

I came downstairs and walked slowly through the dining room, recalling its gracious atmosphere on the night Howard and I had come here for dinner. Then the scratched wood tables were covered with pale chartreuse cloths. Wisely, Mitchell Biekma had resisted any temptation to carry the Plasticine theme into the dining room. When you're paying over a hundred dollars a couple, you don't want your table winking at you. Also wisely, and in the tradition of Berkeley establishments, Biekma had used mismatched wooden chairs, and silverware. The effect had had its charm, and the temptation for a diner to "liberate" a generic fork was not so great as to pocket one engraved with "Paradise." Tables for two to four filled the front and main sections. Only in the rear, along the back wall, were there wooden booths.

Mitchell Biekma had been on one of the afternoon talk shows while I was in the hospital. Then I watched whatever would divert me. In the afternoon, talk shows were the cream of the crop. And Mitchell Biekma was la crème de la crème. He had regaled the audience with tales of the frenetic soap-opera atmosphere that prevailed in gourmet kitchens, where chefs were at once impresarios and czars, where one such tyrant fired his *sous*-chef for using the great one's butter brush, where cooks raced to get twenty individual soufflés ready at once, only to find that the party had left after the appetizer, where romance bloomed near the torrid heat of the pastry oven, flamed near the Cherries Jubilee, and wilted by the greens left out of the fridge overnight. There was the time when the dishwasher and cook were in love with the same waitress; the dishwasher had won out, and in a fit of pique the cook thrust him headfirst into the onion soup. Biekma had told of restaurants, not his own of course, where tips were paid in coke, where snagging a reservation was not the problem, but getting into the bathroom was. And he'd talked about the crises—when a neighboring cat got into the kitchen and lapped the cream off the food critic's almond crème torte, when the white asparagus around which the entire menu was planned didn't arrive, when two waiters fell in love and left without notice for a tryst in New Orleans. He had looked like a rubber man as he leapt up to parody a customer who had arrived at nine on a Saturday night for a seven o'clock reservation, with eight people instead of the four, and was devastated at being asked to wait. Biekma, mimicking him, had dropped his face into a mask of tragedy, smacked his hands to his heart, and crumpled into the chair behind him. The audience had loved it. I had loved it.

I peered through the kitchen doorway. Inside, Lopez, a rookie, guarded the scene.

"What's the word here?" I asked.

"It looked like this when I arrived," he said, waving a hand around. There was a look of proprietary embarrassment on his long, narrow face. In the thirty minutes he'd been on guard here, it had become his room; and admittedly his room was a mess. Soaking pans filled the sink, gummy handles poking up in all directions. The counter next to the sink was nearly invisible under a tower of dishes that looked as unstable as Mitch Biekma in his parody. And the dishes themselves were almost entirely cloaked by mounds of congealed food that had run together and down over the sides. I didn't know Lopez well, but I could guess that no one walked into his kitchen at home and found it like this.

He said, "ID tech hasn't started taking samples. He's only taking pictures. He almost had a cow when the dishwasher wanted to finish up here. He said not to touch anything, literally."

I nodded. Raksen would covet every globule on every dish. "Did someone take the dishwasher to the station?"

"No, he's upstairs, with Murakawa."

So that's who Murakawa was interrogating. He didn't look like a dishwasher.

I glanced down the length of the room, surprised at its size. It ran beside the middle and rear dining rooms, probably thirty feet, and was about ten feet wide. It was, I realized, with a certain amount of shock, nearly the size of the apartment-cum-porch I had just vacated. Kitchens, as everyone was eager to remind me, were not my area of expertise. There was a time when I had made toast for breakfast, but no toasters last a lifetime, particularly ones that come as wedding presents. A toaster can be deemed a success if it outlives the marriage. When mine ceased to pop (long after the marriage had), I considered the options. I could have bought a new one. Toasters were still only ten bucks. But the station had a supply of fresh donuts each morning. So my sole foray into the culinary arts ceased.

I looked around the kitchen. Both the outside wall and the front wall boasted stoves the size of a steamer trunk, with hoods big enough to suck up a lifeboat. Thick latticed rubber mats covered the floor, the spaces between the latticework filled with trampled salad greens, jellied cream soup, and hardened mousse. A giant electric mixer stood next to a wooden cutting board and open shelves holding bowls and stacks of cleaned, but hardly sparkling, pots and pans, as well as implements whose use I couldn't guess. Beside the shelves was a huge gray-metal fridge. Using a handkerchief, I pulled open the door. But if there was something damning in there, it was going to take more than a cursory glance by someone as unknowledgeable as I to ferret it out. The rear of the room held the exit door and the double doors to a pantry three times the size of the closet in my old flat. A couple of patrol officers would devote the rest of the night to checking every can and recording every onion. This was, after all, where Biekma's suspicious horseradish had been kept.

Nodding to Lopez, I walked out the back door, down three steps, and found myself nearly face-to-face with five huge rubber garbage cans that formed the rear boundary of the lot. The only illumination came from a bulb placed over a shed on the end of the building. In the shadowy light the garbage cans looked like a quintet of linebackers wearing sun hats. The thought amused me, but I had no doubt that the brimming garbage did not bring smiles to the neighbors. No wonder they had complained. The trash didn't smell now, but by morning it might. It could also make the day, or the night, of a wandering dog, or a troop of raccoons from the hills.

Next to the house was a small flower garden. Between the garden and the trash cans was an empty space about four feet wide. A rookie stood guard.

Between Paradise and its neighbor, and the two houses behind them, Grove Path ran from Martin Luther King Jr. Way (formerly Grove Street) to Josephine Street, giving Mitch's customers an inducement to park on Josephine, and giving the Josephine Street residents a big headache. I followed the path to Josephine. Despite the commotion at Paradise, both houses were dark. Either the residents had gotten bored watching the rookie stand outside the wine shed, or they were in the crowd on the sidewalk in front. Both houses were protected by tall fences. The one catty-cornered from Mitch's was covered with ivy, the one behind the restaurant was bare redwood. I peered over both fences into the tiny backyards; both were dark and empty. Overcoming the urge to march in and remind Grayson that they needed to be checked, that *I* would have had them checked already if I had been supervising the scene, I sent the rookie in to pass the word. Chances were slim to the point of nonexistent that anything would be found in either yard, still . . .

In less than a minute the rookie tramped back down the steps, followed by Len Parker, the beat officer I'd requested. Parker was one of those people who fit in anywhere, with whom everyone found something to identify—a very handy quality when conducting an interrogation.

"You don't waste time, eh, Smith?" Parker said. "I didn't even realize you'd gotten back, much less you were on a case. You all mended?"

"One hundred percent."

"And staying high up in the hills, eh?"

"I'm going to see how the other half lives. In a week you won't recognize me."

He glanced at my wilted turtleneck and wrinkled cords. "Nah, Smith, you've got your reputation to uphold. Wealth won't corrupt you."

I smiled. "Maybe not. You take the house behind the ivy. Take statements, and check the yard. I'll see the neighbor behind, and tell her to expect you in her yard."

"Wasn't she involved in the protest last winter?"

"Involved? She led it." Mitchell Biekma had given his account of that on the talk show too. The description he had given of his adversary wouldn't be one she'd use as a reference. "He characterized her as a batty academic verging on senility, and self-absorbed to boot."

"From what I've heard of her I'm surprised she let him get away with mocking her like that."

"Slander is damned hard to prove."

"I guess. Well, Smith, maybe she couldn't get back at him then. By now she should have had ample time to stew. And you should be the beneficiary of that stew. I'll bet she has plenty she'll be delighted to tell you."

CHAPTER 6

The gate to the brown shingle house behind Mitch's opened off Grove Path. I climbed two steps to the stoop, rang the bell and waited, trying to recall the newspaper coverage of Rue Driscoll and her campaign to keep Mitchell Biekma from extending his closing hour. It wasn't unusual for neighbors to be wary when a restaurateur applied for a liquor license or a bookstore owner wanted to double his floorspace. Many Berkeleyans had come from cities that had been modernized in the fifties and sixties, and where, before they realized it, landmark buildings had been demolished, row houses replaced by apartments, offices, or shopping centers. City councils had been cozy with developers. The landscapes of their childhood had vanished. They had come to Berkeley determined that that wouldn't happen here. And in their determination, they eyeballed every "Notice of Intent," chewed over every change of ownership, sniffed around every building permit. There were neighborhood organizations in each part of the city. The board of adjustments had heard from nearly all of them, from some many times. But few campaigns had had the vehemence of Rue Driscoll's.

I tried to recall the newspaper stories on Mitch's fight for later hours. Biekma, of course, had had to post a notice of intent. Had there been no protest, the change in hours would have been approved by the board of adjustments automatically. But Rue Driscoll had gathered the signatures of all the neighbors on her block and the one facing it. She had garnered something like sixty percent of the residents along Martin Luther King Jr. Way, a coup when dealing with apartment dwellers on a crowded crosstown thoroughfare. She had convinced a lawyer to check precedents, a teacher to devote half her summer vacation to wading through records in a search for similar cases where later hours had been denied. She even found someone—someone in our department, the speculation went—to give her figures on the increase in crime in places where later hours had been approved. She had brought neighbors to complain about the noise, about the garbage, about the smells from the kitchen; and most effective, she'd picked up the cry that had led to the Gourmet Ghetto Ordinance and complained that with restaurant customers filling the few vacant parking spaces for blocks around, residents couldn't park their second cars near their own homes.

It had been an impressive campaign, and how Mitchell Biekma overcame it was a mystery to me, as it had been to the reporter who covered the hearing.

"It's after three in the morning," a scratchy female voice called through the closed door.

"Police. We're investigating the death of your neighbor. I need to talk to you."

"Show me some identification."

"Just a minute." I fingered through my purse for my shield.

"Slip it through the mail slot."

"No way," I muttered under my breath. "I'll hold it against the window." Two years before, a patrol officer had slipped his shield through a mail slot; it had been mauled by a pit bull. He was still known as "Bull."

I pressed the shield against the pane. The beam of a

37

flashlight framed it. It was a good minute before the door opened, revealing a woman who looked to be in her late sixties. Her gray hair was thick, long, and caught with a clasp at the nape of her neck. Her eyes were closer to gray than blue, and the lids drooped at the sides to correspond to the set of her mouth.

There is a typical retired Berkeley matron like Rue Driscoll—not about to dye her hair or dabble in plastic surgery, but having no intention of growing old with quiet grace either. She can be seen striding along Shattuck or College Avenue in Birkenstocks, on her way to a meeting to preserve public access to San Francisco Bay, to fight Medicare cuts, or to plan another protest at the Diablo Canyon nuclear plant. Or she may be spotted walking to Safeway despite the car that sits in her driveway, or headed to the Yoga Room or the local swimming pool. She lives by the dictum of "use it or lose it." "Little old lady" is something she has no intention of becoming.

Now as she glared at me, Rue Driscoll's lips pressed together in impatience as if ready to denounce me for commandeering the time she had allocated for sleep. I had seen this expression in her news photos when she marched her neighbors to the board of adjustments.

"I'm Detective Smith, Homicide Detail."

"Homicide?"

"We handle all suspicious deaths."

She nodded.

I took down her full name, Mary Ruthe Driscoll. I'd need it to run her through files.

"Who died?" she demanded.

"Mitchell Biekma."

"Mitchell!" she gasped. If her shock was real, it held sway only momentarily. Stepping back, she said, "You'd better come in. This way, to my study."

The layout of her house was the mirror image of Mitch's, except that here the front door lead one off Grove Path into a foyer between the living room and dining room. With a quick glance into the book-strewn oak-paneled living room, I followed her through the dining room to the back. There were newspapers and magazines spread haphazardly on the dining table too, but neither the dining room nor the living room held the array of clutter that overwhelmed her study.

The study corresponded to the rear portion of Paradise where the booths were, but was ten feet wider because the kitchen didn't impinge on it. A wall of windows overlooked her backyard, and Mitch's. Beneath those windows, running the considerable width of the room, was a built-in desk. The wall opposite was hidden behind floor-to-ceiling shelves, with books lined up in tight rows, books stacked in front of those volumes, two or three piles to a shelf. From the look of it, there were books in the back that hadn't been seen in years. The desk, too, was strewn with books, as well as, piles of papers, and notes file cards in four colors.

She motioned me to a captain's chair. I moved a stack of papers to the floor and sat, watching her push two buttons on the side of an electric radiator. "The damp and cold aggravate my sciatica, otherwise I'd never have heat at this time of year," she said almost apologetically. "There were years I didn't turn the furnace on at all."

I smiled. Whereas Minnesotans or Upstate New Yorkers boast about the blizzards they have survived, some Northern Californians demonstrate their heartiness indoors. Clutching cups of hot tea, they sit in their fifty-degree living rooms, wrapped in silk turtlenecks, Aran sweaters, chamois shirts, and two pairs of socks, as they boast not only that their heat is off, but that the pilot light hasn't been lit yet this year.

"Now tell me about Mitchell," Rue Driscoll said in a tone that reminded me she had taught at the university for years.

"He died tonight."

"Here?"

"Yes."

"I didn't see anything. And I've been here in the study since noon. I even ate my dinner in here."

From her study Rue Driscoll had a view of the Paradise backyard and of Grove Path leading to the restaurant's back door.

"Think. Have you seen anything odd here recently?"

"Nothing more than usual. Not unless you mean something like yesterday, when that van pulled up and they tried to deliver health club equipment to Paradise. But there were reporters here before they could get a box out of the truck. Mitch was on the evening news. He was making a show of laughing about it, but I could tell he was furious that anyone would mistake his restaurant for a health club."

I made a note of that. "Was there anything else? Any person who shouldn't have been here, or who was acting odd or suspicious or inappropriate?"

"Inappropriate! Half their customers act inappropriate. They don't have to leave till midnight now, and they don't. I don't know what time they come, whether they just like to eat late, or they sit around after dinner drinking. Restaurants don't hurry them out; that's where they make their money—on the liquor and desserts. I told the city that, for all the good it did." She shrugged. "These backyards are only ten feet deep. The noise carries. But that's not the worst of it. When those people do leave they're laughing and calling to each other. Sometimes they screech out a song. And where do you think they're doing that? On Grove Path, right under my window. The regulation says they have to be out of the restaurant by midnight, but there's no law to keep them from standing there for half an hour. I'll tell you, just like I told the city, many a time when I'm working, like tonight, I keep my shades pulled and my ears plugged. It's when I'm in bed—that's the real problem. They don't care that they wake me up. I've put on my light and hollered out to them, and I've asked them nicely to quiet down, and to knock it off. Makes no difference.

They've spent a fortune for dinner, and had a couple of bottles of wine; they figure they've paid for a big night and they don't care who they bother doing it." Her face was flushed, the gullies in her skin pulled taut, so that the folds of skin between them hung looser in contrast. Her breath came in quick pants.

"But the board of adjustments did decide against you."

"Influence, pure and simple. Wining and dining. Mitchell knew the mayor; he had contributed to his campaign. Mitchell wasn't about to lose."

"Because he needed the extra revenue?"

She shook her head. "It was more than that. Mitchell hated to be beaten. He was like a child, a brat. He'd go into a rage and turn purple. I saw him do that when another student made a fool of him. It only happened once, thank goodness, and that was before the rest of the students arrived for class. There were only two more classes that semester, and he and Laura skipped them both. Laura told me later that if he had seen the young man again, he would have had the same extreme reaction. But by the beginning of the next semester it had all been forgotten, which was certainly good. I couldn't have that kind of behavior in my seminars."

"Mitch was your student?"

"Two semesters. I should have remembered Mitchell's childishness when I went to the hearings. I shouldn't have expected fairness. I should have been prepared for Mitch using every bit of influence he could. He knew how to work the media. He had friends with money. It's the same old story." She shook her head. "I just didn't expect it to happen in Berkeley."

"And it made you angry," I said.

"Not foolhardy enough to kill him, if that's what you're leading up to."

It was. "Without Mitchell Biekma, there'd be no influence."

Wagging her finger at me, she said, "If I'd killed him, I

would have done it before the hearings, not after. It won't do me any good now."

Outside I could see Parker's light moving back and forth against the fence in the neighboring yard. I glanced around the room, trying to get the feel of it, to understand this woman who had swallowed her surprising defeat here. On the desk, she had cleared spaces every three or four feet, but the books and papers had impinged on most of them. It was the desk of an obsessive; it was not the desk of a woman who would give up a righteous cause when one board turned her down. "Why didn't you appeal?"

She leaned back against the chair. She half closed her eyes momentarily, as I'd seen teachers do when choosing a strategy. "I was too sick," she said. "Laura and Mitch invited me for dinner over there. To make up, they said. I was poisoned."

CHAPTER 7

"You were poisoned at Paradise!" I exclaimed to the still extant Rue Driscoll. "How?"

"Food poisoning. I don't think they intended to kill me. But I was nauseous for thirty-six hours. I couldn't leave the house. I regurgitated six times, and I haven't done that in fifty years."

I tried to recall a newspaper evaluation of Rue Driscoll's mental state. Had her obsession with Mitchell Biekma led to delusions? Or could this bizarre accusation have some basis? "And that was after the board decision? Were you planning to appeal?"

She shrugged. "I hadn't considered it yet. I was astounded by the decision. The probabilities had been so clearly in my favor. . . . Foolish as it sounds, I hadn't given thought to proceeding if the board's decision came down against me. In any case, it was only three days after the last hearing that Laura invited me to dinner."

I nodded, trying to conceal my surprise.

I mustn't have been entirely successful, for Rue Driscoll said, "My reaction was the same as yours. I should have honored it. But you can't suspect Laura of anything evil, she's just too fine a person. She was my best student, so quick, so interested, willing to do the research to back up her theories. Laura insisted the invitation was for a reconciliation dinner. She said all the things nice people say in those circumstances, that we'd been friends too long for this to come between us permanently, that they would do whatever they could to minimize the noise, that they never intended to disturb me, that they appreciated me finding them the house the restaurant's in, and—"

"You found them this house? You'd better backtrack to the beginning. Did you first meet the Biekmas in one of your classes?"

"They were in my last seminars on Virginia."

"The state?"

She stared at me in amazement. Then waving a hand at the desk and the bookshelves, she said, "Virginia Woolf, young lady. I taught all the Woolf courses. Apparently, you did not matriculate from the University of California at Berkeley."

I hadn't. My undergraduate days had been in Virginia, the state. I could have told her that my ex-husband had been a graduate student in the English department at Cal, but I didn't. "When, exactly, was this seminar?"

"Six years ago."

"Who was in it?"

"Mitchell, Laura, Ashoka Prem, Marilyn Winters, Dana Arndt, Don Ellis, Jivan Mehra, a young man from Bombay, and Noriko Yamamoto from Kobe."

"Isn't that a rather small number for a seminar?"

"It was the second semester."

"How does the seminar connect with your finding them the house for Paradise?"

She hesitated, and for a moment I thought she was going to say they asked her to keep an eye out. Shifting in her chair, she said, "The seminar met here. Mitch and Laura told me they were looking for a place to live and work. They didn't mention a restaurant or I would never have dreamed of putting them next to me. I have my work to consider. I need uninterrupted quiet. But Mitch and Laura should have been perfect neighbors. Mitch was a full-time student. Laura was taking two classes to finish up. She had taken a job handling customer complaints at the water company until Mitch found work."

"Then what were their plans?"

Rue sighed deeply, the sigh of one who has considered a situation too many times and been stymied every one of them. But the effect of that sigh was more mental than physical. Her back remained erect, her shoulders didn't slump any more than they already had (which was considerable); only her face seemed to slacken, and that in dismay rather than relaxation. "When Mitch got his degree it was to be Laura's turn. She would go to chiropractic school. That was years ago, you understand, before every corner in town boasted two chiropractors. I have friends with back problems—not serious like mine, of course—who have never paid to see a chiropractor. They just check the ads and go for the free visit the new ones offer. They've done it for years."

"So Laura Biekma planned to become a chiropractor," I said, herding her back to the topic. "And that affected your finding them the house."

"They wanted a place where they could live upstairs and use the ground floor for her office. It needed to be on a main street, in a good neighborhood, and not be too expensive. At the time, the house fitted all three criteria."

"Did they spot it on their way to your class?"

"Yes. And they knew right away it was what they wanted."

I nodded, silently noting that Rue Driscoll had taken great credit for this boon of circumstance.

As if reading my mind, she raised a forefinger. "They wouldn't have gotten it without me. The old man who was selling it had lived there twenty-three years. We were good friends. He had other offers, but I convinced him to sell to Mitch and Laura, even though it meant carrying a bigger loan. He wouldn't have done it for anyone but me."

"Surely Mitch and Laura"—I was beginning to think of the Biekmas as Mitch and Laura—"realized that."

"Of course. Then, they had no plans to disrupt my work. Then, I didn't have the same kind of work to disrupt. And for years they didn't make a sound. Mitch and Laura bought the house, and rented the upstairs where they live now."

I was tempted to bring the interrogation back to the question of why she thought she had been poisoned, but I decided to let her follow this train a bit longer. I would have to know about the Biekma's background anyway. "What happened after your seminar ended?"

"They all graduated. Noriko went to graduate school at Columbia. She was a bright girl. She wrote an incisive paper on anti-Semitism and its effects on Virginia's work. Dana left for some monastery outside Katmandu. I think she was planning to hike up there from Calcutta. Jivan went back to Bombay. He was applying to graduate school, but I don't believe he was accepted, at least not then. His family had money; he could wait a year. And he wasn't a dedicated student. Sometimes I thought he just came for the food."

"The food?" Maybe I was letting this go too far afield.

"They brought food. You see, we'd been together the whole year. And during the first semester the eight of them had discovered their common interest in cooking. Jivan's father owned a restaurant in Bombay, quite a famous one, I believe. Noriko was intrigued by Occidental food, and at the time, I thought the others just liked to eat. Whatever their initial interest, they got into the habit of bringing desserts, or hors d'oeuvres, or snacks—not pretzels, but elaborate cooked things like individual pizzas with salmon and sun-dried tomatoes. Exquisite things. I'll tell you, if the topic had been anything less fascinating than Virginia, the focus of the class would have altered."

"So they were already interested in cooking."

She jerked forward. "Don't you tell me I should have known, young lady. I've already heard that from Mitchell. Smug as could be, he was. Laura understood the importance of my work. She was very accommodating. She insisted they'd do everything possible when they opened the restaurant so I wouldn't be disturbed, that I would be welcome to have free meals there anytime. But Mitch, he just said I should have known." Bracing on the arms of her chair, she lifted up an inch, leaned forward, and lowered herself down, presumably settling on a more acceptable part of her anatomy. "I pointed out the fallacy in that argument. How could I have known? They didn't know then. Even when Mitch went off to France, to cooking classes, they didn't tell me they planned to open their own restaurant. I thought Mitch was just going to visit Jivan and Ashoka. I didn't realize till he'd been there for six months that he was enrolled in classes too. And even when he got back, it was three years before he opened here. How could I have known?" she insisted in a voice that made me sure she secretly suspected Mitch was right—she should have known.

"So Paradise opened," I prompted.

She shook her head. Gray hairs that the clasp had bitten through spun like kite tails. "And since that point I haven't gotten a decent day's work done."

"Mitch's is only open for dinner. Couldn't you work during the day?"

"They serve dinner after six o'clock. They get deliveries all day long. The trucks park on Josephine and drivers wheel their carts down the alley, cloppety-clop. Sometimes they come two at a time, and they yell to each other. Or they yell to Adrienne, the cook, to open the door. Some of them even yell to me when they pass. Think they're being friendly," she muttered in exasperation. "The garbagemen come every day, at the crack of dawn. There's no way they can be quiet. And that's not even counting the customers themselves."

"I can understand—"

"*Understand* nothing! Tell that to scholars fifty years from now. Which will be more important, their half-drunken cavorting, or Virginia Woolf's Berkeley letters?"

"This Berkeley?" I asked in amazement. I was hardly a scholar; indeed, for two years after my divorce from an aspiring English professor, I hadn't read anything more intellectual than the L. L. Bean catalogue. But there had been a time before that when I'd read Virginia Woolf, and a time since when I'd picked up the Quentin Bell biography. And even from that bit, I knew Woolf had never set foot in the United States. "Who was she corresponding with here?"

"A woman named Florence Crocker. Now before you say anything, I'll tell you that I know these letters may be apocryphal, indeed *probably* are apocryphal. Nothing in her published letters or diaries mentions Florence Crocker. Nothing suggests she had an acquaintance here, or any interest in acquiring one."

"Then how—"

"According to Florence Crocker's grandson, she met Woolf when she was in London in nineteen thirty-nine, just before the war broke out. They corresponded for the next two years, until Virginia's suicide—that is, according to the grandson," she added. "I know it's a long shot. It's one chance in a hundred, or a thousand, or more. But suppose the letters are not a fraud. Can you imagine what a boon they would be, particularly since they cover that period when she was working on *Pointz Hall*? It's too important to let go without proper investigation."

I knew enough about the competitive world of professors to realize that even after retirement, the possibility of making a mark in their field would be more than many could resist.

"It's very painstaking, precise work, not work you can do half-asleep," she said. "It was bad enough when the customers left at ten. You know, young lady, it's not good for the body to be fed that late. The blood shouldn't still be in the stomach with the digestive juices when you lie down to sleep. Very unhealthy."

Choosing to ignore that—"unhealthy" eating habits were not a topic I wanted to consider—I said, "What I don't understand, Ms. Driscoll, is this. You got food poisoning in Paradise. Did you go to a doctor?"

"Yes, he confirmed it was food poisoning."

"So you had proof?"

"Oh, yes. I am a scholar, young lady. I don't make statements without data to support them."

"So, you could have taken action against the Biekmas. As the owners of Paradise they'd be liable. It would have given you a position from which to negotiate, to get some concessions, maybe even an earlier closing. Why didn't you do it?"

"I probably should have. But Laura came over. She was so apologetic. She really felt terrible. She's such a sweet girl. They're all in love with her over there, you know. And she had put so much into the restaurant. It was just beginning to make a profit. She was just starting to work in the kitchen—training, she said. She realized she had a talent for cooking too. She decided to focus on that. It was too late to be a chiropractor, she said, but she could be a cook, a fine cook. I understood that. It was to her, what Virginia's letters were to me. I couldn't ruin Laura. So I let it drop."

I sat, letting the silence lengthen. Despite the electric heater aimed at Rue's back, the room was cold. It was definitely a heat-for-one setup. I recalled the single-mindedness with which my ex-husband had pursued his Yeats studies.

What would it have taken for him to let them go? More than his attachment to me. Certainly more than one to a friendly neighbor. "I don't buy that, Ms. Driscoll. You wouldn't sacrifice your work that easily."

She glanced around at the papers strewn on the long desk, as if pondering a scholarly spring-cleaning. "You're free to draw your own conclusions."

"Of course," I said firmly. "But that's not the end of it. Failing to cooperate in a murder investigation is a serious offense."

She jerked forward. "Are you threatening me, young lady?"

"I'm telling you that I *will* get to the truth. If you don't cooperate, it will take me longer. I will have to come back here again and again"—I paused—"or have you come to the station."

The small lines around her eyes tightened till they seemed ready to squash the eyeballs back into their sockets. "All right," she said. "It wasn't entirely for Laura, though I was quite honest with you in saying I am fond of her. We spent many pleasant afternoons discussing Virginia and her work. It was Laura whom I first told about the Berkeley letters. She was almost as thrilled as I."

"But that wasn't the reason," I prodded.

"No. Look, the letters aren't scholarly; they're chatty reminiscences and observations. But the work of authenticating them is exhausting. It could take me years, years I may not have. I haven't the resources to hire the caliber of assistants I need. The great Woolf mania has faded. If they're authentic, the letters would be published by a scholarly house; anything connected with Virginia would be. But they would be presented as a small addendum to the great works of scholarship. The more commercial publishers who put out the popular works wouldn't find these letters worth their investment. And even if they were published, they wouldn't get the publicity they deserved. Not unless . . ."

I began to see. "Unless the author creates some interest in them herself."

She nodded, her lips pressed tensely. Even the stray hairs seemed to move reluctantly.

"And nothing increases interest like publicity. Did Mitch offer you his TV connections or his publishing ones?"

The doorbell rang. I held Rue with my gaze. "Which?" I demanded.

"Both," she said, pushing herself up, clearly relieved to escape this distasteful topic.

I followed her to the door. She pulled it open to reveal Lopez.

"It's the sergeant," he said. "He says he's had Earth Man in the dining room as long as he's going to. He says it's too cold with the windows open, but it stinks too much with them closed. And if you plan to talk to Earth Man here, you'd better . . . well . . ."

"Haul ass?"

Lopez grinned. "Close enough."

I glanced back at Rue Driscoll. I wasn't satisfied with her explanation, but like the Woolf mania, the moment to press her had passed.

CHAPTER 8

I stood for a moment on Grove Path, letting Rue Driscoll's house protect me from the fog blowing in off the bay. In the distance I could hear the foghorns, sighing with an intensity similar to Rue Driscoll's. I could hear Parker much closer in the tiny Driscoll backyard, shuffling through ivy, grumbling as he moved his flashlight inch by inch. The staccato burst from the patrol-car radios came from Martin

Luther King Jr. Way. I glanced back at Rue Driscoll's study. The light was still on; she wasn't going back to bed, at least for the moment. I had given her too much to think about. Had she gotten food poisoning at Paradise? Apparently, something in that meal had disagreed with her. Apparently, Mitch Biekma had taken her seriously enough to try to placate her. But there were plenty of reasons he might have done that. Laura, the wife whom "everyone loved," might have convinced him to be generous. He might just have wanted to avoid any more negative publicity. The original battle with Rue Driscoll had been long and tough, and a lot of Berkeleyans had sided with her. The mantle of Berkeley Hero he had come to enjoy had been pulled lower with each skirmish. By the end of the hearings, Mitch Biekma was in serious danger of being viewed as just another businessman. Well, I thought, that was one danger death had spared him. No one would ever recall him now without thinking that the bird of paradise in his front yard had been his road to the ultimate paradise.

Stopping halfway on the stoop, Lopez pulled open the kitchen door.

The pungent aroma of unfamiliar spices greeted me. My tongue mimicked the taste; at three A.M., it had been a long time since the lunch on the plane. At the rate things were going, it would be a long time till breakfast. I climbed the two steps to the stoop and walked into the kitchen.

If I had had any questions about my contest with Grayson, they vanished. By leaving him with Earth Man, I had won. Even in the kitchen I was overwhelmed. The aroma of spices was a thing of the past. All I could smell now was the unmistakable cologne of street living—months of dirt, embedded in months of sweat, smeared with spoiled and rotten food.

As I walked into the dining room, Grayson's fringed lip quivered with anger. Then as he glanced toward the restaurant foyer, the corners of his mouth moved sharply up into a smile. "He's by the door, Smith. And he's all yours."

Had I, by some miracle of nasal blockage, overlooked Earth Man, one glance at him would have corrected that. His floor-length cape was covered with plastic noses. From his well-soiled green cloak protruded trunks, muzzles, proboscises, and snouts in an array of colors. Toucan beaks decorated his shoulders like epaulets. But the most eye-catching was the trunk that protruded suggestively from the general area of his navel.

Earth Man was clearly in his nose period. More than six feet tall, he couldn't have weighed over a hundred and thirty pounds, and a couple of those pounds were accounted for by his thick blond hair. From the look of it, he had hacked it himself. It stood out in clumps two to three inches from his gaunt face, forming an aureole around his boney arched nose. And that, the pièce de résistance of this ensemble, was painted white and accented in glitter. Between the beaks and bills he had pinned a sign—BREATHE FREE, BREATHE DEEP. It was the last thing I wanted to do.

Earth Man had been a fixture of the Telegraph Avenue scene since the sixties. He had discovered LSD early on. Later, he had diversified. He had passed some years in a state hospital before the Reagan Administration closed most of them and sent the inmates home to depend on community mental health facilities that had never been adequately funded. Many of his companions from that era had died. Those who were nominally still alive spent their days leaning against walls, watching day fade to night and night lift to day, or stumbling along the Avenue past the tables and blankets where street artists sold their hand-tooled leather belts and cloisonné earrings. As the end of the month approached and their Social Security checks ran out, they begged for spare change along the Avenue with the same hopeful stance they'd adopted nearly twenty years ago. But times had changed. The days when it was de rigueur to contribute to the Free Clinic and the free clothes box had passed. Twenty years ago, the undergraduates who now traversed the Avenue hadn't been born.

Berkeley wasn't New York. No one froze to death overnight here. But even the most inviting doorway couldn't keep the penetrating Pacific fog from seeping beneath the skin hour after hour. But Earth Man was more together than some; he wasn't dependent on a weekend in the jail or a fortnight in the county hospital, "the poor man's spa," for a break from the street. As long as I had known him, from my days on the Avenue beat, he had had a room in one of the transient hotels, and no matter how spaced out he got, somehow his rent was always paid.

"You want some coffee?" I asked.

He hesitated.

I wasn't sure where coffee fitted into his present campaign. When I had been a beat officer on Telegraph Avenue, I'd seen Earth Man daily. I'd watched as, dressed in a series of appropriate costumes, he'd harangued whoever would listen to protect the trees, save the seals and whales, clean the air. He was more of a town landmark than Paradise, as much a folk hero as Mitch Biekma. He was in his own bizarre but unquestionably sincere way, symbolic of one Berkeleyan article of faith—total commitment to saving the environment. And those who gave less to Friends of the Sea Otter, the Sierra Club, and Greenpeace than they spent on a dinner at Paradise, viewed Earth Man, for all his craziness, with a guilty respect.

Looking at him now, I wondered what was behind those dark eyes that stared so piercingly—eyes that, without seeming to move or change, suddenly lost their power and looked no more keen than the plastic eyes that could have come with any of his snouts or beaks.

"Coffee?" I repeated.

"Fresh brewed?" he asked hopefully.

"Fresh brewed." Only in Berkeley would the street people disdain instant. I nodded to the beat officer, and waited till he brought two cups. Beside the open window, at the rear of the dining room, Grayson grinned. In the bathroom Raksen's flashbulbs went off.

I would have taken Earth Man outside and interrogated him on the stoop, but I wasn't about to give Grayson the satisfaction. Instead, I motioned Earth Man to a table by the front window, and sat down, taking small careful breaths, as if they would keep the air from flowing too far up my nostrils. "You found Mitchell Biekma's body," I said. "Now I want you to start at the beginning. What were you doing here?"

His eyes narrowed. Was he were trying to decide on a strategy, or merely attempting to recall why he was here?

"I was passing by."

"Here? What were you doing in this part of town at midnight? You don't live here."

"I was visiting a friend."

I stared, amazed. In my four years on the force, I had never seen him involved in a give-and-take conversation. "Who were you visiting?"

He shrugged.

I caught his gaze and held it, repeating, "Who?"

He wriggled back in his chair, lifting up the coffee cup with cloak-covered hands. As he leaned forward, a red and turquoise beak on his chest dipped toward the coffee.

"Who, Earth Man?"

"Well, I wasn't really visiting. I was just walking around."

"At midnight?"

"Time's relative."

But it wasn't that relative. I knew which of the Avenue regulars were nocturnal wanderers. Some we kept an eye on, some we made use of. But Earth Man was not one of them. His obsessions were played out in front of people. And by ten at night Telegraph Avenue looked like a movie studio back lot. I shook my head. "Listen, Earth Man, you know me from the Avenue. Look at me. We've talked before."

He stared, his brow wrinkling with the effort of placing me. I wondered how long a thought remained in his head, and if his periods of seeming lucidity were just another mask of craziness. "Remember when you wanted to block off the Avenue to traffic, and that gang of kids tried to rip off your car?" Earth Man had been dressed in a cardboard Toyota, suspended by straps from his shoulders. "I got you away then, remember?"

He leaned in toward me, his dark eyes widening. A smile covered his face. "You were the cop."

"Right. I helped you. You can trust me now. Tell me why you came here."

He lifted his coffee cup, sucked at the coffee, and glanced warily to both sides. Then he leaned closer, inches from my face.

I held my breath.

"Okay," he whispered, "but I don't want this to get around."

"Right." I forced myself not to move away.

"I came for a meal."

I almost said "Here?" Then I realized. "You mean they gave you food?"

He jolted up in his seat. "People leave whole pieces of chicken. They don't eat their corn. People are starving all over the world."

He could have been a mother. *Take a bite for the starving children overseas.* "How many people like you did they feed?"

He shrugged. "Just me. I don't tell people."

Indeed like a mother, with the same lack of benefit for Berkeley's hungry as the children overseas. "So how exactly did this work? Did you just come to the back door and knock?"

"No."

"What did you do?"

"I come at eleven. It's my time."

"But tonight you were here after midnight."

"I came at eleven. But they told me to come back at twelve-fifteen. I did. Twelve-fifteen exactly." He looked up at the Plasticine railing, following it with his gaze down to the end of the stairs, across the front of the desk, and then back up to the door where it started. If Mitch Biekma had wanted to seduce a diner with his glittery décor, he'd found his man. For Earth Man, clearly the sparkling lights had blotted out the rest of reality.

"Who told you to come back?"

"No one."

"You came at eleven. You said someone told you to come back later. Who?"

"No one. There was a note on the back door. It said 'Earth Man, dinner at twelve-fifteen. Come back then.' I remember all the words. I read it four times." He shook his head. "It was a long time since breakfast. It's cold out there. I was real hungry. I was smelling the food, thinking about what Laura was going to make. Yesterday Laura saved me a piece of chocolate cake. I was thinking there might be more. Then I saw the note. I didn't want to wait. But I thought she'd make me something special."

"Why?"

"Laura told me to come back later before, once, because she was making me a quiche, not a slice, a whole one just for me."

"Did she tell you to come back later any other time?"

He frowned. "No. They laughed at her, the other people in the kitchen. I guess she didn't want that. She didn't do it again."

"Does Laura always make your dinner?"

"She understands. She doesn't hassle me. The cook, sometimes she'll let me have what's left over, but she'll yell at me if I sit on the stoop to eat. I have to take my plate into the yard back there, in the dark. And the guy who owns the place, he'd like to hear I'd starved somewhere else, so I wouldn't be ruining the neighborhood here. I ran into him and Laura on the street one day and he started screaming as soon as he saw me. You'd think it was him who was the crazy." Earth Man laughed, such a normal laugh that he could have been any one of us in the room sizing up the situation. Suddenly, he snapped his mouth shut and shrank back in his chair. "Look, Officer, I knew enough to stay out of his way, but that don't mean I killed him."

I nodded. "But his wife gave you dinner?"

His cheeks twitched, and it took me a moment to realize he was smiling contentedly. It was not an expression I had seen on his face often. "She didn't just dump whatever was around on a dish, like that cook did. She fixed me a plate, like she would to take to someone who was sick. She gave me a couple vegetables, more than I wanted, but she told me they were good for me. And she was sorry I couldn't sit on the stoop."

I made a note of that. "So tonight, what happened?"

Again, his eyes narrowed.

"Come on, Earth Man, don't try to second-guess me. Just tell me what happened."

"More coffee."

I nodded at the patrol officer, but didn't let the diversion distract me. "Earth Man?"

"I came up the path from Josephine, like always."

"Why from Josephine? King Way would be closer for you."

Earth Man shook his head. "Biekma told me to. It was part of the deal. I understood. He didn't want a weirdo hanging around. He didn't want his expensive customers strolling out, full of champagne and pâté, and running into me." He laughed.

"And then?"

"I saw the note, and I left. I know not to hang around. I went to the park and waited. I have a watch. One of my supporters gave it to me. It runs good if I wind it."

"So you came back at twelve-fifteen. By way of Josephine?"

"Twelve-*fourteen* I walked up the path, then up the steps. I knocked."

"Do you always knock?"

"Don't have to. She's usually in the kitchen. She knows what time I get there. Sometimes she even looks out the door for me. But tonight she didn't have time. *He* was too close."

"Biekma?"

"Yeah." Earth Man leaned toward me. I forced myself not to move back. "He *was* crazy, you know," he whispered. "He started screaming like I was going to hold up the place. But then the cook screamed at him." He grinned. "She screamed about the noise! He screamed back. There was a lot of noise. Laura tried to make them be quiet, but they didn't listen. Then he charged out."

I stood up. "Show me exactly what happened, in the kitchen."

He took a long swallow of coffee, then sat back staring at the cup.

"Leave it," I said. "It'll still be here when you get back."

Still, he hesitated. In his world a promise like that was a fifty-fifty proposition. Then he stood and followed me around the corner into the kitchen.

"Hands!" Raksen screamed. "Keep your hands off things, off everything. I haven't started dusting or collecting samples, Smith." He was propping the pantry door open with a hip, camera hanging from his neck, as he swung around to face us. He stared in horror at Earth Man. "Don't rub anything."

"I'll be careful," I assured him. "But we do need to be at the back door."

I waited while Raksen dusted the door handle, then called the rookie guarding the backyard to stand at the bottom of the stoop. I put Earth Man outside the door, even though the wind was blowing in our direction. Steeling myself, I said, "So you knocked on the door and Biekma opened it. How close were you to him? Show me. Pretend I'm Biekma."

"Come forward," he said. I took a step. "More." Holding my breath, I inched forward. "Closer."

"Are you sure?" I couldn't imagine Biekma electing to be this near. Earth Man hadn't smelled any better an hour ago. He grabbed my arms through the wool of his cape and pulled me forward. "This close." My face was a foot from his. A beak pointed to my breast, a trunk to my waist.

"Are you sure about this?"

"He was yelling at me. His spit hit my face."

"Okay, then what happened?"

"The cook yelled."

"Where was the cook?"

"At the stove, there." He pointed to the stove next to the sink on the outside wall.

"What did she say?"

"'Shut up, Mitch. Take your soup and get out of my kitchen.' That's a quote," he said proudly.

"What did Mitch say?"

It was a while before he admitted, "I don't remember."

"Where were the other people while this was going on? The dishwasher?"

"At the sink." He pointed to the sink.

"The sous-chef?"

Earth Man looked puzzled.

"The other man in the kitchen?"

"Oh him, the stranger. He was at the chopping block, there by the refrigerator, when Mitch opened the door. But he caught on fast. He went back to the stove where the cook was. He stood next to her, like she was going to protect him. I guess he knew what Mitch was like."

"And Laura?"

"Laura?" He smiled. "She was standing by that table there, by the door to the dining room."

"Are you saying no one was near you and Biekma?"

He nodded. "No one *wanted* to be near him. *I* didn't either."

"Then what happened?"

"Laura told them both—Mitch and the cook—to stop screaming at each other, that they had to give me dinner.

Mitch screamed some more, then he stomped out past her. Then she got a bowl and put some soup in it and then she broke up a couple of pieces of French bread in it, like croutons. Then she spread some Parmesan cheese over it. The cook yelled at her about the cheese, but the cheese smelled real good. When she gave me the soup, she said I could come back for more. I stood outside a while. I had to decide what I should do. Sometimes it takes me a while to think. I have to be careful, you see. I figured I'd better not eat on the stoop tonight. I didn't want to sit in the backyard either, because the cook was so pushed out of shape about the soup and I didn't want her to bring anything out to the garbage and find me there. So I thought I'd take the bowl out front and go down to that empty lot where the gas station used to be." He shook his head. "That was a bad mistake."

"How so?"

"Because I heard this groan—no, more like a grunt—in the front yard and I looked over. I thought my eyes were going. I almost didn't stop, but then I looked again and . . ." he shrugged.

"And?"

"I came up to him. Biekma. He wasn't moving. I almost lifted him up, but I've been in enough emergency rooms to know that you don't move people. So I came to the door and pounded, and the cook opened it. She ran out. She looked at him and screamed. She didn't do anything, she just stood there and screamed until people came running from inside, and someone lifted him off, and then two of them carried him inside."

"And then what did you do?"

"I went around to the back door. See, I'd dropped my bowl."

I stared at Earth Man. Maybe I had been mislead by his seeming clarity. I said, "What made you think they'd feed you then, of all times?"

His eyes went blank.

"Earth Man?"

He shook his head.

"Why did you expect a meal then?" My voice had risen. Out of the corner of my eye I could see Grayson moving closer. Earth Man's lucidity might be like one color in a kaleidoscope, presenting itself by chance, or there could be a core of sanity he could reach when he stretched. I could only hope for the latter.

I leaned back, letting him take notice of Grayson barking orders at Lopez. When the sun rose, Lopez and Parker would begin the task of sifting through the garbage. I let Earth Man watch Raksen as he brushed the powder on the kitchen door. I let him feel the omnipresence of the police.

"Paradise gave free dinners to one person, you, Earth Man. Why?"

He shrugged; his beaks and snouts bounced.

"You said Biekma didn't want to see you here. Why did he keep feeding you?"

He looked down at the red and turquoise beak.

"Earth Man," I snapped. "He despised you; you found him dead. You better answer me—now."

He didn't move.

I grabbed the beak and yanked it toward me. It pulled free of his cloak. He stared at it, as if he had been dismembered.

"Earth Man, now."

"Okay, okay; but don't let this get around. He gave me free meals for a month, delivered to my room. Room service, he said. He was going to tell the newspapers he was doing that. It was after that reporter had said two dinners here cost a whole month of food stamps."

"When was that?"

"April."

"Two months ago. So why was he still feeding you?"

"I don't know."

"Why?"

He shook his head slowly.

"Laura Biekma told him he *had* to feed you. That's not how you describe an act of kindness. Now you tell me what was going on."

He took a long breath, half closed his eyes, then said, "Because in the first month the food made me sick. I got real sick—food poisoning. I know what food poisoning is," he said, catching my eye and nodding.

It was the only time he had made eye contact. I wondered what he was hiding. I said, "Did you go to emergency?"

Releasing my gaze, he shook his head. "Nah, like I say, I know food poisoning. I knew I'd live. I just stayed in bed a couple days."

"But if they'd pumped your stomach—"

"It came on me too sudden. If I could have got to emergency, I wouldn't have been sick. I was too sick to get to emergency. I just stayed home and threw up." He grinned, relaxed now.

"You ate the dinner in your room," I said slowly. "You've still got that dinner in your room, after two months, don't you?"

CHAPTER 9

I sent Lopez for Parker.

To Earth Man I said, "When I'm through talking with Officer Parker, he'll take you to the station so he can get your official statement." I decided not to mention the second half of Parker's duties, the trip to Earth Man's hotel. Knowing Earth Man, he would kick up enough of a fuss just about going to the station.

"What about my dinner?" he demanded.

I stared.

"It's four o'clock in the morning," he went on, as if this were the universally recognized hour for the last sitting.

"Earth Man, you want a meal from this kitchen? Where the owner has been poisoned?"

He considered his options, fingering through the cloak the rubber trunk that protruded from his waist. He reminded me of a naked two-year-old, but it was a safe guess that wasn't the picture he engendered in every citizen's mind. The surprising thing was that we hadn't had more complaints about him. But then, he hadn't been in this particular attire that long.

What might he have been like if he had had decent psychiatric care along the way, if there had been money for private help rather than the county clinics that were too overburdened to offer much more than drugs? Would it have helped? Or would it have been too late even then? I said, "Officer Parker will get you a couple of donuts at the station."

"Donuts!" he said, dropping the trunk. His appalled expression was the same Mitch Biekma might have had.

"The gravy train's over."

"Come on, *donuts*! You know what's in those things?"

"Take it or leave it." Whichever, I just hoped he wouldn't take the last one. I didn't feel like eating now, but by the time I got back to the station a donut might be very tempting. "Earth Man, the note that told you to come back. What happened to it?"

"Gone."

"Did you take it off the door?"

"I didn't need it. I knew what it said. I left it there. When I came back it was gone."

I pressed Earth Man, but the only thing he added was that the note had been tacked on the door. I checked outside. There could have been a note tacked there tonight. From the pockmarks on the door, there could have been five hundred.

Lopez and Parker were standing inside the dining room, Lopez with his arms crossed over his chest in disgust, Parker with an expression that could have meant any of ten conflicting things. "Lopez," I said, "the time has come. Take Earth Man to Parker's car to wait for him."

I thought Earth Man might go into passive resistance, fall to an unappealing heap on the floor. But he shrugged, as if to say he had given a decent meal his best effort and, having failed, was prepared to deal with donuts.

When he and Lopez had left, I motioned Parker to sit. He smiled, and settled opposite me, an average-looking man in an average chair. There was nothing outstanding about Parker—medium brown eyes, light brown hair just long enough to save him from a charge of conformity. He reminded me of the stranger on the bus, the unfamiliar priest in the confessional in a distant parish: the faceless listener.

Parker laughed. "I've had some very strange entrees here. There are times when I think it's all a game in these places, that someone comes into the kitchen in the afternoon, hands the cook any two items, like turnips and maraschino cherries—the odder the paring the better—and says, 'Betcha can't make a main dish from these.'"

"I didn't know you were into gourmet food."

"Sparingly, on a cop's salary. But, Biekma was such a character. Half the fun of coming here was seeing him perform. The word is that 'San Francisco Mid Day' was considering him for a guest host; they were that impressed with him the times he was on. A friend of mine said there were researchers from the show at the next table one night when she was here. She said Mitch was in rare form."

"I'm not surprised. He was great the time I was here." Turning my attention back to the issue at hand, I asked, "How far did you get on the yards?"

"The catty-cornered one's done. Not much in it. Cement, deck chairs. Easy. The other—the Driscoll woman's—is a mess. I went over it but it'll take daylight to find anything."

"This is becoming a very peculiar case," I said.

Glancing at the doorway through which Earth Man had passed, he said, "I can imagine."

"Biekma took poison, then fell over his metal flower. Rue Driscoll says she got food poisoning here, but not till *after* the extended-hours hearings were over. And now Earth Man claims he was poisoned from a handout here."

"Makes you wonder what's been going on in the kitchen, doesn't it?"

"If it were just one of them . . . Rue Driscoll saw a doctor after the poisoning. She didn't exploit the incident publicly, but she did use it to get Biekma's help publicizing her book."

"Was he going to have her on 'San Francisco Mid Day' when he guest-hosted?"

"He said he'd use his connections. Or so *she* said he said. It would have been interesting to see what came of that."

"Right. Somehow I just can't picture Mitch sharing the spotlight."

I nodded. Neither could I. And I wondered if Rue Driscoll, who had already seen Mitch Biekma turn on her three times—in opening Paradise, in extending the hours, and then in mocking her on television—had come to the same conclusion. "Still, Parker, she's an intelligent woman. She didn't gain anything by telling me about the poisoning. All she did was make herself look suspicious." I waited for Parker's assessment. But he said nothing, merely sat, staring at my Styrofoam cup.

Now that Earth Man was gone, the pungent smell from the kitchen struck me again. And the cold, damp breeze flowing through the window Grayson had opened chilled my neck. To Parker I said, "Take Earth Man's statement and give him a donut. Then drive him home and search his room."

"For?"

"The food that poisoned him, two months ago."

He shook his head.

"Or vomit," I said. "Or both. Whatever they gave him he's still got, in one form or the other."

When Parker left I sent Lopez upstairs for Murakawa. He would keep an eye on the dishwasher long enough for Murakawa to brief me, then bring him down.

I called Inspector Doyle, and summarized what I had. For his part he had interrogated the waiters, the busboy, and Laura Biekma—"Seemed like a nice woman, exhausted but trying to hold herself together." We compared notes on the kitchen interchange; Laura Biekma's account squared with Earth Man's. Doyle had the cook waiting. I started to hang up.

"Smith?"

"Yes, Inspector."

"How are you holding up?"

"Fine."

"You don't sound fine."

"Inspector, it's after four in the morning. I'm in as good shape as the next guy here."

He didn't reply. I could hear his labored breathing; *he* didn't sound so fine.

"Look," I said, "you don't need to baby me. If I can't do my job I'll tell you."

"Okay, Smith. No need to fly off the handle. Just watch yourself. You have a history of taking chances."

Like the helicopter crash.

"If you need help, Smith, ask Grayson. He'd be glad to help."

I'll bet he would. "I'll watch myself," I said and hung up. I couldn't let Doyle's doubts get to me. Taking a long, slow breath, and then another, I pushed the thought of Doyle away, concentrating on the sound of radio squeals, of Grayson questioning the patrol officer who had been guarding the front yard, of Raksen's flashbulbs popping.

I pictured Paradise as it looked the night Howard and I had come, with the chartreuse tablecloths, the muted lights, and the glittering Plasticine stair railing that led the eye inevitably to the closed plasticine door.

"Ah, Monsieur Howard," Mitch Biekma had said in the worst French accent this side of Newark. "I have seen you pictured in the paper, *n'est-ce pas?*" By now even he was grinning. "Our own Inspector Clouseau." At which point he had feigned a slapstick stagger. From someone less appealing, to someone with less of a sense of humor, the reference might have been unappreciated. But either Biekma was a good judge of character, or he had checked on Howard. (Howard, at six feet six, with curly red hair, was the department's most photographed officer. It wouldn't have been hard for Biekma to find out that he was also one of its most avid practical jokers.) "*Permittez-moi* to offer you a bottle of wine while you wait on tier three with the lovely mademoiselle." Then, with bottle and glasses, he had shown us to the third step on the staircase, where we sat for the next half hour.

Howard and I had eaten together many times in our four years on the force, but mostly burgers and fries after work, at Priester's on Telegraph. Those evenings we had been caught up in cases, bitching about recalcitrant suspects, or plotting strategies. They were dinners any two buddies might have had. Or almost.

But this had been different. Here, dressed in our out-to-dinner clothes, where people treated us like a couple, we eyed each other warily, searching vainly for the familiar and finding it stifled beneath our formal behavior. We drank nervously, discussing the wine in greater depth than our interest or knowledge supported. And by the time our table was ready, we had finished the wine. And conversation—the type of conversation we'd been having for four years—had run dry. And that was the last dinner we had had together.

The Plasticine door midway up the stairway opened with a squeak, momentarily revealing a scuffed beige wall, and the lanky figure of Paul Murakawa rushed down. "How's it going, Smith?" Murakawa asked, shifting from foot to foot, as if he had just completed the first mile of a fifteen-mile run and was eager to move on. Even at four in the morning, only a few strands of his dark hair had slipped down over his forehead. He had a shallow nose but a wide mouth. When he smiled his grin filled his face.

"What do you have on the dishwasher?" I asked.

"The minimum. It was like he was paying us a buck for every word he uttered," he said in disgust. "Name's Frank Yankowski, age forty-six. Rents a room in the Hillvue Hotel on University. No children, never married. Grew up in Chicago, dropped out of high school, and has been bumming around ever since. Or so he says." Murakawa shook his head.

"Did he shed any light on Biekma's death?"

Murakawa looked down at his notes. "Said he never left the sink from six-thirty on."

"Then he saw Biekma get whatever poisoned him?" I asked in amazement.

Murakawa sighed irritably. "He could have. According to him, he was in the kitchen when Biekma came in. But, according to him, he didn't see anything. Didn't turn around. Didn't pay attention to Biekma. According to him, he doesn't know anything." He flipped the notebook shut. "He's lying, Smith."

CHAPTER 10

Raksen bent over the kitchen sink scooping a glop of brown into a plastic bag. I said to him, "I'm going to bring the dishwasher in here in a few minutes. Anything still sacred?"

His face dropped. "Do you have to, Smith? I haven't finished. Don't let him touch anything. And don't move anything. There are a couple more samples I need to get. And keep him away from the pantry. Can't you interrogate him in the dining room?"

I smiled. "I'll tell him to keep his hands in his pockets."

Two officers hurried in the front door. Grayson was standing by the foyer partition. "Start on the neighbors," he said to them. "Take the ones on either side, Acosta. You, Leonard, go across the street, to everyone who has a view of the front yard here. I want to know any unusual sound they heard, anything they saw out of the ordinary. Be thorough. Let them tell you too much. Got it?"

Acosta and Leonard nodded, and turned, nearly smacking into Lopez and his charge at the foot of the stairs. As one, Acosta and Leonard stopped, stared at the dishwasher, steeled their faces, and moved on out the door. The dishwasher was a giant. He must have been six four, almost as tall as Howard and a good fifty pounds heavier. His light brown hair would have hung from the edge of his bald pate to his collar—had he been wearing a collar. Instead, he had on a gray T-shirt with the sleeves ripped off, exposing arms thick with muscle. He looked like an ex-linebacker, ex for a while. I noted the bleach spots on his T-shirt, his jeans, and even the tan wool cap that protruded from his pocket; he seemed to have spilled with abandon. All in all, he looked like the last person anyone would hire to deal with wet dishes.

Glancing at his hands, I saw my assessment was wrong. His fingers were long, and the veins on the backs of his hands were swollen into the reddened skin. Dishpan hands. Like his hands, his face looked as if it had been grafted on the wrong body. Under his long forehead, thin, pale eyebrows arched over wary brown eyes. But it was his nose that grabbed attention. Perhaps this man *had* been a linebacker—that would have explained the angle of that narrow, highly arched nose. Halfway down it turned right, as if one of the opposing linemen had grabbed it through the face mask and given it a twist—a permanent twist. It was a snout Earth Man would have loved for his collection. Its angle was so sharp that I found myself staring, wondering if it was possible for its owner to breathe out of both nostrils, wondering why he chose a job in a hot, steamy kitchen. "Have a seat, Mr. Yankowski." I motioned him to a table near the kitchen door.

He moved with surprising lightness, as if he were dancing through rows of tires, and settled silently on a straight-back chair.

Yankowski looked like a man used to dominating. It was not the role I intended for him here. Sitting opposite him, I said, "I've just gone over your statement, Yankowski. You're lying."

"About what?" he asked, in that adolescent tone that means *So?* The effect was heightened by the wheeze that accompanied his words.

"You tell me."

He shrugged, his thick neck almost disappearing between the pads of his shoulders. His expression said *Make me!*

"You've got no work history, no family, and tonight you say you were in the kitchen when Mitchell Biekma got the soup that killed him and you didn't notice his movements. Come on."

He shrugged again, this time his shoulders barely lifting.

"We'll wear you down. It's just a question of how long it takes, Yankowski. You've been around the police enough to know that, right?"

He hesitated, then muttered, "I haven't got a record." The wheeze muddied the last words. It was a moment before I realized that rather than a true wheeze, the sound was the result of the odd angle of his nose. It was not quite a whistle, closer to that labored hiss of a teakettle just before it releases and sings.

"Too smart to get caught, huh?"

"What's that supposed to mean?"

"What time did you get to work tonight?"

He just sat.

I had the urge to kick him—and the feeling that I'd break my foot. Few things were more frustrating than interrogating the strong, silent type. I had chosen the wrong tack with him. Straight-on confrontation was what he must be used to. He'd know how to deal with it—strongly and silently. I let a minute pass, then leaned forward, adopting a more relaxed tone: "Look, I was just asking you what time you got to work."

I could see the slight drop in his shoulders. "Four-thirty," he said with not a hint of the hiss.

"Why so early?"

"Pots, pans, mixer bowls, stirring spoons, knives. Cooks can't run out of them. And tonight I was doing prep."

"Is that normal?"

"Normal?" His pale eyebrows shot up into that desert of forehead. "There is no normal in a kitchen. Look, the guy who did prep quit last week. Tonight the sous-chef didn't show. Called at four and said his tires had been slashed. Adrienne's slamming pans around, screaming that nothing's ready for her. Mitch is in the dining room screaming because he can't get anyone to cook on five minutes' notice. If Ashoka hadn't shown up, we'd have been up shit creek." The hiss was back.

"Ashoka Prem?"

"Right."

"Mitch's friend from college."

"Yeah."

I made a note of that, then asked, "Couldn't Mitch have cooked tonight?"

"Not in the same kitchen with Adrienne."

"How come?"

"Two many prima donnas." Again the hiss.

"But this was an emergency, wasn't it, with two people out?"

"Those two couldn't work together even if a representative of the Michelin Guide were coming."

71

SUSAN DUNLAP

"What about the waiters and the busboy?"

"They don't cross the Maginot Line either." I had the impression he almost smiled.

"Maginot Line? What do you mean?"

"Adrienne hasn't let anyone but cooks past the warm table in three months. If they need something farther inside, they ask the prep cook."

"What about Mitch Biekma? He was in the kitchen."

"Yeah, but not until after midnight. If he'd come any earlier, while she was still cooking, he'd have heard it."

"It's *his* restaurant."

Yankowski laughed, a rough, craggy sound that was painful to hear. "Lady, you don't know the pecking order in the kitchen. It may be Biekma's dining room, but it's Adrienne's kitchen. There everyone follows her rules, him included."

"And he didn't object?"

"Yeah, he objected, but it didn't change anything. It just annoyed Adrienne and made her dig her heels in more." The hiss was louder.

How could he stand that hissing? But then what choice did he have? "How did Laura Biekma deal with this animosity between Mitch and Adrienne?"

"Laura? She never boils over. Maybe that comes from all the years she's listened to customers complain at the gas company. I told Adrienne she should take a lesson from Laura. Laura never wastes time creating a scene. She just realizes what needs to be done and gets started. Adrienne could save herself, and the rest of us, a lot of grief if she'd be more like Laura." The hiss was longer. It wasn't there every time he spoke. I started to listen for it.

In the back of the room, Grayson cleared his throat. I glanced warily at him, ready to motion him away. I didn't want any show of authority to inhibit what rapport I'd been able to develop with Yankowski. But Grayson wasn't looking at us.

72

I said to Yankowski, "Tell me what happened when Mitch got the soup?"

Awkwardly, he lifted a foot and placed it on the opposite knee. His legs were thick and muscular, the type that don't bend easily. "Mitch scooped some soup into a bowl and left. He always helps himself to a bowl of soup and sips it while he goes over the night's receipts. Like it was a mint julep."

"Who was in the kitchen then?"

"Adrienne, Ashoka, Laura, and me."

"But the last salad must have been made hours ago. Why was Laura still there?"

"Cleaning up, deciding what can be saved, what can't, labeling what can, noting how much of it there is and how soon it has to be used. The prima donnas will tell you being a chef requires brilliance, but running a restaurant takes organization. It doesn't matter how good you are, if you end up throwing out half your food every night you'll never make a profit."

I nodded. I wondered how long Yankowski had been a dishwasher. He seemed distinctly overqualified.

Standing, I motioned Yankowski toward the kitchen. "Don't touch anything."

"My fingerprints are all over anyway."

"We don't want you covering up someone else's prints. It's for your own protection."

He looked at me as if to say, *In a pig's eye.*

Careful not to react to that, I moved next to the warm table, by the dining room door. Down from it was one stove, across from it the other. Yankowski's pale bulky form looked as out of place here as I had imagined. "Earth Man usually came here at eleven o'clock, right?"

"Right."

"Tonight he says there was a note on the door telling him to come back later. Did you see the note?"

"No."

"Did you see anyone tack it up?"

"Nope." He started to lean back, then caught himself. His thin lips flickered in a half smile.

I smiled in response, anxious to establish the kind of bond that could be more valuable than any verbal assurances. "An hour later the note was gone. Did you see anyone taking a note down?"

"No. Look, at the end of a shift everyone's rushing around. No one's looking at anyone else, we're all just trying to finish up our own work. We've been at it seven or eight hours by then. Earth Man could have wallpapered the door and I wouldn't have noticed."

I sighed. I wasn't surprised at his response. He could easily have missed the note. He could have posted the note himself, in which case he might have good reason not to admit it. Or there could have been no note; I had only Earth Man's word it existed at all. "So what happened when Earth Man knocked on the door?"

"Mitch came flying out of the pantry, screaming about deadbeats."

"Why was he so angry?"

"Moody. He had a cold. He was worried about it. It put him in a shitty mood."

"How bad a cold?"

"Almost gone. Anyone else would have forgotten it, particularly on a busy night like that. But with him you'd think it was pneumonia. He was still using the horseradish. I'm surprised we had any customers left, the way he'd been sneezing and blowing out there all week."

I stared, amazed. Paradise was a small place. Even a delicate, shielded sneeze would resound through the dining room, disrupting the aura of understated elegance that Biekma had been so proud of. A barrage of snorts and blows would have been devastating.

"Why did he work the desk if he was that sick?"

Suddenly his face seemed to close. "Don't know."

I didn't believe that. "What would be your best guess?"

His shoulders tensed and stayed tense. Even though he wasn't speaking, the hiss permeated his breathing. His pale eyebrows were scrunched together, creating a hummock of flesh at the top of his nose. "Okay. Look, Biekma was an asshole. He shouldn't have been in here at all, sneezing and snorting all over the food. He could have infected half of Berkeley with his colds. He got them often enough. Why didn't he take a decongestant like a normal person? But no, he had to doctor himself with his horseradish. And he didn't touch that till he had his soup, after all the customers had left. Fat lot of good it did anyone at that hour. But tell him that. What did he care who he annoyed, who he infected, who he stepped on when he raced over the finish line first? Ashoka offered to host, but Biekma wouldn't have it. Not The Witty Voice of the Gourmet Scene, Mr. Almost Guest Host. No way would he share the limelight."

Yankowski's face was red; his breath screeched; the strong, silent facade was gone. Had Yankowski himself been one of the people Biekma had stepped on? Before he could regain control, I said, "You could have made more money waiting tables or busing dishes. Did Biekma keep you—"

"Nah. I don't want that," he said, breathing through his mouth.

"Why not?"

"Can't be bothered."

"Can't be bothered with what?"

"People. They're a pain in the ass. With dishwashing, I do my thing and I leave."

"Not in this kitchen, not according to you. You can't avoid people here. You can't even avoid Mitch Biekma. And for all that hassle you make, what, five bucks an hour?"

He tried to answer but his breath caught. He gasped. "Don't need much."

"There's more to it than that, isn't there?"

His faced purpled.

"What?"

75

Taking short, labored breaths, he peered nervously through the doorway into the dining room.

"Yankowski, withholding information in a murder investigation is a crime. I don't have to remind you about jail, do I?"

He clenched his hands over his elbows. Even with his mouth open, his breath was shrill. He looked like he'd take a bulldozer to move. I didn't want to have to call Grayson to help get him to a car.

"Yankowski, this is your last chance. Give me an honest answer or you can be silent at the station."

His hands clenched tighter. He hissed louder.

"We'll keep asking you; we'll run you through files, we'll talk to your neighbors and friends, and enemies. We'll send your fingerprints to the computer in Washington. We'll find what it is you're covering up. It'll just take time, ours and yours."

He didn't move. His breath was pitched so high it sounded ready to explode. Then it stopped. He grabbed me by the shoulders, lifted me up, and flung me back against the sink. I landed hard on my ribs. My feet flew out and I hit the floor.

The back door banged. Yankowski was gone.

CHAPTER 11

"Yankowski's gone!" I yelled to Grayson as I ran out the door, my back throbbing with each step. On Grove Path, I paused. Yankowski was nowhere in sight.

"Smith?"

I spun around. The rookie guarding the yard was pushing himself up. Where'd he go?"

Grayson banged out the door.

"Christ, the guy ran right over me," the rookie said. "I never saw him coming. He pushed me over with one hand!"

"Where'd he go?" I demanded.

"Toward Josephine."

"All the way through to the street?" Grayson asked. Lopez and Raksen rushed out the door.

The rookie thought a moment. "Footsteps sounded like it."

I ran for the street, as Grayson spewed orders—he had access to the walkie-talkie and the car radios; he would co-ordinate the search till the sector sergeant arrived. I had only a beeper, useless in a chase. Grayson yelled for the rookie to check Rue Driscoll's and the yard opposite, Lopez to guard the restaurant, and Raksen to get back to work. A light went on upstairs in Rue Driscoll's bedroom.

At Josephine I stopped, gritting my teeth against the pain in my back, and waited for Grayson. The house on the right was dark. Cars lined the curb. Yankowski could be crouched behind any of them. There was no sign of life across the street, no porch lights, no lights in bedroom windows. The people who slept there were too far away to hear Grayson on the radio telling the dispatcher to pull down the units from the north hills.

Through the thin fog I peered to the left. Branches swayed stiffly in the night wind, leaves crackled, and in the distance wind chime pipes smacked against each other atonally. Grayson shouted into the mike for Murakawa to circle south from Paradise. Two houses down, a cat skittered across the lawn. But there was nothing the size of Yankowski. To the right, trees in front yards shaded the streetlights. "How could he disappear so fast?" I demanded. "The guy's the size of a house trailer."

"Got a good jump on you. Should have had someone on the back door," Grayson muttered before pushing in the button on the mike to answer a call from officer 836.

"Mmm!" This wasn't the time to ponder "should haves."

There would be ample time later. I turned to the right again, looking up the street as it rose to a hummock two blocks away. Halfway between, at the far side of the parked cars, a shadow moved. "There he is! Look!"

"Stop where you are, Yankowski!" I yelled.

Yankowski froze momentarily, then raced toward the crest.

"Give me your flashlight."

Grayson thrust it toward me. Grabbing it, I ran full out, up the middle of the street, racing across the dark intersection. A block to the right on King Way, a car accelerated. With each step the pain clawed my back. I pumped my legs faster, pushing off harder. I hit the top of the rise. The block ahead came into view, but there was no sign of Yankowski. In the distance sirens of converging patrol cars singed the night. I pushed on to the corner and stopped, glancing right. No Yankowski. And left. Nothing. I had to choose. To the right was King Way—traffic, patrol cars. Ahead, another residential block. To the left a short block, then Martin Luther King Junior High School, with its three-winged building, its smattering of outbuildings, and a two-acre paved yard that dropped abruptly twenty feet down to the track, playground, and pool on the north side—a fugitive's heaven. A figure moved in the shadows by the school. Turning the flashlight on and off so Grayson would be sure to see, I pointed left. "School!" I yelled.

Grayson would have the dispatcher get units to the four corners surrounding the school yard. Backups on foot would head inward through the underbrush to the east, through the backyards on the west, the track and playground. They'd converge on Yankowski, if they weren't too late.

I ran down Rose, cutting right on Grant. To my left was the dark stucco wall of the school, to my right a smattering of tree-shrouded houses. The gate to the yard was closed, locked. Through the hurricane fence I could see movement in the school yard. Was that Yankowski? I ran for the fence, pulled myself up, flung a leg over the top, and dropped to the macadam. The pain exploded in my sacrum. A cry broke the silence of the yard. I slammed my mouth shut.

Where was Yankowski? Thick shadows hung off the wings of the main building, onto the acre of gray paving behind it, dark enough to hide him. Lights, dim against the fog of the night, looked more like mosquito lamps than beacons. I could make out the big square gymnasium across the yard, but the corners were fuzzy, and Yankowski, pressed unmoving against it, would be invisible. At the edges of the yard, the wind jostled the branches of tall full trees, but between the buildings there was no vegetation to be moved. In the dim light the school yard looked like a black and white photograph shot without a flashbulb—forever still, forever too dark to reveal its secret.

Revolver in one hand, I aimed the flashlight alongside the outbuilding to my right. The beam skimmed the ground till it was eaten by the fog. No Yankowski.

The sirens sounded closer, coming in from all directions.

Gritting my teeth against the pain, I moved forward, my rubber-soled shoes silent on the macadam. As I rounded the corner of the school, the wind whipped loose strands of hair in my face. I pushed it away and stared ahead at the deserted acre and a half of school yard. There were a hundred places to hide here, around the corners of the wings, under staircases, behind dumpsters, behind the outbuildings; or in the woody underbrush on the east side, in the backyards of the houses to the west; or around the pool, the playground, the trees that edged the track to the north. If he crossed Hopkins Street into the residential area with its maze of backyards, we could spend hours—and half the manpower in our department—and still not come up with him.

I flashed the light back into the black vee between these two thrusting wings of the school, but Yankowski wasn't there. The wind iced the sweat on my face and neck. Standing still, I listened for the slap of moving feet, for that labored hiss of Yankowski's breath. On King Way a car screeched to a halt, then started up. I noted the pitch of the sirens, trying to judge how close they were. Murakawa would be circling to the west. He should be rounding the corner soon onto Hopkins and coming up by the pool.

I stepped out farther into the yard. Headlights threw gray-white cones onto the macadam.

I peered across the yard toward the buildings at the north side. They were too far away for the flashlight beam. I could just see outlines through the fog, filling them in from memory. Near the gym was a small garage-sized structure, beside it a smaller storage shed. West of that was a large wooden umbrella with wings extending out on two sides; during the day seventy-five students clustered on the benches there out of the sun, lobbing scrunched-up papers in the general direction of the heavy, weighted metal waste-bins. To the west the earth had been humped up to create two small bare hills. I eyed them, for variations, a suggestion of a head peering over the top. Yankowski could be anywhere.

To my left the headlights of the patrol car threw long fuzzy beams. I paused, waiting for them to come nearer, and bathe the yard in their strong light. They didn't move. The car had stopped. Of course, the gate was locked; the driver would be climbing over as I had. He'd have called Grayson. Grayson would have notified the dispatcher, who would be trying to get hold of the school custodian. Fat lot of good! By the time the custodian got here, Yankowski could be in San Francisco.

A flashlight beam shone around the corner of school wall. I flicked my light. It fell on a uniform. Devlin? He flicked back. He would finish at the building.

My beam just made the unlit yard blacker. Turning it off, I started across the pavement, letting my eyes reaccustom themselves to the dark. I glanced back at the mounds of dirt, trying to see them as separate from the leaves waving in the distance. The mounds sat dark and unmoving. I shifted my gaze to the umbrella, checking along the extension toward the gynmasium. One of the support poles widened. Was there a trash can behind it? I flicked on the light. There *was* a trash can. And behind it, not shielded by the trash can, was Yankowski's thick arm, bare beneath the ripped edge of his gray T-shirt.

I raced toward him. My feet slapped the pavement. The shoulder holster slammed against my ribs. I couldn't make out Yankowski anymore. Nothing showed around the sides of the trash can. I cut to the left to get a better angle, to flush him back toward the main yard. Still, my light showed only the can, the benches, the wooden support poles. Had he moved to the other side? Was he still behind the can? Or had he scuttled behind the shield of the benches? I slowed to a walk. The wind whistled past. Listening for that hiss, I froze.

"Devlin!" I called. "Over here!" Shining the light toward the ring of benches under the center of the umbrella, I moved slowly northward, passing beside the near support pole. Behind me feet hit the pavement as Devlin ran toward me. I closed in on the circle of benches, aiming the light at the hollow in their center. It would be a fool's cover. I stepped closer. It was empty.

The hiss shrilled ahead. Revolver poised, I moved toward the heavy, weighted trash can, twenty feet away. "Stand up slowly, hands raised, Yankowski!"

Nothing moved. Outside the yard a car screeched to a halt. I sidestepped, edging in closer. The light beam caught Yankowski's bare elbow.

"I said stand up!"

Slowly, that bald pate, that thin pale hair, that twisted nose appeared. Then the trash can lifted up and flew forward, at me. I stared, mesmerized, in a world of slow motion, watching it float nearer. I could feel its breeze when I leapt to the side. It struck my shoulder, flinging me back onto the macadam.

I let out a gasp. My hand struck hard against the ground;

the flashlight went flying, but I held fast to the gun. My body shook with pain. I looked up to see Yankowski disappear over the edge of the yard, down the thirty-foot incline to the playground.

"What happened?" Devlin panted.

"Down the hill, there."

"Are you okay?"

"Fine, dammit," I snapped, grabbing his arm to pull myself up. "I'll take the north, you go south." I ran slowly, the pain one great blur. At the top of the stairs I stopped, looking down into the beamless dark. Yankowski could have been anywhere down there, hidden by trees, behind the pool house, or crouched behind the pillars and platforms of the playground.

There was a cement slide beside the staircase. I put on the safety, and holding the revolver with both hands, leapt feetfirst onto the slide, hitting one of the banked walls, ricocheting off into the other wall, going faster down into the dark, keeping my feet together, my hands steady on the revolver, scanning the dark for Yankowski. The slide leveled out, but I was going too fast to stop; I shot off the end and hit something with a thud.

The impact knocked me back, banging my elbows against the cement, crumpling me to the cement as they collapsed. The pain exploded inward. I couldn't stop the shaking. My breath roared in my head. A groan cut through. And another. It was a moment before I realized they were not my own. My fingers tingled weakly. I could barely feel the butt of the gun. From memory I forced myself to tighten my grip. Then releasing one hand, I pushed myself up, and looked down at the mound beneath the slide. What was it I had hit? "Yankowski?" I said with more hope than expectation.

"No," the breathless form forced out.

My eyes were adjusting; the black didn't seem so dark now. I could make out my victim's face. The face was thin, the hair dark and plentiful, the nose shallow but straight. It was not Yankowski; it was Murakawa.

CHAPTER 12

I'd let him escape! I'd had Yankowski fifteen feet from me; I'd had him at gunpoint and he'd gotten away! Again! Maybe Inspector Doyle was right; maybe it was too soon for me to come back to work. Maybe I should put in for a desk job where I couldn't do any damage.

I spent the next half hour looking for Yankowski in the underbrush on the slope; around the pool, the playground, the track; and back in the school yard. If he handled dirty dishes as adroitly as he had eluding me, he must have been the best dishwasher in town.

The sky was growing lighter. But fog shrouded the dawn. At quarter to six I walked back to Paradise. The pain in my lower back had receded to a heavy ache that throbbed with each step. It felt ominously familiar, the same ache that had been there for weeks after the helicopter crash. My ribs and shoulder still stung. Gritty dirt streaked my face and sweat matted my hair. I thought longingly of my house with its many-headed shower, its sauna, hot tub, and Jacuzzi. Great, Smith, just go home and loll in the tub; that's about what you're good for.

I picked up my purse from inside Paradise, fished out a Wash 'n Dri my mother had given me to use on the plane, and wiped my face. Even though the wipe was thoroughly brown after I finished, I suspected that my face still wasn't anywhere near clean. But at least now it wouldn't cause people to stop in the street.

Parked behind Mitch Biekma's vintage black Triumph in the Paradise driveway, the sector sergeant sat in his car. Grayson was leaning against the window. He glanced up. I eyed him hopefully.

"Nothing new," he said. His voice had no note of triumph. He hadn't beaten me; I'd beaten myself.

"I've already dismissed some of the backups," the sector sergeant said. "We'll give the rest of the guys till the end of shift."

I could tell how much hope *he* held out. I shrugged and headed down the driveway toward the front yard and Mitch Biekma's metal garden. In the pale morning light I could sympathize with the neighbors' complaints about this artistic statement. The metal sculptures, which last night had thrown ominously undulating shadows on the dark, fiery wall, now looked like a collection of garden paraphernalia left out in the fog too long. They looked not so much avant-garde as tacky.

"Which one was it Biekma fell over?" I asked the patrol officer on guard. He pointed to the sculpture nearest the door. It looked like a three-foot-high spear whose point had broken into five narrower, but equally sharp, segments—the bird of paradise. Moving closer, I could see the telltale dark stain on the tallest point.

Behind me a car pulled into the driveway. "Not the press," I muttered. Was it possible for this day to get worse? A front-page photo of the bloodstained sculpture, along with an article on the suspect's escape, would do it.

But the car was a black and white. The driver was opening the door for a blond woman who looked to be a few years older than I, maybe thirty-five. She wore faded jeans and a thin white shirt under an overlarge man's V-necked cardigan that seemed to be hanging onto her shoulders by friction alone. Clearly, she was exhausted. Everything about her sagged: her blond hair hung in limp curls; even her freckles seemed to weigh her skin down. She climbed slowly out of the car, and rested a hand on the top of the door. The muscles in her face stiffened as she stared at the metal flowers. "Which one?" she asked the patrol officer.

He looked confused.

I walked up. "I'm Detective Smith. Are you Laura Biekma?"

"Mitch was so proud of this garden." She shook her head. "He saw a beauty—no, that's not it. No, a stylishness—that's it—a stylishness that most people couldn't. At first I wondered if he was just saying that because he'd committed himself and didn't want to look a fool. But no, he really loved it. It's almost fitting that he should die . . ."

Laura Biekma was the one person in the kitchen Yankowski had approved of. She, if anyone, might know where he'd hide. But I couldn't attack her with questions on the sidewalk. "Come inside," I said gently, nodding at the patrol officer. I walked with her up the steps, and stood between her and the dining room as she paused in the entryway. Raksen was gone. Grayson was still outside. The only signs of an investigation were Lopez standing by the kitchen door, and the chalk outline of Biekma's body on the other side of the partition. I didn't want Laura Biekma to see that. She was shaky enough without that kind of shock. I didn't know how much longer she would hold together. Six to twenty-four hours was the rule with family members. When I worked on my first homicide as a beat officer, I assumed the husband of the victim would fall apart as soon as he heard the news. He didn't, not for a full fifteen hours. Then he went to pieces and couldn't be interviewed for days. Laura Biekma had had more than six hours. She had worked a full day yesterday, and been up all night. It spoke well of her that she'd held herself together this long. If she could just make it long enough to give me a lead to Yankowski.

I followed her up the stairs. The bottom seven, beneath the Plasticine door, were thickly carpeted. Behind the door the top six steps had rubber stair-runners. The walls beside them were scuffed and the moldings coated with greasy dust. It was clear that this apartment, where the Biekmas had lived for six years, was tantamount to a place where they stored their off-duty bodies.

"Come into the kitchen," she said. There was a low-pitched drag to her words, almost a hoarseness, as if they were coming from a tape played at too slow a speed. "I'll make you some toast and coffee. It's Acme Bakery bread."

I lowered myself gingerly into a director's chair, at the tiny table that folded down from the wall. Pain clamped my back.

Watching Laura as she poured water through the Melitta and cut slabs of bread for the toaster oven, I could see her relaxing in the arena she controlled. It was almost as if she had forgotten that she was the bereaved.

"Cream?" she asked, setting a sturdy white mug in front of me.

"Thanks."

She set a small bottle on the table, the type of milk bottle I had seen only in nostalgia ads. "It's so unfair. Why did he have to die now, just when he'd finally found his place?"

"What do mean, Mrs. Biekma?"

She sighed, a long shaky sigh that could easily have turned into tears. "Maybe Mitch was too talented. Nothing ever challenged him. In school he went through eight majors. There were always five or six half-done projects lying around our apartment. Before he'd finish, he find something else and be all enthusiastic about it. I thought that's the way our life would be, just scraping by, me working at the gas company all day and making all the practical decisions at home. Then he decided to open a restaurant. And it was as if overnight he grew up. I'll tell you, when he went to Paris to cooking school, I thought it was just another hobby, and when he came back, wouldn't have bet on it lasting a month. But he stuck with it. He even took courses in accounting and business management, and if you knew Mitch you'd know how much he hated stuff like that. And then, just when people recognized that Paradise was the best . . ." She sniffed back tears, swallowed hard, and then, concentrating all her attention, lifted her coffee cup and drank.

I waited until she set the cup down. "I know it's been a long night for you, Mrs. Biekma. There are just a few things that have to be dealt with now."

She nodded slowly. Now that they were no longer busy, her hands were shaking. I decided to ease into the point at issue. "Tell me about Frank Yankowski."

She looked up, surprised. Doubtless it was an odd-seeming question to someone who didn't know about Yankowski's disappearance. I held my breath, mentally backpedaling to prepare for her questions. But the moment passed. She didn't demand to know why. With a sigh, she picked up the coffee cup and held it an inch above the table. She had taken off the sweater. Her short-sleeved white shirt was blotched with tomato and oil stains. Her arms rested on the edge of the table just below the elbow, the surprisingly muscular flesh barely spread by the pressure of the table. "Frank has been with us about six months," she said in that near-hoarse voice. "He's the best dishwasher we've ever had. He never misses a day."

"Where was he before?"

Eyeing the cup, she considered. "He must have had references. We don't hire without them. We have enough problems *with* them."

I checked her hands. Was the shaking greater? How much time would I have? I didn't want to jar her fragile concentration. I'd go with her train of thought. "What kind of problems?"

"Some pilferage, but it's not a big problem with Mitch handling the checks. Mostly, it's just irresponsibility. Like tonight, the *sous*-chef didn't turn up. He said his tires had been slashed. We've heard that one before. We've heard them all. He didn't call till four P.M."

"Couldn't you get a replacement?"

"Not that late. If it had been noon, Mitch or I would have gone through the list."

"Does that happen often?"

"Sometimes they don't call at all. It's one of the inherent problems in the business. In a way, I'm not surprised," she said with a shake of her head. Moving the cup to her lips, she took a long swallow of coffee, and set the cup down with a sigh. This was not the "survivor" exhaustion she had exhibited a few minutes ago, but the in-the-business weariness of one who had dealt with, and complained about, employee problems on a day-to-day basis. Routine—making coffee, or serving coffee, or sitting here in her kitchen where she had had this discussion many times before—was taking over. "There are plenty of responsible salad chefs around. But restaurant work attracts transients. People are always deciding they want to go to L.A., or back to school, or they want to work in the place their lover does, or someplace where they get better money, or better hours, or which is closer to home, or has a different atmosphere. Or they've had a fight with their lover who also works there; then neither of them shows. If you don't feel like coming in one day, well maybe your boss will just have to lump it; if not, there's always another job—if you're young and reasonably presentable."

"What will happen with this sous-chef?"

"I'll hear from him; he's got nearly two weeks' salary coming. Then I'll see if his story is legit. If not"—she shrugged—"I'll have to start calling around."

"So you'll keep Paradise open then?"

"For now, I suppose. I haven't thought about the future."

I took down the name and address of the missing sous-chef, then said, "Frank Yankowski seems like a bright guy."

"He is." Her voice was sharper.

I could almost see the demand forming in her mind. Quickly, I said, "He doesn't seem like someone who wants to spend the rest of his life in the dishpan."

"No question."

"But he said he didn't want to be a waiter. Why?"

Her eyebrows pushed in, creating a hump above the bridge of her narrow nose. "Why are you asking me these questions? Why about Frank? My husband is dead. Why are you asking me about Frank?"

"Because he's disappeared. He ran out of Paradise before I finished questioning him."

"Oh, no."

"We have to find him."

"But you don't think . . . but of course you do, you think he was involved in Mitch's death, don't you?"

"He didn't make himself look good."

She pressed the sides of the coffee cup. "I can understand how you see things, but if you knew Frank . . . he's not a man who would kill. Mitch wasn't holding him back. He wanted him to be a waiter. He told Frank that he could make four or five times what he did now." The hoarse quality was gone from her voice, replaced by a sharp urgency.

"Then what was?"

"I hope this won't cause Frank problems," she said; then, realizing the ludicrousness of that possibility, she said, "I guess things are so bad now, whatever I say can only help him."

I smiled.

"It's Frank's ex-wife—Sarah, her name is. She dragged him into court four times over her alimony. Frank didn't like to talk about it."

"But he did," I prompted.

"Well, he had to, to explain why he didn't want to be a waiter. He didn't want anyone to recognize him."

"His divorce was local then?"

"No, it seemed like it was in the Midwest, St. Louis or Chicago, maybe. I don't know that he ever said."

"Why would anyone spot him here? Back alimony isn't a crime they send sheriffs across country for."

"Someone might have come across him by accident. His isn't a face you'd forget."

"That could have happened on the street, unless he'd stayed inside all the time."

She sighed. "I guess so. But this Sarah sounded like the type who would make it a point to find him."

"Because there was so much money involved?"

"I don't know." She stared down at the coffee cup.

"He lives in the Hillvue Hotel, right?"

She nodded.

The Hillvue was not the type of place that anyone who could afford to live elsewhere would choose. And no Hillvue tenant would merit a nationwide search for back alimony The whole thing sounded fishy.

"Is he using?"

Her pale eyes widened. "You mean drugs?"

I nodded.

"No."

"Are you sure?"

Now her eyes narrowed and in that expression I could see the woman who directed the running of a successful restaurant. "Detective, I make it my business to recognize the signs. Sometimes, I'm wrong. But I'm not wrong for six months. Frank has missed only one night's work. Every other night he's been here, on time. He doesn't take his breaks in the bathroom. He doesn't drop the china. If he'd been using, he'd have been gone five months ago, leaving half the dishes on the floor and the till empty." The force of the statement seemed to exhaust her and she sank back into the director's chair, letting the cup rest on the table.

"What does he do with his free time?"

"Movies," she said quickly. "He has a pass to the U.C. Theatre. He sees both features on his days off." The U.C. changed its bill daily.

"Regardless of what they are showing?"

"He just loves films."

I made a mental note to send someone to the U.C. They

should remember Yankowski. Like Laura Biekma said, he wasn't someone you'd forget. Perhaps he was there to pass his hours innocently, but a large dark theater may provide not only entertainment but also a good place for commerce. Still, he wouldn't be at the U.C. at six in the morning. Trying another tack, I said, "Who is Yankowski friendly with?"

"He's not friendly. He takes a long time to know." The hoarse quality had returned to her voice. How much longer could she hold up?

"What about the staff? The cook?"

She lifted her cup and sipped slowly. "A lot goes on in a kitchen. People are thrown together so much; we're always racing to get the food out. Everyone's wired. It's like the volume's all the way up all the time. Every attraction is great romance, every cooling of affection is tragedy. But Frank was different. He washed his dishes and kept his back to the melodrama."

"Mrs. Biekma, he's running from something. He's making himself look real bad. If we have to spend days looking for him, it'll be worse. Where would he hide?"

She stared down into the cup.

"When they're desperate, people do dangerous things, things that are harmful to themselves. You would be a friend to Frank by helping us find him. You said yourself that he couldn't have killed Mitch. So there's nothing to be gained by his hiding."

Slowly, she shook her head. "I'm sorry. I just don't know."

But she had hesitated too long. I felt sure she had some idea. Yankowski had tossed me aside like a used junk-food bag—twice. I wasn't about to leave him on the loose. "Mrs. Biekma, this is your husband's murder we're investigating. You do want his killer found, don't you?"

She sighed. "Of course I do. But it's not going to change anything. Mitch will still be dead. I'm so tired. I've got so much to do. I've got to talk to Adrienne. We'll have to close for a few days. There are notices to get out, reservations to cancel, orders to cancel so we're not inundated with rotting vegetables. So much to do."

Her eyes were losing their focus. She wasn't one of the ones who would suddenly become hysterical; she would just drift further and further from the topic. I'd get only a few more answers. "Who would want to kill your husband?"

"I don't know. The inspector asked me that. I don't know." She clutched the cup. "Things were just beginning to click for Mitch. He was so excited about his talk show shots. He loved that. And he was good. Have you seen him?"

"Yes. He was a natural. I heard they were considering him for a guest host on 'San Francisco Mid Day.'"

She nodded slowly. "That sounds a little more definite than it was. They did have researchers out here. But what the producers actually said was that Mitch needed a little more exposure to prove himself, to prove to them he could continue to draw an audience. Then they'd consider him. To Mitch it was definite, but, well, you know how those things are." Her breath caught. She pressed her lips together. "It's not fair that he should die. Why him? Why now?"

I shrugged. I'd heard those questions too often. There was no answer. Laura closed her eyes and breathed in— long, calming breaths. When she opened her eyes I asked, "What about the cook, Adrienne? She and Mitch didn't get along any too well, did they?"

"Sure, Mitch and Adrienne fought. They both needed to be in charge. You can't order a great chef around, and Adrienne is a genius."

"Is she above anyone you could have gotten to replace her?"

"Oh yes."

"Did Mitch think so?"

"Well . . ."

"Then if he wanted someone he could have more control over and he thought there were other cooks of her caliber around, why didn't he replace her?"

She lifted the cup and seemed surprised to find it empty.

"Well, it was financial. It takes a lot of money to open a restaurant, any restaurant. No less than a hundred thousand dollars. Paradise, with the building, and the garden, well, it ran a lot more than that. My salary was our biggest ongoing asset. Even with a loan from my father, we didn't have enough. So Adrienne owns a third."

"Of the restaurant and the building?"

"No, just the restaurant."

"Isn't that giving her a lot of power?"

"There was no way to avoid it. In the beginning, we thought we'd have enough money. That was before he finished cooking school in France. We were just naive then. We never considered taking a partner. But when we realized we'd have to, dealing with Adrienne seemed much better than with a stranger, with someone we couldn't be sure would understand what a really fine kitchen required."

"Wasn't Mitch the chef for a while?"

"Both of them were. It didn't work out. To much conflict, like I said."

"Mrs. Biekma, this conflict, how strong was it?"

She laughed, shrilly, wavering on the edge of hysteria. "Adrienne might kill him, but she wouldn't poison him in her own kitchen."

CHAPTER 13

A patrol officer sat at the desk outside Inspector Doyle's office. "He's waiting for you, Smith," he said in a tone that suggested it would be tidy of me to take a box to catch my head.

I rapped perfunctorily on the glass door of the inspector's office, looking through the window in the upper half. His head was tilted down, as if he were studying a microscopic clue poised on the edge of his desk. When I had first seen him his hair had been carrot red, but now, four years later, gray had muted it to unripe strawberry. His liver-splotched skin hung even more limply than usual, as if it were merely tossed over the flesh rather than being attached to it. Compared to him, Laura Biekma had looked ready for the Olympic Trials. Only his jaw showed life, and it was set in anger.

"I thought you'd be here an hour ago," he growled.

"I was interviewing the widow. She could fall apart any minute," I said quickly. Inspector Doyle's tirades were legendary. His enraged voice had often been heard well down the hall, his face still red twenty minutes after his victim had slithered away. He was said to have chewed out two officers involved in a botched knifing investigation so thoroughly that they quit law enforcement altogether, one after nineteen years on the force. I didn't believe that story, but my skepticism provided me little comfort.

"Sit down, Smith."

I sat, careful not to give any sign of the pain that grabbed my back with each movement, or to twist enough to loose the hot, searing knife into my shoulder; I couldn't disguise my reaction to that. I didn't want to give him legitimate grounds to wonder about my health.

His gaze didn't rest on me, and it didn't change, but I suspected he had given me the once-over and made his assessment.

"Did you see the press outside, Smith?"

"I came around back."

"Ah, well, I wish I could *come around back* and steer clear of that mob. The press conference isn't for another hour. By then we'll be renting a hall."

I didn't respond.

"And what is it I'll be telling them then? My detective let a suspect, the chief suspect, wander off. I can tell them we've taken six cars off the streets, leaving our local burglars free to help themselves all over north Berkeley. And what have we turned up? Zip."

I still didn't reply. He wasn't saying anything I hadn't already told myself. Losing Yankowski was no one's fault but my own.

He leaned forward onto the heap of papers that covered his desk. "Holy Mother, Smith, I asked you if you were well enough to handle this, didn't I? If you'd only told me you couldn't—"

"I *would* have told you, if I'd felt—"

"The suspect escaped!"

"The guy was a giant! He tossed the rookie in the backyard aside like an empty sack."

"Smith, you let the suspect escape twice!"

"I chased him. I caught up with him in the school yard."

"And you lost him, again!"

"He threw a garbage can at me!"

"You should have been out of his range."

"That can weighed over a hundred pounds, Inspector. They weigh them down so the kids don't roll them all over the school yard. I was fifteen feet away from Yankowski. I didn't figure I was dealing with Atlas."

Doyle stared, face redder than his hair, cheeks quivering. In the silence I realized we had both been shouting. I didn't wait for him to continue. "I lost him, Inspector. No one's angrier about it than me. But dammit, it wasn't because I'm sick. Or"—I waited till he looked up—"because I'm a woman. Bubba Paris wouldn't have stopped him!"

He stared at me, the loose flesh on his cheeks still pulsing, his breathing almost as labored as Yankowski's had been. As always, his expression revealed nothing. I couldn't tell whether he was convinced by my argument, surprised at its vehemence, or just taken aback by my invoking the name of the 49ers' offensive tackle. Or, more likely, I had hit on the underlying issue of sex, the issue he wasn't prepared to raise.

"Inspector, I know his identity, I've got the charge"—felonious assault, three counts, one for the rookie in the back-yard and two for me—"and we're in hot pursuit. I'll get a Ramey warrant as soon as a judge is in this morning. Yankowski's not going to knock me around and walk off free. You can count on that."

Leaning back in his chair, he said, "All fine and good, Smith. What about Yankowski? Did Biekma's wife give you any leads on where he'd go to hide?"

"She said she didn't know. Whether that's true or not, I can't say."

"You think there was something between the Biekma woman and Yankowski?"

Considering Laura Biekma in that light, I wondered if rather than fighting exhaustion to answer my questions, she could have been drawing out her replies to keep me occupied, to keep me from Yankowski's trail. "Each one of these people saw Laura as an ally. Rue Driscoll told me Laura understood the importance of her research. Laura made a fuss over Earth Man's dinners. And Yankowski gave Laura a story about an ex-wife he's supposed to be hiding out from. According to her, he wasn't one to con-fide, but he confided in her. And he was plenty pissed off about Mitch Biekma."

"More personal than a disgruntled employee?"

"Sounded like it."

"So maybe Yankowski decided to take matters into his own hands, huh? Or maybe the wife did. What's your as-sessment of her, Smith? You think she was playing these people?"

"I don't know. The impression I get is that she was just balancing Mitch's self-centeredness."

"Still, she owns two-thirds of the restaurant now. And she lived right above the kitchen."

"The thing is, Inspector, the poison was almost certainly in the horseradish. And anyone could have gotten to that."

"Which leaves us nowhere. And it's twenty-five to

eight," he said, fingering a sheet of paper on his desk. Quarter-to was Detectives' Morning Meeting.

I didn't move. "There's another odd thing. Rue Driscoll, the woman who led the fight against Paradise's later hours, says she got food poisoning there."

"I don't recall that in the news."

"It was *after* the hearings."

"*After?* How does she seem to you? You buy her story, Smith?"

I hesitated. "That part, yes. There's no reason for her to make it up. Besides, that's not the oddest thing. There's been another food poisoning there."

"Corroborating?" He dropped the paper and grabbed a pencil. "Who's this?"

"Earth Man."

"Mother of God, Smith, what is this, a circus? I'm trying to find some redeeming factors in this fiasco, and you're giving me a crusader, a giant, and a crazy."

I sighed. "I wish there were better facts to give you."

He shook his head, and sighed. Fingering the paper, he looked blankly at it, then looked back at me. "I'm leaving you in charge, Smith, for now."

I stared. I had misjudged the whole conference here. I'd thought we were assessing the case. But he was assessing me!

"But you're going to get me something fast."

"My in-box should be clear."

"And Smith, you're going to have to handle it with less help."

"Inspector?"

"Murakawa. He may have a cracked rib."

As I put my hand on the door handle, Inspector Doyle said, sotto voce, "It's going to make them a great story."

I didn't respond. There was nothing to say. It was indeed going to make great reading in the afternoon editions.

"The city's most flamboyant restaurant owner is impaled

on his own brass flower," he went on. "The suspect gets away, and instead of catching a six-foot-four, two-hundred-and-fifty-pound fugitive, my detective crashes feet first into a patrol officer."

I pulled the door toward me.

"They're going to have one word for this." His hands clutched the armrests.

"What?" I said, holding my breath.

"Keystone."

CHAPTER 14

Detectives' Morning Meeting starts at 7:45 promptly. I checked my in-box—the in-box I had so innocently thought would be empty—and my share of the "in custody"s from last night were waiting. Murder or not, the suspects in the holding cells had to be processed, and it was the four of us in Homicide–Felony Assault who did the processing. Monday mornings were the worst, when the whole weekend load was waiting, but today, there were only two "in custody"s. I picked up the sheets and began the tedious process of checking to make sure I had the right names, then getting personal file numbers, county booking numbers, arresting officer numbers, and case numbers. I looked over the paperwork in each folder. The ID technician's reports were there. The arresting officers' reports were complete, though one was handwritten and barely legible. There was a typed report from Lieutenant Davis, my watch commander when I had been on beat, in the case he had gone out on. That one had two reports, also typed, from officers called on assist. But in the other folder the assisting officer's report was missing. "Damn." I glanced at my watch: 7:40. I headed through the bull pen to the patrol sergeant's desk.

He looked up, his brow wrinkling when he saw who it was. "Welcome back, Smith, if that doesn't sound too sarcastic." He made a noise that was somewhere between a laugh and a snort, as if unsure whether his reaction to my losing a suspect should be sympathy or pretense of ignorance. He then moved on to safer ground: "You get yourself all healed up in the Florida sun?"

"Yes. But it seems like a year ago now." I pointed to his transfer tray. He nodded. And I riffled through. The report wasn't there.

7:42. I checked the transfer tray for Report Review. It was half full. But luck had thrown me a morsel this time; my case was on top. Grabbing it, I headed back to my office, and shoved it in the folder. These two cases were simple assaults. I needed only to drop them off with the liaison officer. With felony assaults, we hand-carried them to the DA's and explained the background information the standard phrases on the forms couldn't relay. Did "serious disfigurement" mean a gash at the hairline that would be almost unnoticeable in a month or two, or did it refer to a slash across the face that could change the victim's life? Had a perpetrator broken a victim's cheekbone with only one punch, or had he aimed on smashing it to paste? Was the eighteen-year-old perp a true first offender, or did he have a long juvenile record? It always amazed me how so much paperwork, which took so much time to complete and required so many copies, could leave so many questions unanswered.

At 7:44, I slid into an empty seat at the conference table. Across the table was Grayson. What was he doing here? He wasn't a detective. It wasn't customary to have the scene supervisor report. A few seconds later, Clayton Jackson, one of the other homicide detectives, took the seat to my left, proffering a cup of coffee brewed by his son Pernell. Pernell and I had initiated a deal in the spring semester, when he had been dropped from the junior varsity swim team: I would coach him swimming; he would make me a thermos of coffee each morning. Between my accident and my convalescence here and in Florida, Pernell hadn't bene-fited much. On the other hand, he hadn't had to get up early to make coffee either. But now, the deal was back in full swing. Tuesday night he would be in the pool working on flip turns. Jackson rubbed his finger across my tanned arm and grinned. "Lookin' good. Another couple of weeks and you'd be one of the family."

"Couple of years is more like it!" Jackson was ebony black.

Howard made it to his chair just as the captain walked in. Howard grinned. I smiled. I hoped he had thought to bring some of the clothes I'd left with him. The turtleneck I had on, which I'd donned yesterday morning in Florida, was streaked with dirt and matted with sweat.

The usual items on the agenda—the hot car report, the "watch-for"s from Night Watch—went quickly. Most of Night Watch had been on the Yankowski search. Givens from Auto Theft gave a recap on the Walnut Square thief. "He, or she, steals a car three days a week, up in the hills. Some days it's near the Oakland line, others it's all the way over near El Cerrito. Old cars, new cars, stick shifts, auto-matics. Looks like he takes whatever's available."

"You mean what's left unlocked." It was Washington from Crimes Against Property. Unlocked doors drove him crazy.

"Or open windows. I figure he just cruises along till he finds his mark. There's no consistency in his pickings. If we have to nab him in the hills, we'll be looking till every car above sea level is parked at Walnut Square. That's where he leaves them."

"Dude must have better luck parking there than I do," Jackson muttered.

"It's not so hard parking there if you're willing to leave your car in a twenty-minute spot or a red zone."

"No quarter in the meter, huh?" Jackson asked.

Givens shook his head. "Too smug. And why shouldn't he be? By the time we get out there, he's sitting on the bus to San Francisco."

"But why Walnut Square?" Washington asked.

"Peet's coffee," came the chorus.

Givens nodded in disgust. "I can just see the smug bastard stealing a car, driving it down the hill, buying a cup of Garuda Blend, and a *Chronicle*, and waiting for the bus to the city."

"A gourmet car thief!"

"So, Givens, you looking for volunteers to stake out Peet's?" Jackson asked, laughing.

"Yeah, Clay, but you're a big shot now, too important for stakeouts. I've got a patrol officer who'll do undercover nicely."

The captain broke up the laughter. "Smith, the Biekma murder."

I glanced at Inspector Doyle, but he shook his head—nothing worth passing on. I recounted the case. "Mitchell Biekma, the owner of Paradise, was poisoned last night," I began. Another time, with a case that hadn't embarrassed the department, someone would have said, "I thought only the prices were poison." But the humor in the room had vanished as totally as Yankowski. I described the scene in the kitchen when Mitchell Biekma got his soup and screamed at Earth Man. I told them of Earth Man's claim that he had been poisoned, and of Rue Driscoll's.

"And now Biekma?" Washington asked. "Same poison?"

I glanced at Raksen, who, like Grayson, was doing a "guest shot" at the meeting. Raksen, edgy any time he wasn't discussing camera angles or processing chemicals, looked small and wiry, like a mustachioed miniature schnauzer set on a chair he's not allowed on, desperately wanting to jump off but afraid to disobey the command to stay. Next to him Howard looked like the family golden retriever who settles wherever he chooses and waits for a scratch behind the ears.

"The lab reports aren't in yet, of course. They won't be back till next week at the earliest," Raksen said.

I nodded. Everyone knew that. "Can you give us an educated guess?"

"Better than that. It's aconite. No doubt about it. I don't know how I missed it last night. The guy was eating horseradish! It's not in the soup, but the jar; it's full of it—straight aconite. Stupid! I can't—"

"Aconite," the inspector prompted before Raksen slipped into prolixity.

Raksen swallowed. He recognized his tendency to get carried away. He knew the rest of us did too. "Aconite is the root of monkshood, *Aconitum napellus*," he said stiffly. "But the whole plant is poisonous. The leaves look like parsley, and the tuber—the root—is often mistaken for . . . horseradish!"

"Bingo!" Jackson said.

Raksen shook his head. "How could I have missed it? It's an alkaloid. Tincture of aconite is a skin irritant in liniments. Initially it stimulates the myocardium, then it depresses the central nervous system. The tinctures and liniments have been used for relieving toothache, neuralgia, and rheumatism. But it's toxic enough to be poisonous when absorbed through the skin. Aconite has a long history; one of the Roman emperors made it illegal for citizens to grow it, and the Greeks called it 'stepmother poison.'"

Gone was the wary miniature schnauzer look. Engrossed in the explication of one of his favorite topics, Raksen balanced on the edge of his chair, eyes glowing, mouth tensed—now like a full-grown standard schnauzer about to pounce on a fat rabbit.

"Raksen, what are the symptoms of aconite poisoning?"

"Nausea, vomiting—"

"Like Biekma," Grayson put in.

"Numbness and tingling of the mouth, throat, and hands, blurred vision—"

"That would cause him to run into that metal bird of paradise in the garden," Grayson summed up proprietarily.

But Raksen wasn't through. "Fall of blood pressure, convulsions, and respiratory failure. And, here's the clincher." He paused, glancing around the table. "With a dose of one to two milligrams, death can come in eight minutes."

"Pay now, go now!" Howard said.

"Raksen," I said. "Did you, by any chance, check on the poison in Earth Man's food?"

Raksen grinned like I'd put the rabbit next to his water dish. "Of course."

"And?"

"Bingo. Of course, you won't hear that from the lab for a while."

"But you're sure they're the same?"

"As sure as I can be without waiting for the test results. But I did some testing on aconite in school. I know I'm right."

"Good work."

He threw up his hands and grinned. "Nothing any obsessive wouldn't do."

"That's fine," Inspector Doyle said in a tone that indicated anything but fine. "But I don't want this *speculation* to leave this room. As far as the public perception of the case goes, we still don't have anything more than a corpse and a missing suspect." Turning to Grayson, he asked, "What's the status of Yankowski?"

So that was why Grayson was here, subbing for the sector sergeant.

"Still missing," he said. "It's like the man vaporized. Doesn't have a car, but he might as well have. The man's too big to miss. No one reported a possible sighting, not all night long. Wasn't on the street, wasn't on a bus, didn't call a cab. We had twelve cars circling King School till seven. I

SUSAN DUNLAP

still have six. I had Morning Watch alert Parking Enforcement and the school crossing guards. I've got a man on his hotel, and"—Grayson looked at me for the first time—"the U.C. Theatre."

I told Morning Watch! *I* got a man at the theater! Grayson certainly took substituting for the sector sergeant seriously. In a minute he'd be denying the sergeant ever coordinated the chase.

"Good work," the captain said. To me, he added, "Anything else we should know about the suspect?"

"There's no record of him in files. He's not known to Corpus—no arrests, or PIN—no warrants. I'll check with DMV as soon as they open."

It was Inspector Doyle who had the last word. "I've got a press conference in half an hour. And I can tell you, what we have here is a lot of speculation, and a lot of manpower to account for. But as for solid leads, we're batting zero." To me he said, "Check with me after lunch."

I had been planning to go home, shower, change, maybe catch a nap. But there would be no time for that. I was just glad I had slept when I got in last night. Doyle might think I was too battered to manage the investigation, but apparently he didn't consider sleep a cure. When I came into his office after lunch, he'd be expecting me to bring something.

CHAPTER 15

I hurried out of the conference room, not that anyone was likely to stop me. The office I shared with Howard was morning dark. The small slatted window on the west wall was closer to a decoration, albeit a tasteless one, than a purveyor of light. And what sun it did admit wouldn't come till afternoon. The room was barely more than six feet wide. If Howard had lain across the floor, his head would have been up the wall. As it was, the desks filled all but a narrow path, and when I pushed my chair back, I first had to turn to make sure Howard's desk drawers were closed.

Leaving the light off, I slumped in my chair, pulled out the phone list, and squinted till I found the number for Motor Vehicles.

It wasn't till I had dialed, and sat listening to the phone ringing at DMV, that I felt the throbbing in my back. Had I blocked it off with fear, anger, determination during the interview with Doyle and the Morning Meeting? If so, it was having its revenge. I shifted my weight to the right; the pain eased momentarily, then seeped back like water wetting a cloth. I shifted again, but it didn't help. Sandpapery fingers squeezed my lower back. Bed rest, the doctor had told me after the accident. But I couldn't rest now.

"California Department of Motor Vehicles," a morning-chipper voice said. It took two transfers and ten minutes for them to tell me they had no record of Yankowski. He hadn't been cited for a violation, hadn't been a victim, hadn't applied for a license.

"He has no California driver's license?" I repeated. "He's lived here at least six months; he should have taken the test."

"Of course he should have," the clerk snapped. "They all should. But these guys drive on out-of-state licenses for years. You'd think we were asking them to hand over the family jewels, instead of a year-old Oklahoma license. They keep on renewing them from parents' or friends' addresses in Enid or Norman. Either they're afraid to take the test, or they're too lazy, or too cheap. And they're not the worst," she said, warming to her grievance. "The worst are the ones from Jersey and Connecticut. They're not about to give up their precious licenses. They think they're worth more than ours. I've had them tell me that to my face."

I smiled, having been one of the holdouts, afraid that if I

returned to Jersey they would scoff at a license from a state like California where wimpy drivers rarely blew their horns, or blocked intersections trying to make left turns. I had no intention of going through the hassle of taking the road test in Jersey again.

I put down the receiver and turned to find Howard sitting upright in his chair. Connie Pereira and Clay Jackson stood inside the door. And Al "Eggs" Eggenburger, senior even to Jackson in Homicide, shifted from foot to foot by the small slatted window. No matter what his surname, with his pale ovoid face he would have been called Eggs. The four of them looked not quite right. Normally, Howard leaned back in his chair, arms folded over his chest, feet angled across the room, so they rested near the door. Normally, Pereira perched on his desk, and rested her feet on the bottom drawer. Normally, Jackson and Eggs didn't come in here together.

"You got yourself a real stinker, Smith," Jackson said. "One way or another it's going to make you one famous lady."

"Infamous the way things are going," I said, shifting in my chair.

"There are enough reporters out front to cover a summit," Eggs said. "And for them Mitchell Biekma is —you should pardon the mundane expression—their bread and butter. He didn't lift a spoon without someone writing a column. Last month he broke one of his metal flowers in that garden of his and the trauma was reported on the six o'clock news. Wednesday someone delivered health club equipment there by mistake and it made page three in the *Chronicle*."

"That was on the evening news too, or so Rue Driscoll told me."

"I saw it. Biekma said at first he was affronted that the delivery drivers hadn't heard of Paradise. Then, he said, after they left he got to thinking maybe he should convert his upstairs into a spa so his customers could work off dinner." Eggs smiled in reminiscence. "The guy did a great interview. He even had the reporters laughing. The press is going to miss him, or they would if his murder weren't such a great story."

"I get the picture. I know the longer this case takes, the greater the pressure, from the press, the city council, the chamber of commerce. Like you always say"—I looked at Howard—"it could make the department, and me, look real good, or real bad."

"You think Yankowski's your man, Jill?" Howard pushed a pile of papers back from the corner of his desk.

Connie Pereira settled on the cleared spot. Her short blond hair was slightly curled, and her makeup so skillfully applied that only someone who had been in the bathroom with her would realize she was wearing it. Her tan uniform was crisp and fresh, and she looked eager and interested. She looked like the "After" photo, compared to me as the "Before." Of course she hadn't been up all night either. She'd barely been at the station long enough to discover I had commandeered her, and to get a handle on the case. "Why would he poison Rue Driscoll, Earth Man, and now Biekma?"

"There some connection between these three?" Jackson asked.

"I don't see them as Athos, Porthos, and Aramis," Eggs said.

"Or Rhett, Scarlett, and Ashley," Howard said.

"The only similarity," I said, "is that I can't imagine any one of them deigning to be in the same room with the other two."

"But someone poisoned all three of them," Pereira insisted. "And Earth Man was worried enough about being poisoned to save the dish for two months." She waved Parker's report on the retrieval of the dish. "In case any of you are considering cryogenics, Parker tells me the marvel of refrigeration can only do so much."

"The smells coming from Earth Man's room must have made a hit with the neighbors," Eggs said.

"La Maison's not that kind of hotel," Pereira put in. "Believe me. Spoiled food is like a continental breakfast there. Parker says when he went for that revolting plate of green fungus Earth Man was saving, he couldn't be sure which one it was. Earth Man had three dishes sheathed in Saran Wrap. Parker took them all and left Earth Man with his beaks flopping up and down in fury. He swore that two of those plates were from this week. But according to Parker, they all looked the same—like dog food left on the counter for a week."

"According to all the witnesses, Mitch hadn't touched the horseradish since he'd doctored his soup Wednesday night. He used it only in the soup; he ate that only after the customers had left. So the poisoner had twenty-four hours to add the aconite to his jar," I said.

"But he couldn't just mosey into the kitchen and make the switch. He'd have to have watched for the right moment. That might not have come for hours. And when Mitch was in the kitchen, no one was near him and his jar," Howard said.

"No one but Earth Man. He was standing nearly on top of Biekma and his soup," I said.

"Could have dropped that poison right down through his trunk, huh?" Jackson laughed. "Police work. You do get into the nitty-gritty."

Howard could barely control himself enough to speak. "Take the press, Jill. They'll be impressed with how thorough you are when they see you with your finger up the trunk."

"Okay, out, all of you. I've got paperwork to do. And for the first time, paperwork looks good."

When they had cleared out I started on the affidavit for the Ramey warrant. The advantage of the Ramey is that the judge requires only enough documentation to support the charge, in this case the felonious assault charge. If I'd had to present all the paperwork from the Biekma case the judge would have left for the day before I'd been ready. As it was, it took me forty-five minutes, and another half hour to check it over with the DA, before I took it to the judge's office. I was prepared for his questions—hot pursuit can be a touchy issue—but this time there were none.

It was ten-thirty before I walked back to the patrol car. The morning fog still wedged itself between buildings, holding the night-cold air close to the earth. On the plane I had hoped that June would still be spring here, with spring's warm, clear days. Too late. It was already summer, with nights of fog that didn't burn off till ten in the morning or—like today—even later.

I turned west on University Avenue, which connected the campus to the bay, slowing down as I passed a Volkswagen beetle decorated with bright blue paint, life-sized fruits in place of bumpers, and on the roof a globe topped with a wildly spinning windmill. On the sidewalk a street person pushed three supermarket carts tied together, each lined with four-foot-high cardboard and crammed to the top. Whatever was on the bottom of those carts probably hadn't been seen since in months. I smiled, suddenly flushed with delight at being back in Berkeley, in a city intent on protecting its harmless eccentrics.

For years Telegraph Avenue—with its array of head shops, Asian import outlets, and street artists who sold tie-dyed shirts, incense, and feather earrings—had symbolized Berkeley. But Telegraph had changed in recent years. Now cookie franchises, sportswear franchises, computer franchises were the norm. And it was University Avenue that preserved the essence of the Berkeley that had drawn so many of us: University, with its used-clothing stores, its sari shops and Indian outlets, where you could buy garam masala or statues of Shiva, the Destroyer; University, where you could take your wheelchair in for repair, or have pipe tobacco blended specially; University, where you could find a bookstore-café combo, or the U.C. Theatre, which changed its bill daily. It was here that people like the cart pusher and Earth Man felt at home.

I was halfway to La Maison before it occurred to me that while I had kidded with Eggs and Jackson this morning, and had stopped by Pereira's desk on my way out to ask her to go over the Paradise books, I hadn't said anything to Howard. I hadn't said I was glad to see him. I hadn't even asked about my clothes. Lumping him with Jackson, Eggs and Pereira, I had simply shooed him out of the office—the office that was half his.

CHAPTER 16

La Maison was known to its inhabitants as La Maison de Flop. It was a rectangular building that occupied half a block on Addison Street, backing onto University. The facade had once been painted green, but that had been some time around World War II. In the intervening years fog and wind and pollution had worn through the paint to reveal splotches of beige stucco. But La Maison was a clear example of the adage "Sloth pays." With more years of neglect, dirt and exhaust had covered the building so completely that it was impossible to distinguish the stucco from the paint.

La Maison extended back nearly to the edge of the property line, as did Yankowski's hotel. There was just space to walk between the buildings. And there were two common airshafts about the size of the Paradise kitchen, long and narrow. A lot went on in those airshafts. They were known as the chambers of commerce.

An unmarked car pulled up across the street from La Maison. I recognized Heling at the wheel. Even at this distance I could see her familiar sigh as she settled back against the seat to watch the hotel doorway. I walked to the car. "I'm going to need a backup on this."

"Sure, Smith, any diversion." She followed me across the street, kicking a broken green bottle out of the way. Had it been in Jersey City, or Newark, the exterior of the hotel would have reeked of urine; paper cups, napkins, hamburger bags, and Styrofoam boxes would have matted against its walls. But here, the strong winds that pulled the quilt of fog in off the Pacific at night kept the air clean and dispersed the litter.

But the wind didn't reach beyond the door—to the stench of dried urine and ammonia, to the dirt, dust, and grease that covered the floor and walls. There was, of course, no desk at La Maison. The manager's apartment was next to the door. I knocked. I wasn't surprised when there was no answer. The television continued to chatter. I pounded. "Police, open up!"

Footsteps approached, and slowly the door opened to reveal a man in his fifties or his eighties—there was no way to tell. His long curly unclean gray hair hung over the shoulders of his work shirt, and the shirt hung loose over his fragile frame. Once he might have been nearly six feet tall; now he wasn't much more than my five seven. Whether the cause was age, drugs, ill health, or, more likely, the coming together of all three, I couldn't guess. He didn't bother to ask for my ID. He probably hadn't bothered in twenty years.

"What room is Earth Man in?"

"Earth Man? You don't want him."

I was in no mood for this. "What room?"

"Listen, lady—"

"*Detective.* Skip the defense. What room is he in?"

"Okay, but you're making a mistake. It's one eleven," he said, slamming the door.

I had been in my share of seedy hotels when I had the Telegraph beat. In some of those places families lived in the

one or two rooms meant for offices. They used the toilet by the
stairs. For their children the hallways were the Indianapolis of
big wheels. But there were no children here, no smells of
garlic or cilantro. The smells here were ones Earth Man would
feel at home with. The walls were no cleaner than his cloak,
and there was a puddle in the stairwell that didn't bear too
close examination. With each door I passed, I had the sense of
flipping from one radio station to another.

Room 111 was at the end of the hallway, facing one of the
airshafts. Automatically, Heling moved to the far side of the
door. I knocked. There was no sound inside. I waited, then
knocked again. "Earth Man, open up!"

It was the door behind me that opened, a crack. Whiny
sounds of country music flowed out. Three feet away I
could smell the cotton-candy perfume. Mixed with the La
Maison smells, it was nauseating. From the darkness a
gravelly female voice said, "Whadya want with him?"

"It's okay," I said, leaning closer to Earth Man's door,
listening for footsteps.

"He's gone."

"Gone where?"

"Gone. With him, who knows?"

But I figured with her I didn't know either. I knocked on
Earth Man's door again, four times, the police knock.
"Open up, Dana!"

"You're wasting your knuckles," the woman said, and
slammed the door, sending the perfume toward me in a
final gust.

I sighed. Chances were she would be proved right.

I was about to leave when the door opened a sliver.

"Did you get your donuts last night?" I asked.

"Oh, it's you." The door opened. At first I thought Earth
Man was standing by the opposite wall. But it was just his
cloak standing by that wall—draped on something life-
sized, I fervently hoped. I didn't want to think how dirt-
encrusted it would have to be to actually stand alone. With
its beaks and snouts and elephant trunk, it wasn't a gar-

ment to be folded in a drawer. Earth Man himself was wearing a gray sweatsuit. If it hadn't been for the aureole of blond hair surrounding his thin face, if it hadn't been for the residue of white paint and glitter on his thin, high-bridged nose, he might have looked like any Berkeleyan ready for an afternoon's run or read. I realized, with amazement, that unlike the odoriferous cloak, his hair was clean, and he didn't smell at all. How he tolerated being inside the cloak was something I would find out soon enough.

It was clear from a glance at the rumpled bed that we had indeed awakened him.

"I need to see your cloak, Earth Man," I said softly.

"You saw it last night."

"I need to look at it again."

He scrunched his eyes in thought.

The longer we stood in the hall, the greater the chance of a hassle. "Earth Man, now!"

He stepped back. I followed him in and walked to the cloak. But it wasn't supported by grime alone. As soon as I touched the chest, I could feel the form beneath it—a dress form. The type grandmothers had in their bright, starched-curtained sewing rooms. I almost laughed. But I should be thankful for small favors, I reminded myself. The cloak needed all the airing it could get.

Turning away, I took a breath, and bending down, peered up the inside of the elephant trunk. Darkness. Feeling much the same revulsion I would have in dealing with a real elephant, I stuck my finger up the trunk. Beside me Heling pressed her lips together hard. "Cloth," I said. "Solid cloth at the end."

"The hole could have been sewn closed," Heling said, her voice breaking as she tried to control herself.

To Earth Man I said, "I'm going to have to see this from the inside."

Earth Man looked as appalled as I felt.

I didn't dare make eye contact with Heling. "Take it off the dummy," I said to Earth Man.

For a moment he didn't move; then, frowning with worry, he took the shoulders of the cloak and inched it up over the dress form. Halfway off, the fabric caught. Earth Man's eyes widened in horror. Swallowing her grin, Heling grabbed the hem and lifted the cloak free.

Then she handed me her flashlight. I took a last breath and ducked inside. It was close, hot, and smelled like a bear cave at the end of winter. I flashed the light slowly, systematically back and forth, inch by appalling inch. I took short breaths, as if their shallowness would filter the smell. Sweat beaded my forehead, ran down my back and sides, adding nothing to the congeniality of the environment.

"No holes," I said when I emerged.

"Oh, no," Earth Man said. "I'm very careful with it. It's very fine wool, you saw that, didn't you?"

"Yes," I said. I had expected him to be offended or even frightened by my invasion of his garment, but instead he continued to smile as if my sojourn in the cloak had created a bond between us.

To Earth Man I said, "Is this your only cloak?"

Heling stared in amazement. But Earth Man merely nodded.

A survey of the room would have answered the question. There was no place to put another cloak. The one tiny closet would have squashed one.

La Maison hadn't been converted from apartments, or toned down from a tourist hotel. It had never been much more than it was now. Earth Man's room was about ten by fifteen. To say that the two dirt-encrusted windows provided light would be serious exaggeration; they just added two paler gray rectangles to the bare floor. Against the inside wall was a bed covered with a Madras spread, its orange, red, and purple having run together so many times that it was virtually a homogeneous shade. At the foot of the bed was a small TV—black and white. On the near wall, by the door, was a bookcase stuffed with pamphlets. Earth Man must have collected every one ever issued on air pollution in the state. And between the bookcase and the bed, next to the TV, was a sink and a hotplate unit that sat atop the world's smallest icebox. Looking at it, I realized that it couldn't have held more than the three dishes Parker had taken, which meant that Earth Man had considered the dish from Paradise worth a third of his fridge space.

Any dinner from Paradise would have been worth a third of this fridge. How had Earth Man come by that dinner and the others he was given? Paradise didn't feed other poor people, Earth Man had admitted that himself. What did he have that the rest of the poor lacked? A friend in the right place.

I dismissed Heling, then said to Earth Man, "There are a few more things I need your help with."

He sat on the bed and motioned me to a padded chair by the window. The chair was covered with a piece of cloth that vaguely resembled the bedspread. I settled gingerly on the edge.

"So Yankowski arranged for you to get dinners at Paradise," I said conversationally.

"Yes." He smiled.

"Why did he do that?"

"We were friends. He supported my work."

"Financially?" I asked, suppressing my amazement.

He nodded, his blond corkscrew curls bobbing. In the light that filtered through the windows, a smattering of gray hairs was visible amid the blond. "Sometimes," he said. "But he didn't have much money either. They don't pay dishwashers much. Some places split tips—he told me that—but not Paradise. We talked about that, being poor. He doesn't like it either, but he's not really poor, you know? He's just passing through poor. But me, like I told him, I'm lifetime poor. Even without my work, I couldn't wash dishes all night. I'd go crazy in one place like that."

"About the dinners," I prompted.

He nodded. The muted sunlight reflected off the gold flecks on his nose. "We were talking one night about what we would buy if we had a hundred dollars. And I said I'd start with a really good meal. You know when you're poor, you don't get healthy food. Not if you don't cook. You get a lot of junk with lots of sodium, and red dye, and grease and sugar. Like those donuts you cops tried to fob off on me."

I forced back a smile.

"I used to eat that stuff. I mean, I'm poor, and I'd get hungry and I'd see half a donut left on a plate. Or someone would give me a candy bar as a donation. And I ate it. It was very bad for me; my stomach suffered. That's why I sewed the handholes closed on my cloak." He pressed his arms to his sides. "See, no temptation."

"So what did Yankowski do for you?"

"A couple of days later, he told me the restaurant would bring me dinner every night for a month."

"In return for?"

"Nothing."

"Earth Man, nobody brings you dinner for nothing."

"She did."

"Laura Biekma?"

"Most times. Sometimes she couldn't get away and someone else brought it. Twice it came by cab." He grinned, showing two rows of even, surprisingly white teeth. "You should have seen the driver's face when he got here."

I could imagine.

"Did they have a reporter come out?"

"No. No one came except the people who brought the food."

"Are you sure? Last night, you told me they fed you for the good publicity."

"The only person besides her and the cab drivers was one of the waiters. I saw him at Paradise later, after they stopped bringing the food here."

"What about on the street? Did reporters ask you about dinner there?"

"No, no! I told you no reporters talked to me." His face reddened around the white nose. It looked like a ball of red salsa with a blob of sour cream. "I was waiting. I thought they'd come. I had things to tell them."

I could imagine that too. Still, it was a puzzle. Why would Mitch Biekma have fed Earth Man, if not for the publicity?

"What did Frank Yankowski get out of this?"

Earth Man stared me straight in the face. "The pleasure of helping a friend," he said. "Frank got his meals at work."

I decided to drop that line of questioning. Whatever Yankowski got from this deal, he wouldn't have gotten it from Earth Man. "Where is Frank now?" I asked, hoping to slip that in.

"Isn't he in his room?"

"No. Where else would he go?"

"The movies."

"Besides that?"

"No place. He's poor."

"He could be visiting friends, couldn't he?"

Earth Man's face lighted up. "Oh, yeah," he said, pleased to be able to offer something. "He's got a friend down the hall."

"Who?"

"Sam, the manager."

I pressed Earth Man, but clearly there was no more to squeeze out.

On the way out, I pounded till Sam, the manager, answered; but if he had any idea where Yankowski might be, he was playing dumb.

I walked back to my car, wondering what had brought about those unpublicized dinners. Had Yankowski made the arrangement out of the goodness of his heart? Had he paid for them himself? Not on his salary as a dishwasher. But even if the dinners had been paid for, I couldn't imagine Mitch Biekma sending his food to La Maison de Flop. How could Yankowski have convinced Mitch? And why did he do it?

As I started the car, I thought of Earth Man standing nearly nose to nose with Mitch Biekma and his bowl. He was close enough to pour the poison in. Close enough, but his hands were sewn inside his cloak. Besides, the poison was in the horseradish, and Earth Man didn't have access to that at all.

What had gone on between Mitch Biekma and Frank Yankowski? Frank had vanished and Mitch was dead. But Laura was still around, and Laura, who had been willing to discuss her murdered husband, had been strangely reluctant to tell me about Yankowski. And now it might be too late to question her.

But it might not. Pereira was at Paradise going over the books. She could give it a shot. I called her.

By the time I got off the phone, I realized that what I really needed to do was talk about Laura, and Yankowski, and Biekma and Earth Man, and the cook, and the temporary *sous*-chef, and the string of poisonings. How many breakfasts had we downed while we hashed over our cases? There was a time when I'd feared that was about to end. But it hadn't. If I called Howard, odds were he'd be sitting in Wally's Diner when I got there.

CHAPTER 17

I stopped at Yankowski's room in the Hillvue Hotel, which backed up to La Maison. I'd called from outside the judge's office, to notify the manager of the warrant. By now, whatever was inside room 209 would have been viewed and catalogued. Whoever was guarding the room would be delighted to have company.

I knocked. "It's Jill Smith."

The door opened. Sapolu, a patrol officer the size of Yankowski, smiled wearily. Beyond him I could see a room no bigger than Earth Man's, furnished in the same manner, minus the television, bookcase, and standing cape. "What did you find?" I asked Sapolu.

"Not a whole lot. But what we've got isn't going to make your day, either. You want the grand tour here?"

"Sure."

The closet was small. Yankowski would have had trouble hiding in it. But his clothes didn't fill half of it. On hangers were a navy pea jacket and a dark ski sweater, the thick kind meant to be worn outside. Suspended from a hook was an insulated ski cap, and on the floor were duck boots. I looked more closely at the sweater. There was a sharp dip at each side where the hanger ended. If I took the sweater off the hanger and held the sleeves out, there would be bulges. "What we've got here is Yankowski's storage closet. He's packed away his winter clothes. He must be wearing his summer whites."

Sapolu stared, mystified.

"You didn't grow up in the East, huh?" I said.

"No. San Francisco."

"So you never put away your winter clothes on Memorial Day and dragged them back out on Labor Day?"

He looked at me as if I were crazy. "What happened if it got hot in October?"

"You sweated. It's not like here, where you just wear fewer layers in the spring and fall." And more on the summer nights and mornings like today, when the fog can be thick enough to make Yankowski's pea jacket an appealing sight, I could have added.

The dresser was empty, as was the tiny refrigerator. On top of the fridge was a mug, and a nearly new bottle of instant coffee.

"Moved out, huh?" I said.

"Looks like it." Sapolu sat down in the chair. It was coverless, but the black Naugahyde had been ripped and taped back together. "No one used to drinking coffee at Paradise drinks instant at home."

"Not unless he just wants something here in case he needs a cup when he comes to check on his winter clothes. Did you find any hint of where he's living now?"

"Nada. The neighbors"—he motioned toward the nearby rooms—"haven't seen him in two months, and when they did, he didn't say more than 'How you doin?' There wasn't one scrap of paper in here, not a Kleenex. Your perp travels light. And careful."

I spotted Howard loping across University Avenue, his long strides seemingly effortless, his curly red hair bobbing with each step. The fog was gone, and the sunlight sparkled off the window panes across the street, off the Volkswagen that cut sharply right to avoid Howard, off the Mercedes convertible that slammed on its brakes three feet from him, and off the big gold ring on the finger next to the one the driver flipped at Howard.

"Hey, fellow, there are laws against jay-running," I yelled at Howard.

"I'm above the law," he said as he stepped up on the curb. The light turned amber; the Mercedes driver raced his engine and shot across the intersection, coming as close to a van making a left turn as he had to Howard. Howard winced; no one had to tell him he'd set that up. Then his grin returned. "So, Jill, how was Earth Man's cloak? Give me the inside story."

"It really makes you appreciate clean air." Before he could probe more deeply, I said, "What about your sting last night?"

Howard's grin widened. "Well, Jill, just let me say that it was a masterwork. Arlo is in cell nine."

"Whew!" Arlo was Berkeley's most successful drug dealer. Howard had been after him ever since he was assigned to Vice and Substance Abuse. Arlo hadn't bitten on two previous sting attempts, a rarity in the history of Howardian setups. This last sting was a grudge match.

"So?" I prompted.

"So." He was grinning so wide he could barely talk. "I got the word that Arlo had a big shipment in. I kept the heat on Arlo. Tails any hour of the day. Bushy tails."

"Bushy tails" were the kind the suspect can see—more for show than work.

"He couldn't open the door without spotting us watching him, much less conduct business. Arlo's no fool; he isn't about to take chances. He knows all those tails cost a fortune. So he was laying back, figuring he'd wait me out. But he was also getting antsy. No merchant likes to carry big inventories. But he didn't figure on the number of favors I called in and the number I asked. I'm in debt all over the department. He also didn't know that some of the tails were guys taking twenty minutes off patrol. By the end of two months he was doing my work for me, seeing cops everywhere. And he was worrying about his inventory, see?"

"And?"

"I waited till the last moment, I mean the last moment. Another day and he'd have split or been carted off to the Highland psych ward. Then I just eased the word out about a big buyer, a very nervous, suspicious buyer."

"One who wouldn't deal with him because he was hot."

"Right. I trained you well, my woman."

"And then?"

"And then I reeled him in. But here's the clincher, Jill. I set up the buy for Telegraph and Ashby. Then at the last minute I had my man change the location to Ashby and Roosevelt, and then again"—the corners of his mouth were tickling his earlobes; he could barely contain himself—"to Roosevelt and Acton."

"A block from the station! Did you take a car, or just decide to walk him back?" I laughed.

Howard grinned and pushed open the door to Wally's.

At eleven, only two customers were sitting at one of the Formica tables by the windows. The counter, which filled two thirds of the floor space, was empty. Behind it Wally perched, Raksen-like, on a short stepladder, leaning precariously over the grill while balancing a four-by-three blackboard framed in orange. Wally's was to Wally what Paradise was to Mitch Biekma. Whereas Mitch spent his time charming the viewers of television talk shows, Wally devoted his free moments to redecorating and redefining. None of his dishes were so pedestrian as to be called "Two Eggs, Any Style." On Wally's menus, two eggs might be a "Pair of Specs"; two eggs with ham, a "Groucho"; a jelly donut, a "Gusher." The names were rarely inspired, but it didn't matter, because Wally changed them at least once a month. He replaced the menu boards nearly as often. One week he had had three different signs out front. I couldn't imagine how the man turned a profit.

We walked in silently and sat at a table. But if we'd had any fear of startling Wally, we'd misjudged him. He was entranced with his blackboard.

"We could have *driven* in unnoticed," I whispered.

"We could have called that health equipment company that tried to deliver to Paradise. They could have unloaded their whole truck in here without worrying about being interrupted."

Howard picked up the salt cellar, assessed it, and set it down. Wally continued to shift the menu board. Howard moved the pepper shaker. His blue eyes sat deep in his head. Above them a wrinkle moved up from the bridge of his nose. There were wispy lines around his eyes I hadn't noticed before—smile lines, but lines nevertheless. Had they etched themselves in during the last month? Howard asked, "Your trip back okay?" He sounded different, too formal for Howard.

I hesitated, recalling that sweaty landing. "Fine."

"I've got your clothes in my Land Rover."

"Great. All I've got with me are loud flowered shirts and white shorts."

"You'd make quite a hit with the press. You do have good legs. And quite a tan."

"I'll give it some thought. I can use all the help with the press I can get now." I felt like I was making conversation with a stranger. It would be a relief when Wally took our orders.

"That bad, huh? Look, Yankowski's not someone who'd get lost in a crowd. If he stays in Berkeley you'll get him."

"That's a big if. Yankowski's no amateur who panicked and ran last night. He watched what he said to his neighbors at the Hillvue, which is not exactly a place where residents are dying to chat up the cops, anyway. His room was a roadblock to anyone looking for him. A dead end."

Howard shoved his chair back and leaned his elbows on the table. "He must have done that before Mitch Biekma's murder, right?"

"He hasn't been back there since."

"So he cleared everything out before. In preparation for hiding out after murdering Biekma?"

"The thing is, Howard, if Yankowski had planned to kill Mitch Biekma, he would have been prepared for the questioning that followed." This was the same type of conversation we'd had at breakfast, at dinner, in our office, on the phone for years. At times when we weren't sure where we stood with each other, we had slipped into the tell-me-about-your-case talks for security. But this time it wasn't bridging the distance.

"But suppose he killed Biekma on the spur of the moment?"

"Possible," I said slowly. "Yankowski didn't strike me as a spur-of-the-moment guy. But even if the murder was unpremeditated, I don't see him losing his cool in the middle of an interview. I wasn't pressing him that hard."

A bang came from behind the counter as Wally aimed the menu board for the two support nails. The hanging-from-nails look was too indecorous for Wally; Wally's nails would be hidden behind the board. And it would take more luck than Wally had to find them.

Howard jumped up. "Let me give you a hand, Wally."

"Over here," Wally said, without turning around. When it came to his first love, the identity of his proposed helper was secondary to the project.

Standing, I watched as Wally reached up trying to balance the menu board with the aid of Howard, who had to be nearly a foot taller. Howard could easily have done the job himself, but he didn't. He eased the board back and forth across the elusive nails, the sun highlighting his green turtleneck and his jeans, the movement accenting his lean back, his long muscular legs, and his not-half-bad buns.

"There it is," Wally exclaimed, releasing the board and stepping back with proprietary appreciation. "What do you think?"

"Looks good. Now how about a little service in this joint," Howard said, turning toward me.

I jerked my gaze away from his derriere. Maybe I had been convalescing too long.

"Hey, you're back," Wally called to me. "Bet he's glad to see you, huh?" he said, eyeing Howard. To him he said, "She looks pretty good, huh? All tan. A little thin, maybe." Wally followed Howard out around the counter, his gaze steady on my face. "Tired, that's what she looks. You been keeping her out too late?"

"We've got criminals for that," Howard said, careful not to meet my gaze.

"What'll you have?" Wally demanded. "We have two fine specials today." Wally pointed to the menu board. On it was "Wally's Daily Specials" in baby blue letters. Underneath were four lines, well smudged in the hanging-up process.

"Read them to us," I said.

"You can't see that? That's what happens when you leave your vegetables on your plate, if you order them at all."

I didn't bother to acknowledge that. Wally didn't expect me to. From him, chidings about my eating habits were akin to "Hi, how are you."

"First up, we have the 'Cow in the Pasture.' That's a third of a pound of beef mixed with lettuce, tomato, carrot, red cabbage, and cucumber. Your choice of dressing."

Back before I left, Wally had offered it with Thousand Island dressing and called it "Mexicana Suprema Salud."

"And the second?" Howard asked.

" 'Fox in the Hen House'—"

"Let me guess," Howard said. "Egg salad."

Wally's face dropped. "With pimento."

I kicked Howard under the table. "Give me the cow, with Thousand Island, and a Coke," I said.

"Guacamoleburger, large order of fries, salad, and a Coke."

"No pie?" Wally demanded, clearly insulted.

"Later."

To me Howard said, "So Yankowski?"

I picked up the fork, fingering the points of the tines. "Yankowski. Maybe I pressed him harder than I thought. What was it I said to him just before he shoved me into the counter?" I hadn't thought I was tired. I'd slept all last evening. But now, trying to recall that interchange with Yankowski, my mind flitted over the surface. I pressed the tines into my fingertips. "I told him we would check his background, question his friends, find out all about him."

"Sounds like that was what he wanted to avoid."

"Howard, if you want to avoid drawing attention to yourself, you don't plan to kill a man."

"So you're saying it was spur of the moment?"

I pressed the tines harder. Why didn't that seem right? "He didn't strike me as the spontaneous type. And anyway, it's hard to poison someone on the spur of the moment. Even the best prepared of us don't carry packets of aconite around just in case."

Howard fingered the ketchup bottle, steering it between

the metal cream pitcher and the salt and pepper. He nodded thoughtfully, his blue eyes half closed. I knew that look, it was the one he had when he got down to the issue. "So how's your house-sitting working out?"

I felt myself tense, unsure about leaving the safety of shop talk. "Okay," I said tentatively. "It's just going to take me a while to figure how all the electric gadgets work. They've got every comfort electricity can provide."

"You need help with all those stimuli?" His eyes had opened and his grin was the same one he'd had as he started to describe his sting. It was the old Howard grin.

"You angling for an invitation?"

Wally set down the drinks. "Entrees coming up pronto."

Howard fingered his glass, the grin set. "I could—"

The door slammed. "I was afraid you wouldn't be here." Connie Pereira rushed in, grabbed a chair from the next table, and plopped down in it at ours. "I called the station. When you were both out I took a chance. Then, I was afraid you'd have come and gone, and I'd have to call the station again."

"Hey, calm down," Howard snapped. "We're here." He stared in amazement at Pereira. In three years I had seen Connie Pereira this agitated only a few times.

Ignoring him, she said to me, "When I looked at those books at Paradise, I could see there was something a little odd. Another time I might not have caught it so soon, but we'd just been talking, and I was thinking about the string of poisonings and why anyone would poison Rue Driscoll and Earth Man, and maybe those were just practice runs to see how much they'd need to kill Biekma. I mean, we don't know if they used more in Earth Man's food than in Rue Driscoll's, do we?"

"No. I never considered that."

"Well, I was thinking that if the killer did a couple of practice runs, he couldn't have learned much, because Earth Man, at least, didn't tell anyone how sick he was. So the killer probably figured, 'Screw it,' and tossed the rest of the poison in Biekma's horseradish. I mean, if Biekma got too much, so what, right?"

I nodded.

"So it seemed like the best thing to do was to see what had happened around those dates. I mean, I was checking the books anyway."

Wally set down the dishes. Howard's guacamoleburger filled his plate. The fries covered another. His salad a third. It looked like a smorgasbord.

Wally eyed Pereira. She waved him away.

Picking up the burger, Howard said, "What did happen, Pereira?"

"Nothing. Then. But listen to this. Driscoll was poisoned the third of April. Earth Man, the fifth of May. On April eighteenth, the books indicate two free dinners, on May third two more. Then on May twentieth and twenty-first, two each. And six in June. And," she said, picking up one of Howard's fries, "those dinners are carried as a loss."

"Free dinners for customers who'd had meals that weren't up to Paradise's standards?" Howard asked.

"Standards of nontoxicity," Pereira explained.

I swallowed a mouthful of salad and asked, "How was Laura Biekma, Connie? Could you get anything out of her?"

"She was in bed. I don't often feel bad about waking up a suspect, but she looked like she was the one who'd been poisoned—you know that jaundiced look you get when you've thrown up?"

"But you didn't let your better instincts inhibit you, right?" Howard said, spearing olive, tomato, and lettuce.

Ignoring Howard's jibe, she said, "I started in about Earth Man. Even half-asleep, she gave me the line that she and Mitch had given him dinner as a publicity gimmick, to counter the view that they were elitists."

"But they *didn't* publicize those meals," I said.

"Earth Man didn't exactly fit the image Mitch had had in mind when he concocted the idea. Mitch, it seems, had a few failings, like getting carried away with an idea and leaving the work involved to someone else. He wanted to be seen giving meals to the deserving poor. He just didn't take time to check out his recipient."

Howard laughed. "Afraid Earth Man would steal the show?"

I said to Pereira, "So Yankowski set up Mitch, huh?"

"Got it. How come, you may be asking? Well, it seems that Biekma was on this talk show with two nationally known chefs. Each of them had his cookbook out on the bookstore shelves—Biekma's is only in the manuscript stage—and Biekma was hot to score over this big-time competition. So he pulls out all his best stories, and adds a few new ones, and one of those includes a description of their giant dishwasher with the twisted nose cowering in the kitchen."

"Clear enough description for his ex-wife to recognize him?" I asked, forking a piece of cow. It tasted better as "Mexicana Suprema Salud."

"Apparently Yankowski thought so."

"And so," Howard said, gleefully, "he gave Biekma Earth Man to get even!" This was right up Howard's alley.

"Mitch couldn't fire Yankowski because he was the most reliable dishwasher around," I said.

"And not only did Biekma never get his publicity for being a good guy, but he couldn't stop feeding Earth Man for fear Earth Man would complain to the press about him breaking his promise, right? It's a masterwork," Howard pronounced.

"But," I said "even if there came a time when the threat of bad publicity wasn't enough, Mitch couldn't get rid of Earth Man, because Earth Man had the evidence of the poisoned food. I'll bet it was Yankowski who told him to keep that food."

Pereira grabbed the biggest fry on Howard's plate. "Wait. Here's the clincher. If Earth Man had gone public, you know what would have come to light?"

I nodded. "All those dinners the Biekmas wrote off! The ones you found in their books."

"Exactly," she said triumphantly, scanning both our plates before helping herself to Howard's pickle. "Seems people have been getting sick there every couple of weeks."

I put down my fork. "So what did Laura say about that?"

"Said they were very upset, for one thing. Seems Mitch went wild trying to find the culprit. Fired the waiters, the salad chef, the *sous*-chef, the busboy, everyone but Yankowski and the cook—"

"Who he couldn't fire because she owns a third of the place," I said.

"So Mitch starts poking around trying to figure out who's behind it," Howard said.

To Pereira, I said, "We've got to get a list of which staff members were there the night of each poisoning."

She grinned. "I'm way ahead of you. Mitch had the same idea. Here's the rundown. Laura was there on and off. Ashoka Prem, last night's *sous*-chef, helped out a few of those nights. There were three salad chefs and four waiters during that time. Yankowski was there all but one day. And Adrienne the cook was there every single night. And here's another interesting thing," she said, plopping the remainder of pickle in her mouth.

I waited while she chewed.

"I had a look at the partnership agreement. Not only do all three of the partners have right of first refusal if the others choose to sell, but each one has veto power over any prospective buyer."

"So no one would get greedy and sell their share to a burger chain, huh?" Howard asked.

I took another bite of my salad, then put down the fork and pushed the bowl in front of Pereira. "I'd say it was time I had a talk with Adrienne."

CHAPTER 18

"Poison!" Adrienne Jenks shouted. She was a tiny woman with shoulder-length brown hair that stood out from her head in bursts of thick wiry curls. Even the net she would have to wear in the kitchen wouldn't hold that mass down much; and wearing it, she would look like a saint whose halo had darkened with age. But now, a saint was the last thing she resembled. She glared at me with dark eyes, and in a startlingly deep and loud voice, demanded, "Poison? Are you crazy? I'm the chef. Food is my art. Do you understand what that means?"

"But you know about the food poisonings at Paradise," I said. We were in her studio flat, a large room that had once been a partial basement of the house above. The Berkeley Hills, part of the Coast Range that run the length of the state, rise from the fault line gently in some places, abruptly in others. This house had been built at a corner, on a downslope so steep that the front door was at street level; but here in the back, Adrienne had to climb down six steps from her converted basement to the yard. Unlike the "garden" that had been outside my old flat, one forever in the planning stage, Adrienne's yard sported a bed of day lilies, two tall pines, and a four-foot-high hedge beside the sidewalk. A walkway bisected the hedge. "You do know about the food poisonings at Paradise," I repeated.

"Know, of course I know. Everybody knows."

"There was nothing in the papers."

"Oh, that," she said, dismissing the media with a wave of the hand. "Everyone in the business knows. It's a disaster. They're all talking about it. Our business is way down."

"How far?"

She paused a moment. I had the feeling that figures and specifics were too pedestrian for her. Great flourishes of emotion seemed more natural. Lowering her voice, though there was no one around to hear, she said, "You could almost get in without a reservation."

Like dinner at Wally's, I restrained myself from commenting.

"It's all people talk about," she declared. She was wearing a red smock with huge purple flowers, and pipe-leg jeans. She looked like a Popsicle. Smacking each small foot against the floor, she began to pace briskly across the twenty-by-thirty room. It was not to be an easy journey. To one side of the doorway, where I was still standing, a red and purple print sofa and three stuffed chairs covered in sea blues and bright green were grouped around a low oak table. Straight ahead, a potted ficus the size of a family Christmas tree stood like a traffic cop. And to the left, a violet and green double-bed sized sleeping mat lay between the front wall and a large worktable—a board balanced on two two-drawer file cabinets. Strewn behind it were a padded office chair and two stools. To make it from one wall to the other required a couple of moves worthy of a wide receiver. "And you know what people are saying, don't you?"

"No."

"No?" She flung her arms in the air. "They're saying I've lost my touch, that's what. It could kill me. Do you know how I've worked to get some recognition?"

"Sit down and tell me," I said, motioning her to join me on a soft couch with throw pillows that reminded me of her smock.

She sat. "I don't have money like Ashoka."

"Ashoka Prem, Mitch's friend from the English class?"

"Yeah. Ashoka's family has oodles. Had it for years. Being a chef is a hobby for Ashoka. Hell, life is a hobby for him. He can dabble till he's eighty and it won't matter. And Mitch, well, he had Laura to support him. I wish I'd had a wife to stay in California and work her tail off so I could spritz around some tourist cooking school near the Left Bank. Those places cost a fortune. Rich American dabblers come to spend money, they figure." She threw up her hands, looking very French.

"That's where you went?" I asked, amazed.

She jumped up. "Not me. Mitch and Ashoka."

I motioned her down again.

"I went to the best school in Paris. I saved for five years to pay for tuition, and fare, and living expenses. I applied three times before they would consider me. I took French classes for years; they don't speak English. I had to hock my soul to start Paradise. Look, this is the best place I've lived since I left my parents."

"But it's worth it, isn't it? You've been written up in the paper. Everyone in Berkeley knows your name."

"I'm not after fame. I'm not looking to write a cookbook like Mitch. I'm not hot for the talk show circuit. I want people to savor my creations and to know that this is the best it can possibly be." She assessed my reaction. "How can I make you see. It's like art. I don't want to be just El Greco or Modigliani; I want to create the Mona Lisa. Or in music—"

"I take your meaning."

"Oh, okay," she said, deflated.

"About the poisonings . . ." I prodded.

"I might as well never lift a crepe pan again." She sank back into the pillows, her small drawn face looking paler and sharper in contrast to their lush shades. Pushing herself back up, she rested her elbows on her thighs and stared directly at me. "It would be one thing if people had really been poisoned. If they'd died. Then everyone would know that there was a lunatic loose. But what I've got is the customers complaining that the food tastes funny. Funny! They feel lousy later on. What's that? It doesn't sound like a lunatic. There are homicidal lunatics; there aren't indigestive lunatics. 'Funny' sounds like the milk has gone bad, or the spices came out of a jar. 'Funny' is how dinner tastes if your kid makes it. So no one's going to think of a conspiracy. Everyone just assumes the problem is with me. Of course they're not saying it to me, but I can tell. People shy away. It's like I'm, well, poison."

I knew the feeling. "Why would anyone indulge in that type of poisoning?"

I was prepared for the type of tentative reply Pereira had gotten from Laura Biekma, but Adrienne didn't hesitate. "To destroy me."

"What about Mitch, it couldn't have done him any good."

"He wasn't the chef. Everyone in the business knew that. He never came in the kitchen till after the customers had left."

"Because you wouldn't let him, right?"

She gave me a quick nod.

"Why?" I insisted.

"Why? Because there can be only one chef in the kitchen. He hired me to be chef. I'm the chef. I can't be bothered with him futzing around tasting the soup, tossing in a handful of cilantro—he did that once, in *my* soup! Or he'd say the wine sauce needed scallions instead of shallots. I can't put up with that."

"But if you had an agreement . . ."

"*Had* is the word. For Mitch, the agreement lasted while he was making it." She reached out and put a hand on my arm, then, as if remembering the nature of our interview, drew it back. "Look, Mitch and I got along, in our way. He didn't mean any harm, far from it. Mitch thrived on being liked. That was the problem. He was so busy concentrating on being liked *now* that the past slipped away."

"Criticizing your food was hardly the thing to make you like him."

"But the customers, if he made their dinners better by adding cilantro, they'd like him. And they did, they loved him. He was on their side, making sure they had the best dinners in town. If the food did taste funny, the only question they had about him was why he didn't get rid of me. And then, they excused him that because I own a third of the place. He couldn't fire me."

"Couldn't he have bought you out?"

She shrugged, "He might have thought about it, but he didn't have the money. Besides, I would never have sold. Not the way things were. That's what I'm telling you; now I couldn't *get* another position. No one would hire me even as *sous*-chef, much less give me free rein."

"Free rein?"

"Look, Mitch might have been an egomaniac, but he wasn't a fool. He caught on real soon in Paris. He knew he'd never be great. Ashoka never understood that. He still thinks he'll open a restaurant that will transform Indian food. But Mitch got it quick. He knew if he was going to make a splash he needed an artist. And he knew enough to realize I was an artist. So we had a deal."

"So Mitch was never the chef?"

For the first time Adrienne hesitated. "Not really. No. He cooked. He even created some dishes, sometimes they were good, but just *good*, not superlative. And good's nothing. In Berkeley, good is what you get on any corner."

"Then what is it he put in his cookbook?"

"What do you think?"

"Your recipes?"

"You got it."

"Why did you allow that?"

Scowling, she squirmed, reached behind her, and yanked out the offending lump—a bleach-spotted tan wool cap—and tossed it angrily to the floor. "Stupidity. Greed. Innocence. Take your pick. It was part of the agreement. I wanted security, a place where I could create, where no one would tell me what to cook or how to cook it, and no one could fire me. And I got that. No matter what happens, I stay at Paradise."

"Suppose Mitch and Laura had decided to sell their

shares? You have right of first refusal. Would you have bought them out?"

"Before this poisoning business, I'd have jumped at the chance. I could always have gotten backing. People would have been lined up for the honor."

"And now?"

"Now only an insecticide company would take the chance."

"And if the Biekmas had wanted to buy you out?"

"They wouldn't. I am Paradise. Without me it would be nothing."

"But suppose."

"They could shove it. Particularly now."

"What did Mitch get out of the deal?"

"Fame," she said with disgust. "He got his restaurant. He got the notice of being the cook there. The deal was that for publication we were both chefs for the first year. And he got the recipes. I didn't care. What's one year? I'll be cooking for the rest of my life. What I created last year is gone. I'm not interested in that. I care about what I'm creating now. So as long as Mitch presented the recipes right, and he did do that, he was welcome to them. He could have his picture on the cover, he could do the signing circuit, he could hold press conferences, he could angle for Johnny Carson: that was all fine. I didn't want any of that, and frankly, he was damned good at it. Talk shows were his thing. I saw him on a couple. He loved being the guest chef. But he could as easily have been the guest lion trainer. He wasn't a chef, he was a personality."

"So you are saying the deal worked out for both of you?"

"Yeah, until the poisonings."

I shifted on the cushion. "Adrienne, you've given this a lot of thought. Do you have any suspects?"

"Of course."

"Of course! Who?"

"Ashoka."

Ashoka Prem, the guy with all the time and all the

money, the friend who had helped out as *sous*-chef last night. "Why?"

Adrienne looked at me with the same expression I had seen on the faces of people catching their first sight of Earth Man. She looked like I had just descended from outer space. "The ordinance. The Gourmet Ghetto Ordinance that limits the number of restaurants. Ashoka's had his restaurant ready to open for ages. He's got every cent tied up in it. And he's next on the list."

CHAPTER 19

Ashoka Prem was first on the list to open his restaurant in the Gourmet Ghetto, an enviable position to the fifty or so restaurant, boutique, or produce-shop owners who crowded behind him. But perhaps it didn't seem so desirable to him as he sat around month after month waiting for an establishment to fail, or an owner to die. How was he handling the good fortune of Mitch Biekma's death? I wanted to observe him in his own restaurant. But it was already one o'clock, time for my "after lunch" appointment with Inspector Doyle.

The fog had cleared; the sky was that unbroken birds-egg blue so characteristic of the West. But as I drove down Spruce I could feel my throat tightening and a line of sweat forming at my hairline. It was the same sweaty fear that had clutched me in the plane. *Get hold of yourself!* Glancing down the steep, winding street only enough to drive, I focused frantically on an oak-beamed English cottage, on a wispy blue-violet–flowered jacaranda tree, on a date palm, as if I could lower myself from one to the other down the hill. I glanced furtively at the empty road, then back to a

Spanish villa, to a wooden split-level. They were all the rage in Jersey when I was a kid.

I clutched the wheel. My throat throbbed. *Check the road; not much traffic now. Relax your grip.*

I slowed, barely moving. The afternoon breeze hadn't picked up yet. The leaves were still. Their steady shadows accented the glimmer of the sunlit stucco houses.

A van passed; I swerved to the left, my heart pounding. Why was I panicking? This wasn't the helicopter. I'd driven last night; I'd driven up here an hour ago. What was going on?

But I hadn't driven downhill.

I unclenched my fingers, easing up on the wheel, and drove on, staring at the pavement ahead. *What about Ashoka Prem? Think about him!* He was in the Virginia Woolf seminar with Mitch and Laura. He must have been there when they found the house Paradise was in. *What else?* He was in Paris with Mitch, and with Adrienne. Paris, where the one-of-a-kind horseradish jar came from.

I braked at Marin Avenue. I could turn right here, down the hill; it would be just as fast; faster because it was steeper. I swallowed, let my eyes shut, gathering all my control behind them. *One more breath, then I'll go—forward. Spruce is steep enough for today. One more breath.* An engine raced behind me. I checked the rearview mirror. Three cars lined up.

I stepped on the gas. *Prem.* He trained as a chef. He's sunk his money, all of it, Adrienne said, into a restaurant that can't open till one goes under. And he just happened to call Mitch yesterday afternoon after the regular *sous*-chef had called to say his tires had been slashed.

I braked at Rose, and looked ahead, feeling my breath ease. The hill flattened to a gentle grade here. I would be okay. For the moment.

Sweat still coated my forehead, and my turtleneck stuck to my back when I pulled into the parking slot. I turned off the ignition and glanced in the rearview mirror. It wasn't as bad as I'd thought. I didn't look like someone who had panicked; I just looked like I'd been up all night. My gray-green eyes, always the bellwethers, reflected the gray of my skin. My brown hair was sticky and clumpy. A wash, a combing, a little makeup to replace what I'd sweated off, some clean clothes—they'd make me look less like someone recently exhumed. But if I couldn't shake this ridiculous panic, it wouldn't make any difference.

I got out, slammed the car door, and strode across the lot. "Detective Smith!" Three men raced toward me. Reporters. "You're in charge of the Biekma murder, right?"

"No comment."

"Do you have any leads?"

"No comment."

"No leads at all?"

"I said, no comment!" I walked into the station and slammed the door.

I stopped in the bathroom and made what repairs I could, and headed on to Doyle's office.

Inspector Doyle was hurrying out his door. He paused, hand on the knob. "No time, Smith. Phone's been going all day. Half the city council's been on the horn. Reporters from New York, St. Louis, Miami, New Orleans, Toronto, and even Paris. And now someone from the mayor's office is coming down. I don't know how they expect us to get anything done." Releasing the knob, he said, "And I've got the press in half an hour. What do you have for me, Smith?"

"Only suspicion."

"Smith, I need facts. I can't give these people suspicions. I need to show them progress." He shook his head. "I could take Eggs off rotation—"

"It's my case, Inspector. I'm handling it!" I snapped. "I haven't been home since last night. In the last four hours I've done two interrogations, conferred with Pereira twice, and stuck my head up inside Earth Man's cloak. What more do you want?"

Doyle's thin lips quivered. "Okay, give me this suspicion of yours."

I told him about Ashoka Prem. "He's been a friend of the Biekmas for years. He probably knew about the salad chef quitting, and how tight things were at Paradise. It would have been no problem for him to find out where the *sous*-chef lived."

Inspector Doyle nodded. For the first time I saw a hint of a smile on his face. "And he probably knew how to slash a tire too. Right, Smith?"

"He called Paradise just after the *sous*-chef told Mitch he couldn't get to Berkeley. That does seem a great coincidence."

CHAPTER 20

My office was empty save for two cardboard boxes of clothes Howard had left, and the growing pile of papers in my in-box. I poured myself the dregs of Pernell Jackson's coffee and stood while I dialed the bullpen for Murakawa; he'd meet me at Prem's restaurant. I wasn't going to take the chance of interrogating such a likely suspect without backup. Still standing—tired as I was, it would be fatal to sit—I read through Doyle's report on Ronald Struber aka Ashoka Prem.

Ashoka Prem had been born Ronald Struber. That he had changed his name didn't surprise me, hundreds of Northern Californians had changed their names in the last decade. Animal rights advocates called themselves Laughing Otter, the ecology-minded became Singing Rainbow or Green Meadow, and those who found gurus switched from Jim, Jane, and Jerry to Ananda, Jyoti, and Ram.

And it didn't surprise me that Struber had maintained his chosen name of Prem so long as no one thought to mention the change. I doubted whether someone like Adrienne Jenks had ever heard the name Ronald Struber.

Ashoka Prem—I found myself thinking of him as Prem— had been cooperative with Inspector Doyle, albeit too distraught to be much real use as a witness.

His account of the activities in the kitchen had fit with those of the others. He had stated he lived on the premises of his own ready-to-open restaurant and was there, alone, all the previous day until he went to help the Biekmas. The initial papers indicated that Prem had been a disciple of a guru in Maharashta in central India. He had been to the ashram there on and off for some years. Now that he was back in Berkeley, he rose at four every morning to do esoteric breathing exercises. If he had been distraught last night, I had no idea what shape he would be in this afternoon. I hadn't been to India, though I had friends who had (you'd have to look hard in Berkeley to find a person who didn't have friends who had). But I did know that breathing exercises done without guidance could be dangerous. How dangerous in the hands, or nose, of one already distraught was anyone's guess.

Murakawa was waiting when I pulled up in front of Prem's.

"How're your ribs?" I asked.

He shrugged. Murakawa had assisted me on a number of cases. He was young, eager; had stamina that would have awed Inspector Doyle in his prime. I had yet to hear Murakawa complain. "I'm okay. But I'll keep an eye on you from now on, especially on slides." Glancing toward Prem's restaurant, he said, "I can't wait to see the inside of this place."

Like Paradise, this building had originally been a house. However, there the likeness ceased. What had once been a five-room dwelling on a residential street now looked like an Indian stupa—a white stucco building that blended upward into a dome and culminated in a golden spire. It hadn't been finished a week before it was christened the North Berkeley Boob.

"It looks like a place you'd go for hotdogs in L.A.," Murakawa said as he walked up the white path.

There was no sign outside, no windows. It took me a moment to find the white stuccolike door, so closely did it blend into the facade. I knocked.

There was no answer. "Asleep?" Murakawa suggested.

"If he's asleep, it's in here." I knocked again, louder. To the right, beyond a shoulder-high hedge, neighbors stared through their windows.

"Maybe he breathed himself into oblivion." Murakawa grinned. At twenty-three, he was too young to have been pulled into the Eastern mysticism that had left Berkeley with Buddhist establishments from Thailand, Tibet, India, and Japan, with Moonies and Rajneeshis, and with yoga classes of all varieties. For Murakawa, life was sinews and muscles, stakeouts and deductions, and the pull that spurred most cops—the chance to make a difference. "You want me to guard the back, if I can find it?"

"I'll give him one more chance." I pounded hard. Almost immediately footsteps were audible.

The man who answered the door was what I might have expected of Ronald Struber–Ashoka Prem. He was tall, robust, with dark hair curling off his bare chest, a thick pelt of dark hair on his forearms and the tops of his feet, and no hair, dark or otherwise, on his head. He wore blue drawstring pants with *Om* stenciled on the right hip. With an asthmatic-sounding wheeze, he pulled the air in through his nose and down into his expanding chest. I waited for him to exhale, but he kept taking in air; the pale skin on his chest kept stretching out to the sides, blowfishlike, the dark hairs springing to attention. His pale blue eyes shone; they may have reflected a surge of enthusiasm, but it wasn't for anything here. There was no question that only Prem's body had come to the door. His mind might be anywhere between here and Varanasi. Just as I was wondering how soon his face would match the color of his pants, the wheeze lowered in pitch and the skin began to pull inward.

"I'm Detective Smith, Homicide, and this is Officer Murakawa," I said before he could begin another breath. "You're Ronald Struber, also known as—"

"Ashoka Prem," he said with a great sigh. His chest looked like a punctured balloon.

"Right. I need to talk to you. Inside."

"It's the middle of my practice. I still have my *pranayama*—breathing—and two more hours of *pratyahara*—what you might call meditation—to do."

"We're here about Mitchell Biekma's murder."

His dark pelted arms crossed. "I'm sorry, but I just finished the *asanas*, the yoga poses. My chest is supple now. If I wait, I'll lose it. In an hour—"

"Now! This is murder." Already, I could sympathize with Adrienne Jenk's exasperation.

He began inhaling again, his eyes moving toward Varanasi.

I had the urge to pinch his nose. "Prem!"

"Oh, very well," he snapped. He turned and stalked inside, into the center of the room.

The interior must have been gutted in the reconstruction. From five small rooms it had been transformed to one large windowless square with double doors that led from the middle of the rear wall to what was presumably the kitchen. The walls were white, the marble-tiled floor looked worthy of the Taj Mahal, and in the center of the room was a four-foot-high sandstone post that resembled a thick, stubby pencil—eraser end up—with faces protruding in four directions near the top.

"You like it?" Prem asked with sudden eagerness. "It's a *pancamukhalingam*, from East Rajasthan. It's over a thousand years old."

"It must have cost a fortune."

His lips curled; then clearly by will alone, he forced himself to begin another inhalation. I had the suspicion that "yahoo" was the term for me that had crossed his mind. But if so, he restrained himself from acknowledging it. Maybe breathing exercises did nourish self-control. What he said was, "The five-headed lingam is a Hindu fertility symbol, a symbol of the structure of the world. The five faces of Shiva."

Murakawa stared at the huge sculpture. "Shiva have a few children?" he asked with a straight face.

Prem glared at him. "The idea," he said, "is that the *sadhaka* or seeker learns practices like *pranayama*, the breathing techniques, and through them he learns to transmute the sexual energies at the lower chakras at the base of the spine, up to the seventh chakra here." He tapped his forehead. "Spiritual energy," he said, his eyes resting on the giant lingam with an expression that suggested he viewed transmutation with mixed feelings. There was an intensity in his eyes, eyes that had stared at one spot for hours or years, eyes that had resisted seeing normal life so long as to become strangers to it, eyes that looked lustfully at the stone *pancamukhalingam*. Had I not been a cop, I would have felt damned uncomfortable with him. Even being a cop, I wouldn't have picked him for a weekend guest.

I looked from him to the *pancamukhalingam*. "Five-headed?" Four heads looked out, and three of those had the same pleasant, if not seductive, expression. The fourth had the look of a cutthroat. There was no fifth face at all.

"The fifth head," he said, caressing the top of the sculpture, "is symbolic." He sank down on a folded blanket and sat cross-legged. His breath was thick.

Along the walls, tables the size of those in Paradise were pushed together. But unlike Mitch Biekma's utilitarian wooden tables hidden under his colorful tablecloths, these tables were marble. And like the multifaced Shiva, they must have cost Prem a bundle.

His breathing had grown louder. Looking down at him, I

asked, "How long have you spent creating this." I waved my hand around the room.

He exhaled, the sides of his chest sinking into the spaces between his ribs. "Three years. I supervised all the work myself. I made two trips to India to find the right lingam. The whole effect would be destroyed if that were wrong."

I looked back at the sturdy faces under the stylized mounds of hair at the top of the lingam. "You've succeeded. It's magnificent, and it does set off the room. Still, this is a great deal of work and money to put into a restaurant without being sure when it can open."

"I wasn't that foolhardy," he said with an unconvincing laugh. "I had an opening date. Ten months ago. August twelfth. I had hired the staff from the Indian community here; I'd ordered flowers arranged just like they are in India. The advertising was already cut and pasted." He fixed his gaze on the symbolic head of the lingam, and began an inhalation. His eyes half closed, he drew his mouth into a laconic smile; his torso shivered as he inhaled.

Behind him, Murakawa shook his head.

When he had exhaled, Prem's expression returned to normal, and he said, "It was my own fault. I was so busy supervising the plasterers and cabinetmakers, so concerned with getting to India to find the lingam, and to check out the restaurants that I had heard of since my last trip, that the Gourmet Ghetto Ordinance was law before I realized it. Oh, I'd heard about the possibility, sure"—the tenor of his voice was rising—"but it never occurred to me the city would pass it. I mean, you'd think people would be delighted to have a great restaurant close enough to walk to." He took another breath, but this time there was only a lowering of his pitch, a slowing of his words. "Someday Bhairava"—his glance moved from the ominous face on the lingam around to encompass the restaurant—"will open and it will be even better. Time is nothing more than time. I can wait."

But I noted that his voice had risen again as he announced his patience. "And for now you're first on the list to open?"

"That's true. It could be any time—ninety percent of restaurants fold in the first year."

"But not in the Gourmet Ghetto," I said.

"No. But I'm not impoverished. I'm willing to wait. I wouldn't want to open if that meant one of my friends had to close."

It all sounded good, too good, particularly for someone who had all his assets tied up here. "So you don't have any idea when you'll be able to open?"

"No."

"But if Paradise closes . . ."

"Mitch was my friend," he snapped. After another, shorter breath he said, "We went to school together. I helped him plan for Paradise. He heard every idea I had for Bhairava. I was there helping out last night."

"Fortuitous," I remarked.

But if he caught my sarcasm, he gave no indication. "They'd been short-staffed. It was Mitch's own fault. You can't go around firing people wholesale and expect to be able to find decent replacements. Reliable people don't want to work where the boss is capricious."

"And where the customers are poisoned?"

He hesitated. His chest, which had been reacting rhythmically to his breathing, became immobile. Then he said, "I'll tell you, I wouldn't have wanted to be the poisoner when Mitch uncovered him."

"You think Mitch would have?"

"Oh, yeah," he said without hesitation. "Mitch had energy like I've never seen. If I didn't know better, I would have thought he was on something. But he wasn't; didn't need to be. No drugs, no exercise, no spiritual practices: zilch. The guy must just have had good heredity. And he was obsessive. That's why he was so good at so many things. That's why he could be so funny when he was carrying on about the customers and the cooks and the waiters and Rue and everyone on those talk shows. He knew obsession from the inside. And when he got his teeth into something, he never let go, not till he devoured every bite and there was nothing left."

I pictured Biekma rather like the ominous lingam head. Returning to my question, I said, "You just happened to call Paradise yesterday afternoon. Are you in the habit of calling the Biekmas right before they open?"

"No. Of course not. But yesterday, when I was doing my P.M. practice, I kept getting thoughts of them. I knew things were tight there. Everyone was stretching over his limits. Laura has a female problem. And Adrienne had a rash on her hand—"

"A rash?" I asked amazed, barely restraining myself from asking if they stayed home with pimples too.

"In this business, a rash is serious. You can't work in the kitchen without getting your hands in all sorts of acids and irritants—chili peppers, alkalis. You keep working and your rash will get infected. Just a matter of time. Do you know what the biggest cause of injury is in a kitchen?"

I thought a moment. Hot grease, slippery floors? "Knives? Cutting yourself?"

"Close. But no. It's boiling water. The most common injury is burns from water. And the bitch of that is that it happens midshift, and then you're a person short. It's like last night. Even with Laura and me helping out, things were strung as far as they could go. Laura was sick; she shouldn't have been working at all."

"Sick? How?" Had she gotten a taste of the poison?

"She has something the matter with her uterus. It can give her a lot of pain, on and off. That's the reason I called yesterday, to see how she and Adrienne were."

I leaned back against the nearest table. "You and Adrienne were in France together. Are you closer than just friends?"

Prem shrugged. "Taking that at face value, yes. Everyone

in this business is closer than just friends or just enemies. There are no casual relations in the kitchen. But you don't mean that, do you?"

"Lovers? Maybe you were lovers in France?"

He laughed. "You're thinking of long, lazy afternoons on the Left Bank? Let me tell you, it's not like that. Well, maybe at the school Mitch and I went to—the Rich American Klutz Classes. But Adrienne went to the best. They work till midnight there. It's like being in a monastery. If Adrienne had had any free time, she would have spent it in bed, asleep. Mitch and I ran into her one Sunday at a leftist rally. We couldn't believe it, but it turned out that her school was closed that week."

"Still, if Paradise does close, you will get to open."

His smile faded. "I wouldn't have killed Mitch for that. You don't spend years feeling every breath in your nostrils, in your lungs, your ribs, your intercostal muscles, on the inside of your skin, and then throw it all away and kill a friend so you can serve curry a month sooner."

"But it could be a year, two years. It could be never."

He shrugged. "I have to accept what is."

"And make payments here while you do. How long can you do that?" Adrienne had told me Prem had money. But he'd already put enough into this building to keep an Indian village for a century.

"A while," he muttered. "I can hang on a while."

"How long?"

He shrugged.

I repeated the question.

"Three months," he said in a voice as quiet as it had been when he first sat. But there was none of that lassitude now. There was no faraway look in his eyes. He looked like any guy who had just about lost his dream.

But there was no way to know whether that was because he had come to the end of a long fruitless wait, or because he'd tried to turn the odds in his favor.

CHAPTER 21

It was nearly three o'clock when I got back to the station. I clarified my notes on the Prem interrogation, and glanced over the others to see if they were still clear. I wouldn't get around to dictating till at least tomorrow. Things I thought were unforgettable could slip into the unknown by then. Two inches thick, that was the average homicide folder. Two inches equals about a hundred fifty sheets of paper, a hundred fifty pages I hadn't begun to dictate or gather up from Inspector Doyle, from Pereira, Murakawa, Grayson, Raksen, Parker, Lopez, Heling, the sector sergeant, from the guys on surveillance—when they all got around to dictating. And it wouldn't be top priority for them, not unless I got on them. And I couldn't do that with my own reports undone.

There were times when dictating helped me sort my ideas, but I knew this wouldn't be one of them.

I dialed the office at Paradise. Pereira answered.

"I called with a gift," I said. "How're the books going?"

She sighed. "It's good for me to do this once in a while. It reminds me why I didn't become an accountant. I could make a lot more money that way, in creative accounting."

"You could go to jail, too."

"I'll tell you, Jill, when you're not halfway through books like these, it's a hard choice."

"Come up with anything yet?"

"Such as?"

"A big order of aconite?"

148

"From the River Styx Supply Service?" She laughed. "Hey, Jill, what about this gift you were offering?"

"Dinner. I owe you. How late will you be there?"

"All evening. Tomorrow's my day off. I'm not going to spend my Saturday with my nose in profit and loss."

"Nine o'clock okay?"

"Very continental. Sounds like this gourmet exposure is improving your social graces."

I snorted and hung up.

I leaned back in my chair. If I didn't watch it I'd fall asleep here. My back, which I'd ignored since morning, throbbed. It had been like this when I got out of the hospital. It would just get worse unless I rested it. Maybe the hot tub, and the Jacuzzi. Maybe just bed.

I grabbed the nearest of the cardboard boxes Howard had brought—I'd make do with whatever was in it. I was too tired to root through it here. Any choice was preferable to what I was wearing now. I could be home by four, in bed by four-oh-one.

But when I got there the draw of the hot tub was overwhelming, particularly when I realized that it sat under a skylight, and next to a one-way picture window that looked out on the bay. I fished out the thermometer, recalling tales of the hours necessary to heat these tubs. It read one-oh-four. Wasteful of them to keep the heater running. Superbly wasteful. I stripped off my clothes, and washed my hair. Then I slid slowly in, savoring the bite of the water as it rose over my hips, up my ribs, over my breasts, to my shoulders.

It was like coming home to a hero's welcome—the steamy embrace, all those little bubbles cheering. I settled back, propped my feet against the wooden bench at the other side, and watched while the fog nestled against Twin Peaks in the city, as if a Great Pyrenees were settling its bulk against the back of a couch.

Why was I seeing dogs everywhere? Was it the residue of

149

a month with my parents, looking at old pictures of us and our succession of dogs?

I looked back at the fog, squirming there at Twin Peaks, scrunching a massive shoulder, shifting a furry leg. I could almost hear the strained snores from a snout pushed into the sofa cushions. Then, sleepily, tentatively, a paw reached over the edge, hovered there; then another paw reached over. Like the Great Pyrenees tumbling off the constricting couch and sprawling comfortably on the floor, in half an hour the fog would flow over the ridge of Twin Peaks and cover the city.

I turned on the Jacuzzi, centered the small of my back in front of it, and let the needles of water massage the pain away. The picture window was steamy. Drops of water began to meander down, like sleds on a snowy hillside. Maybe like Great Pyrenees on a snowy hillside, or tiny sleds on a Great Pyrenees. Smiling, I leaned back and rested my head on the side of the tub. It was so warm, so comfortable. My eyelids were closing. So what? I had five hours. Lazily, through my lashes, I watched the drops mosey down the foggy glass. I reached languidly for the Jacuzzi switch, flicking it to low, resting my fingers on it, sinking back, releasing my fingers. The pulsing water drawing me down. Deeper.

Reaching for the collective lever to bring the helicopter up. Where is it? Keeps moving away. Too far. Can't reach. Rain battering the windshield. Nose down. Too sudden. Rotors stopping. Ship plunging. Into the Bay. Down, down. Crashing. Water rising, closing around my head—

I gasped for air, grabbed for the edge, frantically pulling myself up, half out of the tub. My heart was slapping my chest. I could see the mounds of my breasts pulsing. Hell and damnation, couldn't I even deal with a hot tub? What a great headline it would make if I drowned: HOMICIDE DETECTIVE STEWS OVER RESTAURANT MURDER. Adrienne could toss in some spices and serve me for weeks. I stayed poised there till the shaking stopped, then dragged myself out, yanked a thick terrycloth robe off its hook, and wrapped my wet body in it. Looking back at the once-inviting tub, I grabbed my clothes, yanked open the door, strode to the bedroom, and set the clock for seven-thirty. That would give me an hour and a half before meeting Pereira, ninety minutes to drive down Marin Avenue—the steepest street in town—back up the hill and down again, until I'd beaten this fear.

It was the telephone that woke me.

"Jill, what about that dinner you promised?" Pereira demanded. "Restaurants don't stay open all night."

9:15. "Sorry. Be there in ten minutes." I jumped up, splashed some cold water on my face, did a world-record makeup job, rooted through the box and pulled out a not-too-wrinkled Eddie Bauer black sweater and L. L. Bean brown cords, grabbed my Land's End jacket, and raced out the door. As the engine warmed, I remembered for what time I'd set the alarm, and why. What had happened to the alarm?

My car was pointing south, toward the more gently sloping streets, the ones I had to take driving uphill in the old VW. Taking a breath worthy of Ashoka Prem, I hung a U toward Marin Avenue.

Marin doesn't plummet straight down, but close enough. I made a left, and sat there in the middle of the intersection, poised at the top of that mile drop. The fog curtained the streetlights. Two red dots—taillights—pierced it, maybe a block ahead. I waited. The street had to be clear. No one in the way in case I panicked. The lights sank into the fog and were gone.

I turned the radio on loud, and rolled the window all the way down to let the wind wipe the sweat off my face. I stepped on the gas. The Volkswagen cleared the level intersection and jolted downward. My stomach lurched. I clutched the wheel, singing, shouting with the music, trying to drown out my fear.

When I reached the Marin traffic circle, relief washed over me. I pulled to the curb and sat to savor it. But I had barely pulled up the emergency brake before it melted away. *This* ordeal was over. But I knew it would be no better the next time. Panic throbbed out against my skull. But it wasn't the panic I'd come to know, it was a new, deeper one. It was more than the fear of crashing down; now it was fear of the fear. I had never dealt with a fear I couldn't handle. Face them, conquer them. But this one—I kept staring it in the eyes and it didn't blink.

Connie Pereira was bent over the Paradise books in the upstairs front room. To her right a beige corduroy sofa huddled in a corner facing a small television and stereo. One speaker was on the wall, the other functioned as an end table. The arrangement had more the aura of a warehouse than a living room. Clearly, it had been squeezed into the few square feet left over from the mammoth oak desk, typewriter table, desk chair, two oak visitor's chairs, and three file cabinets that made up the office.

"How's it going?" I asked.

She stretched her arm forward. "Look at that. Bureaucrat's elbow!"

"What's that?"

"It's been bent over forms or books so long it won't straighten." Setting the offending joint down on the desk, she leaned back and sighed. "All those strength and agility tests to get on the force, Smith, what were they for? I'm just going to sit here hunched over garbage bills and wine receipts till my eyes cross, my shoulders touch in the front, and my butt spreads wide enough to wedge me in the chair. I can't . . ." She looked up at me. "What's the matter, Smith?"

My neck tightened as I battled between the urge to hold down my squalid tale of terror and the urge to spit it out. Connie Pereira was my closest friend on the force, next to

Howard. Surely, she would understand. "Have you ever been really afraid, Connie?"

"You mean other than when I face these books?" She grinned, then shrugged it off. "You mean it, don't you?"

"Yeah."

"Okay. Lots of times. When I was a kid I was afraid all the time. Afraid when there was a knock on the door that it was the landlord, or the sheriff. Pop was always behind on the rent. At night I lay in bed listening to Ma and Pop screaming at each other, terrified their anger was going to boil over onto me or the boys. When I walked to school I was afraid the girls would make fun of my clothes. Later, I was afraid of every decent guy I met, that he'd be the one that trapped me into a life like my mother's. Why do you ask?"

"I don't know." My own situational fear seemed even more embarrassing next to Pereira's history of legitimate ones, ones she had overcome. "How about a walk to Fatapple's?"

She hesitated long enough for her silence to say that wasn't an answer. But she didn't press me.

Fatapple's, renowned for their burgers, muffins, and pies, was a block and a half away. It was a rarity not to find a line out the front door. But Berkeleyans appreciated good food and took it as a statement of their own discriminating taste that they were willing to stand in line for it. What was half an hour in the evening fog when the perfect mushroomburger and ollalieberry pie awaited? But perfect was not a word I associated with food, and waiting was something I had little patience for. Fatapple's *was* one of the few places in town where I was willing, albeit ungraciously, to stand in line while other people ate.

But we were lucky. There were two empty tables. We ordered burgers, cheese for Connie, mushroom for me, and café lattes.

"So how's it been today?" I asked.

"Quiet. When I started, Laura was calling the newspapers to run a notice that Paradise would be closed till the end of the week."

"It'll open Monday?"

"Tuesday. It's normally closed Mondays."

"That seems rather soon."

"That's what I thought. I didn't say anything, but she must have picked it up from me. She said she had the staff to consider. They can't be without work too long. And the routines are set; it's easier to keep going than make all the calls necessary for a month's lull."

"After she gets a new *sous*-chef, salad chef, dishwasher, and host. That in itself should take her the rest of the week."

"Well, she didn't do that today. She hit the sack as soon as she made that call. She hasn't been seen since. But the books are clear enough that I haven't needed to ask her anything."

"Mitch did the books," I reminded Pereira. Despite the new touches of makeup, she still looked exhausted.

The waitress put our burgers and drinks on the table. I added a long pour of sugar to the latte and stirred. "Aconite comes from a plant called monkshood. You know anything about that?" I asked, not having much hope. Pereira's interest was in only one kind of greenery, and that didn't grow, at least not for her. Her parents and brothers kept her financial plants closely trimmed; no fruit ever dropped to the ground to reseed itself.

"Nope. But I know where you can find out. I've got the name of the florist Paradise got their arrangements from."

"Great." I took a bite of the burger; it was great too.

"The records are pretty straightforward. But there are one or two puzzling things, Jill."

"Such as?"

"The receipts have fallen off in the last month, but I guess that's not surprising. There's a check from a David Whitney of something called Bump and Grind that makes up the difference. It could be to take over the place for a night, for an employee dinner. It's big enough, but there's no record. It's a good thing, though, because Mitch paid the leasing company that handles the kitchen equipment a double payment this month."

"How come?"

"I don't know. If the books were done by a professional, there would be a lot more clarification. What they've got here is a competent job, but a job by someone who was still learning the ropes."

"Could there be something in the contract, like a balloon payment?"

"I haven't found the contract. But balloon payments aren't likely in equipment-leasing contracts."

"Any ideas?"

"The logical one would be a prepayment penalty. If the Biekmas decided to lease from another company before the term of this agreement was over, they might have to pay an extra month's fee to get clear of this one."

"Is that normal?"

"I can't say for sure. I do know that different companies which lease their own equipment vary in their servicing. Maybe Mitch and Laura found a better deal."

I took another bite of the burger, chewing thoughtfully. "What else is odd?"

"The employees were paid once a month. Most places go on the biweekly or weekly schedule. It's not a stable enough industry to assume that all your help will still be there at the end of the month. And it's a hassle to terminate midmonth, what with notifying the health care carrier, Social Security, et cetera, and then start someone else, much less do it three or four times during the month. It's easier to pay more often."

"So Paradise must have had a pretty stable employee situation."

"And employees who could wait till the end of the month."

Pereira swallowed the last of her latte. "So what are you going to do with your supposes, Jill?"

"It keeps coming back to Yankowski." I shoved the last bite of burger in my mouth. The first of the month was Sunday, which meant that Frank Yankowski hadn't been paid in four weeks. Yankowski might have friends who were willing to help him; but there was a limit to friends' help. And there was nothing about Yankowski's life to suggest he had groups of friends, or even a few friends. According to Laura, he didn't make friends easily. So far the only one we had turned up was Earth Man, and he certainly wasn't in a position to bankroll anyone. A month's salary would be a temptation, if I could work it right.

CHAPTER 22

It was nearly ten-thirty when we got back to Paradise. I left Connie Pereira to put a note on the kitchen door telling Earth Man to come back at midnight. Then I climbed the stairs to the Biekma's office, settled in the desk chair, and dialed Homicide.

"You have reached the Homicide Detail of the Berkeley Police Department. At the present time no one is in the office to answer the phone. If your call is an emergency. . . ." The answering machine, the price we paid for direct phone lines.

I depressed the button, then dialed Inspector Doyle at home. "Doyle here."

It didn't take a genius to tell I'd woken him up. Quickly, I relayed my plan.

"You're hot to catch this guy. Only natural. But your plan's damned iffy, Smith."

"I know that. Still, every curve leads back to Yankowski. The whole case is on hold till we find him."

"May be, Smith. The question is, with this scheme are you going to find him?"

"I don't know. What alternative is there?"

He sighed. From the background came a soft moan. Presumably Mrs. Doyle had adjusted to interrupted sleep.

"Pereira's wiped out. So I'll need two other—"

"Holy Mother, Smith, you've got men watching La Maison and the Hillvue. You had Parker last night, Pereira all day today, and now on overtime. You've had Murakawa. You can't have the whole damned department."

"Inspector—"

"The plan's not worth it."

"Fine," I snapped. "I'll just make do with what I have."

"Call me if you get him. If you don't, I'll see you in the morning." He hung up.

Pereira flopped on the couch. I hadn't been exaggerating her condition. Yankowski could have run out from behind one of the stereo speakers and she might have spotted him, but she'd never have caught him. Still, I couldn't handle this surveillance alone. Who owed me? Whom did I not owe? The answer to both questions was virtually no one. There was only one choice. I dialed Howard's number.

I didn't have to worry about waking him at this hour. Howard shared a six-bedroom brown shingle house south of campus with five guys and their ever-changing girlfriends. It was every college senior's dream, a perpetual party. No matter what the hour, there was someone in the living room with whom to watch the tube, drink beer, or share a pizza. A variety of music wide enough to suit any taste, loud enough to block out unwanted thought, flowed from all directions, frequently accompanied by the howls of the basset hound in the bedroom nearest the stairs.

Howard had been low man on the rental agreement when he moved in six years ago. Since then, he had risen to the top through attrition, like a name on a form letter. By now he should have been lord of the house, levying the rent, setting the rules, filling the bedrooms with considerate adults. But the kind of housemates he wanted weren't willing to put up with the chaos; no one else shared Howard's passion for the house; no one was willing to wait months or years till the party animals moved to other dens. And now, rather than controlling the house, Howard was finding that it controlled him; he could neither afford the rent alone nor bring himself to move. Someday, he insisted, he would buy the house. The same way he asserted he'd make chief. But even if the latter happened—and I had my eye on that job, or at least I did before I'd become too timid to drive downhill—he would never be able to afford a six-bedroom house south of campus.

"I need a favor," I said when he picked up the phone.

"What?"

"Tailing."

"What kind of tailing?"

I explained the plan.

He didn't respond. Behind him the bass of a stereo boomed in something akin to four-four time. The basset howled, not in four-four time. Howard, I knew, was howling silently, asking himself why I couldn't get someone from Patrol to do my tailing. Tailing was the second rung from the bottom; only surveillance was worse. But Howard didn't question me; he realized my call to him meant Patrol was unavailable. "I'll get an unmarked car and be on Josephine Street by midnight."

I drove to the station to change cars. When I got back to Paradise, Laura Biekma was in the upstairs kitchen, brewing coffee for Pereira. Pereira was still in the office, but she'd given up trying to focus on the books. She was just baby-sitting Laura for me and it was taking all her energy to stay awake for that. Laura Biekma's coffee wasn't going to make a dent.

But it could help me. Accepting Laura's offer of a cup, I took a moment to watch her. Although she had slept during the day, she looked almost as tired as Pereira, albeit in a different way. Hers was the internal exhaustion of shock, fear, and deadening sorrow that requires months of sleep to ameliorate. She had washed her blond hair. It hung in fine waves. She hadn't bothered with makeup, and now her pale skin seemed to have lost what color it had before, and her freckles stood out as if her face had been splattered with Day-Glo paint.

"Cream?" she asked me. "It cuts the bitterness this late at night. We have real cream, from the farm. Yesterday it was still in the cow."

I felt I couldn't refuse, though the picture of that cream oozing down inside the udder last night did nothing to tempt me. I like to think of cream as divinely created in little half-pint cartons. "Thanks," I said. I took the cup from her and propped myself on a stool. "I need your help," I said.

"Yes, of course. What can I do?" She rested her hips against the counter and leaned forward, as if her concern for my problem was drawing her toward me. "I feel guilty having slept all day while strangers worried about who killed Mitch. He was *my* husband."

"Don't. This is why you have professional investigators. All you need to do is keep yourself together, so when we do ask for your help you're in shape to give it."

She nodded slowly. "What is it you want from me?"

"You haven't paid your employees this month."

If she found that comment strange, she gave no indication. Twenty-four hours into a murder investigation, most witnesses have given up trying to differentiate strange questions from the merely obscure but necessary ones. Laura shook her head.

I said, "Frank Yankowski must need his money. I want you to give it to Earth Man."

159

"And let you follow him? You want me to set him up, right?" It was the first flash of anger she'd shown.

Had she and Yankowski been lovers? The question had arisen before. But a lover should have been frightened rather than angry. Was she protecting a lover, or just reacting to being used?

She wrapped both hands around her coffee mug. "I can't do that."

"This is your husband's murder we're working on."

"Frank didn't kill him."

"How do you know that?"

"I know Frank."

"How well?"

"What? Are you suggesting. . . ?" Her mouth quivered, then set into a hard line. "I don't like that inference. My husband hasn't been dead twenty-four hours and you're accusing me of infidelity."

I didn't respond. Let her answer my question.

But she didn't. What she said was, "You're assuming Earth Man knows where Frank is."

I nodded.

"But suppose he doesn't know? Six hundred dollars is a lot of money to Earth Man. It's unfair to tempt him like that."

"In most cases it would be unfair, and foolish. But Earth Man has his own set of ethics. He's not going to steal from a friend."

"You're asking me to betray his friendship."

"Only if Yankowski killed Mitch. If he's innocent, there's nothing to betray."

She stared down into the coffee as she sloshed it slowly around the sides of the cup. In the harsh white kitchen, the light showed up the myriad fine lines around her eyes. "Can you guarantee I'll be reimbursed if it never gets to Frank?"

I restrained a smile. Ah, ethics versus economics.

"Give him two hundred, and if he skips the department will make good."

She took a long drink of coffee, thinking. I wondered whether she was considering how to alert Yankowski. There were phones up here in the office and the bedroom. Downstairs the only one was at the front desk, behind that Plasticine-covered strip of twinkling lights.

She set down the cup with a thump and—resistance clear in every leaden step—walked into the office and unlocked the safe, and counted out two hundred dollars. Pereira stared blankly as if dazzled by a sleight-of-hand act, but Laura Biekma seemed to have forgotten she was there. Putting the money in an envelope, she said, "I'd better fix Earth Man something to eat up here. I don't think there's any food downstairs."

"Make a sandwich he can carry with him, so he doesn't have to hang around and return a plate."

"Goose on black bread?"

"Fine."

She cut two thick slices of ebon bread, spread them with a paste that resembled butter only in the broadest sense, laid on the meat and some greens I couldn't name. The result looked like a sandwich that should have been consumed on the Left Bank with a bottle of champagne.

"Earth Man usually comes at eleven, right?" I asked as we walked down the stairs. Neither of us suggested that he might think Paradise would be closed tonight and there would be no handout. I wasn't sure the possibility of closing would occur to him, and even if it did, I was willing to bet he'd decide the trip was worth the chance. Earth Man took comfort in the traditions he'd created, in occupying his spot at Sproul Plaza every day regardless of the weather, delivering his spiel regardless of the reception. Dinner here was a tradition he wouldn't let go of easily.

By now Howard would be parked at the Josephine Street end of Grove Path.

Dum de dum dum, a tape played as the clock hit midnight. "One of Mitch's innovations," Laura said with an embarrassed shrug. "It always amused the crowd. Then Mitch would go into his routine about the city insisting we throw them out. He was good, you know. No one ever complained. Other places practically have to shovel the dawdlers out, but Mitch, he always had them on his side." Her face flushed, as if all the control that had supported her these last twenty-four hours was about to shatter. Again, I wondered if it was the realization that Mitch was dead or the fear of exposing Yankowski which was getting to her. She pressed her eyes closed. When she opened them she said, "Should I wait in the kitchen, where Earth Man will see me?"

"Why don't you put something on the stove nearest the door." I followed her into the kitchen and stationed myself inside the pantry, next to the back door, where I could see her as she filled a pot with water and put it on the burner.

It was twenty minutes before he rapped on the door. "I made you a sandwich," Laura said as she pulled opened the door. "It's goose, you'll like it."

"I appreciate that. You've been real nice to me all along," he said in a tone he might use with a small child. There was no remnant of his public stridency, or the confusion and fear that emerged when he'd answered my questions. He sounded as normal as any of us, more sincere than many. Laura flushed. She stared down at the sandwich—her own thirty pieces of goose—as if frozen by her impending betrayal. Then, she thrust the sandwich at him. I wished I could have seen Earth Man's reaction. But from my vantage point, only the front of his cloak was visible, moving toward the sandwich. It looked as if he were going to inhale the sandwich through his elephant trunk. "I have to ask you a favor," she said to him.

"For you? Of course."

She pulled an envelope from her pocket. "I didn't get a

chance to pay Frank. He's going to need his money. I know you're his friend."

"You want me to take it to him."

She swallowed. I wondered if Earth Man recognized the shame in her face. Would he catch on that she was deceiving him? As I had so many times before, I wished I knew the state of his mind better.

"Tuck it in my boot," he said, extending one foot.

She bent down, lifted the hem of his cloak, and wiggled the envelope down inside his well-scuffed boot.

"Thanks," she said in almost a whisper when she stood up.

Earth Man didn't answer. Was he lifting an eyebrow in question? Was he looking toward the corner around which I stood, tacitly asking Laura if they were being watched? If she responded, it was too subtle for me to catch. Finally, she said to him, "Is something the matter?"

"No. I'm just sorry this happened to you. I'm glad to be able to help. Are you going to be here tomorrow?"

"I don't know. But we'll be open Tuesday."

"But I can come tomorrow, right? This is where I have my dinner. Even if no one else shows up, I'll be here," he assured her, as if his continued patronage were the key to Paradise's financial survival. He pulled the sandwich closer to him. The cloak covered it almost completely.

"Yes, you can come tomorrow," she said as she closed the door. She turned to me, but I held my finger to my mouth, and listened to Earth Man's footsteps. I had hoped he would head toward Josephine, toward Howard, and give me time to get to my car. But he was going east, to Martin Luther King.

CHAPTER 23

I waited till Earth Man had time to reach the street, then opened the kitchen door of Paradise and walked quietly down the steps. There was no sign of him. I raced up the path, my running shoes silent on the cement. Pausing at the edge of the building, I looked left. No movement. At the end of the walk, I peered around the hedge. There he was, heading north on King.

Keeping on the grass, as near to the buildings as possible, I ran the hundred feet south to my car and waited to open the door until Earth Man started into the intersection. Once inside, I keyed in the mike with my thumb and called the dispatcher to get a car-to-car channel. The dispatcher would notify Howard and would route anyone else to another channel. Only someone wanting one of us would be referred to our channel, and in this instance, with both Doyle and Pereira in bed, that meant no one.

"I'm here on two," Howard said in a minute. "Where's our boy now?"

"North on King, going away from his hotel. He just crossed the street. You take him."

"Any guesses where he's headed?"

"Could be the Bhairava, Prem's place, or to Adrienne Jenk's flat. Could be some secret hideout known only to him and Yankowski."

"Wherever, he's not headed there fast. He ought to have a turtle beak in place of some of those snouts. Or maybe a few more trunks."

"Leave a message for his couturier."

"I've just passed him. He's crossing the street, still moseying north."

"Okay, I'm starting up." I hung a U. The fog was thinner than it had been last night, barely a filmy veil. I could make out Earth Man's conical form a block ahead. "You're certainly right about turtle steps," I said to Howard. "I hope he's not having second thoughts about delivering the money."

"Or considering bankrolling a ten-day vacation in Acapulco."

"With the money I authorized, it would be a weekend in San Jose." I sighed. I passed him at twenty miles per hour. Any slower would be an invitation, if not a demand, for him to notice me.

"Five bucks says he's just scouting around for a spot to sit and eat his sandwich. How long has he been coming here for meals?"

"Two months."

"He must be an expert on moonlit al fresco dining in this neighborhood."

"You take him, Howard. He's three houses from the corner."

"What about the fiver?"

"Listen, if I have to tell Doyle that I spent two hours trailing Earth Man just to watch him gobble goose, I'm going to lose a lot more than five bucks. Doyle already has reservations about me handling this case."

"Reservations?" Howard demanded. "Hey, how come? He didn't have *reservations* when you delivered your last killer. He thought you were pretty hot stuff then."

An AC Transit bus passed. Its bright interior lights shone against the dark night. Inside, one man sat in the back, staring ahead like the last patient in a dentist's waiting room.

"Jill?" Howard demanded.

"He keeps asking me if I feel up to handling the case."

"Well, you have been on sick leave."

"He asked me four times, Howard."

"Maybe he's just concerned. Earth Man's midblock. I'm past him."

"Okay." I drove in silence, toes pulled back to keep the speed down. When I spotted Earth Man he was nearing Hopkins Street. "If Doyle's concerned, it's not *for* me, it's *about* me. Each time he asked, I told him I could handle the case; he doesn't really believe me. Howard, the thing is I don't think he can bring himself to believe me."

Howard hesitated. "Well, you were in a bad crash. You could have been killed."

"Howard, damn it, don't defend him. Look, suppose it were you. Suppose you'd been out on sick leave; suppose you'd come back with a medical release. Suppose he'd asked you if you could handle a case, and you'd assured him, and then he'd asked again, and again, and again."

"He wouldn't do that."

"Exactly."

"Oh." A van passed heading south. A cat darted half way across the lane, froze, then spun around and leapt for the curb. "Jill, Doyle probably thinks of you as a daughter."

"He should think of me as a cop!"

I could hear Howard's sharp intake of breath. "Oh. Well, you know, Jill, it probably doesn't even occur to him he's treating you differently. It's the generational thing."

"The generational thing that could bounce me out of Homicide. Howard, he wants me off the case, and he thinks he's doing it for my own good. I'd be better off dealing with Grayson, who's just after my job."

"Jill—"

"Howard, you're not even mad."

"I am."

"You don't sound it."

"What do you want, a growl?"

"Skip it," I snapped.

"Hey, I'm trying to look at this thing logically. You want

166

me to go charging down to the station, to Doyle, to protect you?"

"I said skip it." Earth Man paused at the corner of Hopkins. He turned east, toward the hills, toward the hills, toward Adrienne Jenk's flat, but he didn't start walking. Then he turned south, for a moment looking directly at me. "Earth Man's at the corner," I muttered, "facing back south. I've passed him."

"Fine," he snapped.

The north branch of the Berkeley Library sits on a triangle of land at the northwest corner of Hopkins and King. I pulled around it and stopped.

"He's heading west," Howard said. "He's crossing Josephine, picking up his pace, going toward the running track. Maybe he's warming up to run a few laps." I could hear the unsureness in his voice, but I was too angry to deal with it.

"Umm."

"He's still walking. I'm past him now. You better start. That hurricane fence isn't very high. It'd almost be worth the chance of losing him to see his beaks chirping on top of the fence."

"Maybe to you. I don't have the luxury of losing another suspect." I turned right onto Hopkins, my hands clutching the wheel, my teeth clenched. A block ahead, Howard's car moved slowly. Earth Man ambled along staring at the track as if he were watching the Olympic Trials. He passed the end of the track, walked behind one of the shade trees at the curb. Then he disappeared. "He's gone!"

"Gone? What do you mean gone? Where could he go? He has to be in the park."

"I'm twenty yards shy of where he disappeared."

"I'm heading back toward you. You see anything?"

"No movement. Nothing. He has to be in the park; there's nowhere else for him to be."

"Maybe he's just taking a leak."

"Right." I wanted to step on the gas, but I forced myself to keep the pace steady, not to chance alerting him by gunning the engine. I stared to the left. Despite the occasional streetlight, the park was dark. Too many trees. Scores of places to hide, in the playground, in the bushes, by the pool, up in the school yard. I scanned the track, the bushes, the macadam walkway into the park. Then I spotted him. I sighed, feeling simultaneously relieved, furious, and foolish. "There he is, on the path to the playground. He's sitting on a bench." I slowed the car and stared, the relief gone. Now I felt only angry and ridiculous. "Goddamn it, Howard, he's getting out his sandwich."

Howard laughed. "Five bucks, lady."

"He's sitting right under the 'Park Closes at Ten' sign, eating his fucking goose sandwich."

Howard roared. I was surprised Earth Man couldn't hear him. "So what are you going to do, Jill, arrest him? Or should we just bring him a bottle of Chardonnay?"

"Not funny," I muttered. "Maybe tomorrow it'll be funny. After I figure out a way to explain it to Doyle. But now I'm too furious to laugh." Across the street, a van screeched to a halt. Taking advantage of the diversion, I pulled to the curb, doused the lights, and adjusted the rearview mirror. "I'm across the street. I've got him in view."

"I'm at the corner. I could cut in on foot at the far end of the playground, if you promise not to attack me at the slide. Murakawa was good and sore this morning."

And no one suspected he was too lame to work, I thought. But there was no point in prolonging my complaint. Howard's silence had said it all. Even he, my closest friend, could understand Doyle's reaction. I should have felt justified, knowing my assessment was right, but that only made matters worse. I hadn't even told Howard about my panic driving downhill. I was too ashamed. Now I was glad I had kept silent. And if Doyle ever found out about it, that would be the last straw. He wouldn't just take me off the case. He'd nod knowingly, mutter a few fatherly words about not risking my safety, and add that city insurance wasn't about to underwrite a panicky driver. Then he'd ask me if I could type. "Stay in the car, Howard. I'm close enough if Earth Man runs. He's barely into his sandwich. He'll be a while."

"Listen, Jill, what have you got with this case? Give me a rundown."

How many times had that question offered needed diversion in the last four years? It wouldn't cover this difference; it would just let us put off dealing with it. This wasn't the time for a philosophical discussion, much less an argument, I knew that. But I couldn't let it go, either.

"Yankowski," Howard speculated. "Why did he run? Because he killed Biekma? Why would he kill Biekma? Biekma had already mentioned him on TV, right? The damage was done. And Yankowski had gotten his revenge foisting Earth Man on him."

I tapped my finger angrily on the steering wheel.

"Jealousy?"

I didn't say anything.

"You know not all feelings are obvious, Jill. Yankowski could have been willing to chance incriminating himself like this because he loved Laura. Maybe he just didn't show it." Howard paused, and when he continued there was a catch in his voice. "Not everyone gets a chance, Jill."

"Maybe," I said, feeling my face flush. "I can't decide." I wanted to reach out to him, but I didn't know whether it was to hug him or throttle him.

"What about Rue Driscoll?"

"Rue Driscoll?" I said slowly, drawing my attention back from Howard to the case. "Listen, I'd almost rather not find Yankowski than discover he was hiding in the house right behind Paradise. But there's no connection between him and Driscoll. Rue Driscoll's got a good motive for killing Mitch. With him alive she'd have been kept up six nights a week. Her work, the research that could make her a name in her field, might never get finished."

"Did you find any monkshood in her garden?"

"No. There was nothing but weeds there. But even if she did have the poison, I don't see how she'd have gotten it in Mitch's horseradish jar."

"How long a time would she have had for that?"

"Since the previous night. Mitch put horseradish in his soup after the last sitting Wednesday night. After that the jar sat in the pantry."

"Just waiting for the killer to add the poison, right?"

"Presumably so."

"And once that was done, Jill, then the killer sat back and waited for Mitch to use it, right? Didn't matter when."

I hesitated. "That makes sense, Howard. But, somehow, I just can't buy it."

"Why not?"

"I don't know. I just can't believe that the timing didn't matter. Earth Man was instructed to come back later; that had never happened before. And when he came back, Mitch died. It's just too much of a coincidence."

"So?"

"I don't know yet, Howard." Earth Man stared down at the remains of his goose sandwich, held awkwardly in a fold of his cloak. Without rising from the bench, he appeared to shimmy. His beaks and snouts bounced. The dark mounds of his cloak swayed forward. What *was* he doing? When the motion stopped I could see more of the sandwich. He had repositioned it. And having done so, he leaned forward and thrust it into his mouth.

"Okay, what about Prem-Struber?" Howard asked. "He's my favorite suspect anyway. He was in Paris with Mitch, right? There when Mitch bought his horseradish jar."

"Rare and unique horseradish jar, Howard."

"Maybe so. Maybe that's just what the merchant told him. Or maybe rare, but not quite unique. Maybe instead of just one in existence there were two."

"Or three. Adrienne was there too. And for motive, it's a real toss-up between those two." The mound of Earth

Man's cloak pressed against his face, then fell to his lap. "Earth Man's finished his sandwich."

"Jill, don't forget what Jackson always says."

"What?"

"'Yet and still, Smith, you've got the wife.'"

I smiled. Jackson was indeed famous for his devotion to mariticide.

Earth Man stood up and shook. His cloak looked like a cupola from which a flock of pigeons was about to take flight. "He's up." I said. "Wait. He's not going into the playground, he's coming back to the street, starting down toward you. He's moving fast. Looks like he's made his decision. I can cover him for a while."

"Right."

"He's going in, through the next gate, the one between the pool and the playground." Leaving the lights and engine off, I released the brake. "There, I'm rolling. Okay, I can see him. He's using the phone."

"How? What's he using to dial?" Howard asked, amazed.

"Hand coming out through the neck hole. The hole's not that big; it must be just about choking him. He's hung up the receiver."

"Either he warned Yankowski in a minimum of words, or he told him where to meet him."

In contrast to his purposeful stride of the last couple of minutes, Earth Man ambled slowly to the curb. I pushed the seat back and scrunched down below the windows. "He's right across the street."

"Maybe he wants a ride."

"Keep me posted." The wind rustled the leaves. What sounded like a Styrofoam cup clattered up Hopkins. From the residential side of the street came a dog's howling. I shifted, taking the weight off the injured spot in my back. Who was hiding Yankowski? It wasn't Laura, not in Paradise. And there was no record of her having any other property. If she could be believed, Yankowski had no outside friends. He didn't have friends at his hotel. He wasn't even living there. The only things in his closet were winter clothes, and not even all of them. His wool cap, at least, he kept with him. He had had that in his pocket when I first saw him. Of course, for a bald man in Berkeley, a wool cap can be an all-season garment.

"A cab, Jill," Howard exclaimed. "Earth Man's called a cab!" Howard laughed. "You think you had problems before. Wait till Doyle hears you authorized two hundred dollars for Earth Man's cab fare!"

"Damn, damn, damn!" I smashed my fist into the seat, pushed myself up, and whacked the steering wheel. It quivered, and for a moment I thought it was going to crack and allow me to add a broken steering wheel to the rest of the night's misspent expenses.

"He's turning south at Sacramento, Jill."

I started the engine. Yankowski's wool cap was tan. It had bleach spots. There couldn't be two like that.

"Due south, Jill. He's passing the BART station. Too flush to take rapid transit, huh? Made the light at Hearst. He's turning on University. Okay, he could be headed to the freeway," Howard said, getting into the spirit of the chase.

I stopped wondering about Earth Man. I had seen a tan wool cap this afternoon, one with the bleach spots.

"Jill, the cab's slowing. It's making a U. Ah, shit. You know where he's going?"

I was still on Sacramento, but I knew. "La Maison. Earth man's riding home in style. I'll pass the word to the guy on surveillance, not that they'd miss a sight like that. I doubt Earth Man's going out again tonight."

"Damn. There he is climbing out of the cab, and Jill, every one of those snouts and beaks is laughing at us."

"It's okay," I said, recalling just where I had seen that wool cap. "Betcha that five and five more I know where Yankowski is."

CHAPTER 24

Adrienne Jenks had filled her flat with splashy hot pinks and purples, South Seas blues and greens. Her clothes echoed the theme. A plain tan wool cap was something she wouldn't use to clean her car, much less put on her head. With her thick mane of curly hair, she'd need outside help to pull it on.

But Frank Yankowski's head was a different matter. He had a thin fringe of blond hair around his sizable bald pate. His was a head in danger of sunburn in spring, windburn in summer, and being damned cold any night of the year. His head needed a cap. He had had one in his pocket when I interviewed him, a tan wool cap marked with bleach spots. How could I have missed that? I was looking all over Berkeley for the guy and there he had been, probably hiding in the bathroom while I interrogated Adrienne on the sofa.

It was not Laura Biekma but Adrienne Jenks who was Frank Yankowski's friend or lover. That explained why Adrienne wouldn't allow Mitch in the kitchen for the last three months—to keep him away from Yankowski. It explained why Mitch hadn't fired him. And while it told me where Yankowski might well be hiding, it did nothing to shed light on why he had fled.

Whatever the reason, he wasn't going to get a chance to try it again. I turned onto Spruce, flipped on the pulsers, and hit the gas.

I turned off the pulsers a block before Adrienne's flat, and stopped the car on the side street. Howard arrived less than a minute later. He had a wary half smile—the smile for the prospect of a collar, the wariness for me. "You got your Ramey warrant?"

"I haven't been without it all day. This asshole is not going to run out on me again."

"Let him try," Howard said.

"Yeah." I hoped he would try. We were ready for him. I could almost feel my knees in his back, and the victory of yanking his arms behind him and snapping on the cuffs.

"We'll get him," Howard said. "See what Doyle says about this one."

"Ready?" I asked. He followed me through the break in the hedge, across the tree-shaded backyard, and up the six steps to Adrienne's door. The flat was dark, but I had the feeling that Adrienne and Yankowski were awake. Standing to one side of the door, I knocked. "Police!"

I was just about to knock again when Adrienne called, "It's the middle of the night. What do you want now?"

"Yankowski."

"He's not here."

"Open the door."

From inside I could hear cloth rubbing cloth, then bare feet slapping against the hardwood floor. The feet stopped, then moved quickly back the way they had come. Did I hear whispers or was I imagining the scene I hoped was being played out in there? "Do you have a warrant?" Adrienne called, her voice defiant, but not controlled enough subdue a noticeable quiver.

"You bet!" I called. "Now get this door open!"

There was silence inside the flat. Across from me, Howard bent into a slight crouch, ready.

"We can kick this door in!" I shouted. "You want that? You've got five seconds to decide, Yankowski." I crouched down, ready for him. "One . . . two . . . three . . . four . . ."

The door opened and Yankowski walked out, hands raised. I pushed the door shut after him, banging it against the moldings with all my unspent anger. Howard moved down two steps. "Okay, Yankowski," I shouted, "turn around, hands high on the door!" I patted him down, crisply. Then I yanked his hands back and slammed on the cuffs.

"Hey, not so tight. You're going to cut off the circulation."

"You'll live. Turn around, down the stairs." I knew what I was doing, taking out my revenge in petty bullying. Out of the corner of my eye I could see Howard, looking straight ahead; he knew too. Leaving him to deal with Adrienne Jenks, I followed Yankowski down the steps and gave him a shove, a restrained shove, because I was already feeling like a jerk, and because Yankowski was so much bigger than me.

The process of booking him took less time than the usual half hour. I had run him through files last night. I knew we had nothing. Still, when it came time to take his prints, he yanked his hand back.

"Worried about the prints, huh?" I said. "You're not Frank Yankowski. Who are you?"

"You're disgusting," he said. The hiss accompanied his words. "Look at my wrists; they've still got marks."

"You want to see a doctor?" I said, controlling my sarcasm. "It's your right to file charges, say I roughed you up."

"Yeah sure." His pale eyes narrowed, leaving his sharply twisted nose the only marker on his big, pale round face. "I'm still not answering your questions," he said.

"Look," I snapped, "you can make every step of this more difficult, but that's not going to change the outcome. You're in jail. You're going to stay there till we find out who you are. You're going to stay till we know why you killed Mitch Biekma."

"I didn't kill him."

"You ran."

"I didn't poison Mitch."

"You're guilty, Yankowski."

"I knew you'd think that. As soon as I saw you there in Paradise, I knew you'd come after me."

"You were just a witness, like any of the others, until you ran. You made yourself stand out."

He shrugged.

"So explain. But first the prints."

With a sigh, he held out his fingers and allowed them to be pressed into the ink pad. Then I took him to one of the interview booths, sat him down across the table, and started the tape. "Detective Jill Smith, interviewing Caucasian male calling himself Frank Yankowski."

"Okay, it's Martin Goodpastor."

"And where did you get the name Yankowski?"

"From a cemetery. A dead child in a cemetery."

"Very considerate. His parents could have been in for a nasty surprise if Mitch Biekma had mentioned your name on television."

"I thought of that," he said, the hiss more pronounced than before.

"And, of course, the parents would have tracked you down and exposed you eventually."

"Maybe not. It's not that uncommon a name."

"Why did you run, Martin?"

His hazel eyes opened wide; he almost smiled. "You mean you don't know? You really don't know?"

"Tell me."

"The bombing at the Seattle Induction Center."

"During Vietnam?" I asked, echoing his amazement.

He nodded, his eyes saying that any literate should know that.

The Vietnam protests were twenty years ago. By now he'd be lucky to find anyone who could name the Chicago Seven, much less remember someone connected with the Seattle Induction Center.

"So you bombed the induction center—"

"*I* didn't."

"Okay, we'll deal with that later. What I want to know is why you killed Mitchell Biekma."

"*I* didn't."

I leaned back in the chair. "You hated Biekma. You told me that."

"But I didn't kill him. The world's jammed with assholes. But you don't kill them. Look, I was in the peace movement in Seattle. I didn't set that bomb. I didn't even know there was a bomb there to go off. I wasn't into violence. I was there to stop the killing. I could have given myself up and gone to jail. I'm a big guy, an ugly big guy. I'm not the type who gets raped in prison. I would have survived, but I would have had to bash heads to do it. I chose not to. *Chose.* Do you think it's been easy living on the run all these years. If I'd stood trial, I could be clear by now. But I would have lost my principles." He stared at me, demanding a sign of belief.

But I wasn't about to give that. "Go on."

"You think I'm lying. Dammit. I knew it. You gave me no choice but to run."

"*Go on!*"

"Okay, but if you've decided I'm a killer, it won't make much sense. I didn't murder Mitch. Sure, I wanted him to keep quiet about me. But I didn't have to kill him. I'm a lot bigger than he was; I'm in a lot better shape. I just pointed that out to him."

"And?"

"He backed off. He wasn't out to blow my cover. He didn't care that much. It's just that I made a good story. And he was the kind of asshole who lived for that moment of glory. When he was on—working the customers in the dining room, or on a talk show—that's when it was the worst. He'd do anything for a laugh. And if that meant telling the world he had a crooked-nosed giant doing dishes because he was hiding out from a crazed ex-wife, that was fine. Then he could carry on: 'The guy's six four, he weighs two fifty, how big is this woman he's afraid of? Is she an Amazon?' And on and on. He did it in the dining room once. He had them in stitches. Half the house was peeking around the door into the kitchen before they left. That's what Adrienne told me. I was gone." The hiss almost drowned out his last word. "The next day I made things clear to him. And he never mentioned me again."

"But he could have."

"I wasn't kidding. He knew that."

"But you weren't worried about an ex-wife. There was no ex-wife. That was just a cover story. You weren't worried about some sheriff from the Midwest coming across you, you were afraid of the FBI finding you. Even after twenty years a description of your face could ring a bell." I didn't have to wait for a reply. Yankowski's tortured breath told me I was right. "You had a lot to lose, if Mitch got carried away. . . ."

It was a moment before he controlled his breath enough to say, "Yeah, I did. But with Mitch it was out of sight out of mind. And Adrienne kept him out of the kitchen. He probably forgot I was there."

"I don't believe that and neither did you."

"I still don't know how Mitch found out about the induction center. Maybe someone here recognized me. Maybe Adrienne let something slip. She denies it, but who knows? Maybe I slipped by telling even her." He shrugged. "I did what I could to keep Mitch quiet. And even taking Mitch as a factor in the equation, it was safer for me here in Berkeley than it would have been anywhere else. Turning me in would not have been a popular move for Mitch. He didn't give a shit about me, but he was shrewd enough to know what would hurt him."

That made sense. If he had betrayed Yankowski, liberals would have derided him. If, somehow, he had managed to picture himself as Yankowski's protector, he would have courted the wrath of conservatives in the wider TV market. Still, for publicity-seeking Mitch Biekma, the temptation to find a middle ground and still expose Yankowski must have been nearly overwhelming. And Yankowski was too bright not to have figured that out. I said, "Mitch was poisoned with aconite. Customers got sick from it. Someone put it in their food, eight different times. The only people who were there all those times were Mitch and Adrienne. But you were there seven."

He stared at me. "Why would I poison people? I told you I wasn't into violence. Besides, something like that, it would just bring the cops out, and reporters. Listen, that's the last thing I'd want."

"Then who was the poisoner?"

"It wasn't me and it wasn't Adrienne."

"Then who?"

"I don't know who killed Mitch. But if you want the guy who dosed the food those other times, you've got him. In the morgue."

CHAPTER 25

I stared at Frank Yankowski—Martin Goodpastor. "Do you really expect me to believe that Mitch Biekma was poisoning his own customers?"

"Believe it or not. It's true."

"Martin, you are in far too much trouble to play around here."

He shook his head. "I knew there was no point in telling you the truth. I knew you'd never believe it."

Ignoring that, I said, "How could Mitch poison the food? He wasn't even allowed in the kitchen."

"He came in far as the warm table. That's where the food

was waiting. All he had to do was pour on a drop of poison."

"What makes you think he did?"

"I saw him."

I stared at him, but he had neither the agitated look of an unaccustomed liar nor the defensive mien of one whose normal reaction is to lie. He looked nearly relaxed. And, for once, his breath was almost silent. "Okay, Martin, give me the whole story. From the beginning. How did you come to suspect him?"

"Then you believe me?"

"I didn't say that. I'm just giving you a chance to convince me."

He nodded. Outside in the hallway a high-pitched male voice was insisting he was not a burglar, but had been hired by an absent friend to help a guy move.

"Moving out his TV at two A.M., eh?" an officer demanded.

"Yeah, man, he wanted it in his new place for the morning news."

A door slammed. To Yankowski I said, "So convince me Mitch poisoned the food."

He took a breath. The hiss was back. "Look, I told you what Mitch was like. Well, you can imagine the big stink he made about the supposed poisoner. He was slamming around 'investigating,' making a big to-do, firing everybody in sight. So no one there could help but be aware of the poisonings."

"Go on."

"Well, a couple of months ago he had one of his colds. We were short-staffed because he'd fired the salad chef. Adrienne was in a temper. And about ten o'clock Mitch came in fussing for his horseradish. Suddenly he had to have a cup of soup with the horseradish. The sous-chef's got to drop everything and run for his horseradish jar. Mitch makes this big production about how he needs his horseradish and he can't even get in his own kitchen for it.

Then he stands over the warm table, pours the horseradish in his soup, and stands there and eats it. Of course, he set Adrienne off, which was what he intended. By the time the last meal was out, everyone was snapping at everyone else. It wasn't a night you'd forget. And then the next day I got there early and I heard Mitch on the phone with a customer saying he was sorry the customer had gotten sick last night."

"Are you saying the poison was in his horseradish jar then?" I asked, amazed.

"Of course not. He poured the horseradish into his own soup and he didn't get sick. He could have had the poison in any small container. It wouldn't have taken much, would it?"

"No." Even diluted, a drop or two could have been ample.

"He was just using the fuss about the horseradish for a reason to hang around the warm table."

"Did you *see* him pouring poison?"

"Not then. Then, I just coupled the events in my mind. But the next time Mitch had a cold, he was in the kitchen mixing up his horseradish and putting it in his jar before Adrienne started to work. And the jar reminded me of that awful night. I told Adrienne not to let him get to her, that he'd be at his worst that night because he had a cold. I told her to watch out."

"And was Mitch at his worst?"

"Oh yeah. He kept coming in to the warm table making comments. This wasn't done enough. That sauce was too thick. I made a bet with Adrienne on the number of times he'd be in, you know, to try to make a joke of it as much as I could. Adrienne has a pretty short fuse. But you probably know that by now, right?"

I didn't respond.

He straightened up. "The thing was," he said, the hiss becoming louder, "that we were watching for him. I was watching more than she; my work doesn't take much thought. I saw him pour a drop of something white on one of the dinners. The sauce was white. I almost said something to him, but I just caught myself in time. I was thinking if Adrienne knew he'd put horseradish in her sauce all hell would break loose."

"But he didn't have the horseradish then, did he?"

"No. That's my point. He poured something else. I was thinking about the horseradish because of the last time he'd been in a temper. So my reaction was to think it was horseradish he had poured. But, of course, it wasn't. The horseradish was still in the pantry, where it always was when he had a cold. Whatever he poured just looked like horseradish."

"Then what?"

"When I heard that a customer had been poisoned that night, I put two and two together."

"And you just planned to let him go on poisoning people? You didn't report him?"

"Come on, would you have believed me?" The hiss almost drowned his words.

"No more than I believe you now! What about Rue Driscoll, how could he have poisoned her?"

"Easy, he carried her food to the table."

"And Earth Man?"

"Easy again, if dumb. Laura wasn't there. Adrienne can't be bothered with Earth Man. She was doing a chicken dish that night and she had a few pieces too scrappy to serve the customers, so she plunked them on the warm table and plopped some soup on them as a sauce. The dish must have sat there an hour. It was probably too big a temptation for Mitch to resist."

I sat back, fingering the edge of the table. "Suppose what you say is true, just suppose. You know what that makes me think?"

"What?"

"That someone who had seen Mitch poisoning the customers' food with a substance that looked like horseradish would be curious enough to check on poisons and find out that aconite can be mistaken for horseradish. And then, he would find it a great temptation to put aconite in his horse-radish jar. That would appeal to the same type of person who found it amusing to arrange for Earth Man's free dinners."

He slammed his fist onto the table. The tape recorder jumped. "The truth means nothing to you. What do I have to say to convince you?"

"Mitch drove you crazy. He drove your girlfriend crazy. He was in a position to send you to prison. It's hard to beat that for a motive. But, for incriminating evidence, add the fact that you assaulted two police officers and ran to avoid having your identity discovered."

He shook his head. "I ran, but not because of that. Because of this. I knew if I had to tell you this you'd suspect us."

"You had a great motive for killing Mitch. Maybe you poisoned the other people to camouflage his death. I can believe that a lot more easily than to think Mitch Biekma capriciously poisoned his customers. Why would he do that? Rue Driscoll and Earth Man were the two people most likely to cause trouble. Why would Mitch go out of his way to poison them? It just doesn't make sense."

"Of course it doesn't make sense. It only makes sense if you remember that Mitch was an asshole. He did it out of spite. I'm sure he never considered the consequences. When he'd lost, all he could think about was getting even. Emotionally the guy was a three-year-old spoiled brat. He didn't care who got hurt; he didn't even restrain himself when he was in danger of screwing up his own plan."

"And what was his plan?"

Yankowski's breath caught. He gasped for air. Staring down at the table, he drew his breath in through his mouth. Finally, he said, "To poison the customers. To keep Adrienne from taking over."

That, of course, was a variation of what Adrienne herself

had told me. She had said Mitch poisoned the customers to destroy her reputation. Yankowski's version couched it in more practical terms.

"You're telling me he cut off his nose to spite his face. It was *his* restaurant."

He shook his head. When he got enough air to speak, he said, "Adrienne hadn't let Mitch in the kitchen for three months. That was common knowledge. Anyone who heard him kicking up a fuss at the warm table knew it. Everyone in the business knew it. Three months."

I nodded. "About the same length of time the food poisonings were going on."

"Yeah," he squeaked out.

"Do you believe him?" Inspector Doyle demanded.

I had called him from my office. I had woken him up, again.

"I don't know. He could have poisoned Mitch. He had both motive and opportunity."

"They all had the opportunity, Smith. They had all day to get to that jar and fill it with poison."

"I don't want to believe Yankowski. But I just can't see him killing someone, even Mitch."

"You got some basis for that, Smith, or is it just a feeling?"

It was more than a feeling, but you learn to trust your feelings after a while in police work. But I was not about to tell that to Inspector Doyle now. At least he hadn't called it intuition.

I recounted Yankowski's background. "He might have wanted to kill Mitch. But think about Yankowski. The guy's managed to hide out from the FBI for twenty years. He's learned to second-guess everything. He wouldn't blow it all for the whim of killing Biekma with his own horseradish container, no matter how much the idea might have appealed to him. He might have been a spontaneous type twenty years ago, but he's not now. If he'd been determined to kill Mitch, he could have found plenty of other ways that wouldn't bring suspicion on the kitchen crew." I was clutching the receiver so tightly that my arm was stiff.

Doyle yawned. "So, Smith, you woke me up to tell me that not only do you not think you have Biekma's killer, but now you don't even think we have a suspect in the food poisonings."

"I'm not saying that, Inspector. I checked with the lab. The tuber in the wine cellar is monkshood. Mitch had the only key. He poisoned the customers. I believe his killer knew that and was attracted by the horseradish jar. I just don't think that killer was Yankowski."

"So who was it?"

I hesitated. "Inspector, I know you want facts."

"And I want them soon. I'll give you the rest of the day. Either you get me the killer—whoever you've decided he is—or you stop looking all around, and concentrate on making a case against Yankowski. Because, Smith, you've got your feelings, and I've got mine, and my feeling is Yankowski's our man."

CHAPTER 26

After my conversation with Inspector Doyle, I didn't feel much like eating. But, as Howard reminded me, I owed him plenty. The least I could do was provide breakfast. And since Wally's was closed at four-thirty in the morning, our destination would be my kitchen.

Howard had been anxious to see the place in which I was house-sitting, but he wasn't so eager to deal with my cooking. We had a meeting of the minds there.

By five o'clock Howard was leaning over the stove in my

kitchen, stooping to avoid the throng of twisted and slotted implements suspended from one of those metal things that look like a cutout of half an umbrella. He poured olive oil into the iron skillet. It was extra virgin olive oil, a concept that might have amused me, had I not been so preoccupied. What was "extra virgin"? Was it from olives tended only by prepubescent boys with monastic aspirations?

"Where are the onions?" he asked.

"Fridge?"

"Curry powder?"

"One of these cabinets, I guess." I pushed myself off the low-back wooden stool and pulled open the nearest cabinet door. Inside were plastic bags of variously colored grains of rice, and beige, gray, and maroon beans. Pushing the door shut, I reached for the next.

Howard turned, grabbed my shoulders, and steered me back to the stool. "I can see you're over your head here. Just sit. I'll work with whatever I find." He began to pull open drawers, extricating a can of olives, an onion, garlic, a bag of dried tomatoes, and three small bags of herbs.

I sipped my coffee. Pereira's acquaintance who owned this house had six pounds of coffee beans in the freezer—Sulawesi-Kalossi, Aged Sulawesi (none of this "we serve no [bean] before its time" in Kalossi?), Ethiopian Fancy, Tanzania, Viennese Blend, and Aged Indonesian Decaffeinated. I'd chosen the Aged Sulawesi.

"Jill, at least Doyle should be pleased you got Yankowski, or whatever his real name is."

"He would have been if I'd said Yankowski was the murderer. *He* thinks he's the murderer. I don't. He's just giving me the rest of the day to see if I can prove otherwise."

Pereira's friend must have been about four feet tall. The counters here seemed low even to me. Howard looked like he was cooking on a play stove. Bending, he tossed a bunch of vegetables into the pan, plunked two pieces of bread in the six-slice toaster, and said, "What about Biekma? Are you sure he poisoned the customers?"

"There was a monkshood tuber in the wine cellar. But there's no monkshood in the garden. Monkshood grows four to six feet tall. The garden is tiny; the flowers are small. Mitch wouldn't have been hoarding one tuber, to grow one plant to tower ludicrously above the little ones. And here's the clincher, Howard: Mitch had the only key to the wine cellar; it was on a chain around his neck. He never gave it to anyone, under any condition."

Howard broke four eggs into the pan. "So he had the key, Jill. The rest of the staff couldn't get at it. What about his wife?"

I shook my head. "Not even her. The word is he never took it off, not in the shower, not in bed."

"If the murderer hadn't been in such a hurry, he could have waited till Biekma choked himself in his sleep," Howard said, laughing. Turning back to the eggs, he added spices, murmuring approvingly with each addition. "Okay, so where'd Biekma get his tuber from? Did he yank it out of a neighbor's yard?"

"Nothing so violent. He could have gone to a garden store and bought tubers, which is probably what his killer did. But Mitch didn't even do that. He got his the easy way."

Howard scooped equal mounds of egg onto each plate, and pulled the toast from the toaster, batting it hand to hand till it reached the plates. "The easy way?"

"He ordered them, with the birds of paradise, from the florist who made the restaurant arrangements. I called him after I finished with Doyle. He was none too pleased to be woken up at that hour. But he did check his records. He'd had three orders for what he referred to as Francis of Assisi."

"Saint Francis?"

I nodded. "Monks and birds—monkshood and birds of paradise. Griffon, the florist, must have laughed for a minute and a half over that one. You know, Howard, a man can spend too much time snapping thorns off roses. When he could speak again, he did tell me the dates the monkshood was ordered. They were three of the evenings customers got sick."

"Real gourmet, Biekma. Only fresh poison for his customers." He held up our plates. "Where do you want to eat these? You said we had about six choices."

I was tempted to tell him right here, at the counter in the kitchen. I was too wired now to bother with comfort. But Howard was leaning, just slightly, so slightly I doubted he realized it, toward the dining room. I picked up the two coffee cups and led the way.

The dining room was large, dark, with a working fireplace. A mahogany table for twelve stood between the fireplace and a sideboard. It was the type of room where you could imagine King Edward VII settling for an eight-course dinner. Still holding the plates, Howard looked down the length of the table. "I suppose the owners wouldn't approve of putting the plates on newspaper?"

"I haven't been home long enough to find place mats." Setting the coffee cups on the floor, I turned the chairs nearest us to face the windows, then shoved them up a foot and a half from the padded seat beneath the bay window. I pulled my shoes off and sat. Howard went back into the kitchen and returned to put a stool behind our chairs.

"Not bad," he said putting his feet up on the window seat. The sun hadn't risen. But the black had lightened to charcoal. In the distance were some variations that might, if the morning did not turn out too foggy, become discernible as the San Francisco skyline.

"Not bad either," I said, taking a bite of the scrambled egg mixture. "Pretty darned good. How'd you learn to cook like this?"

Putting down his fork, he patted my hand. "It's one of my many hidden talents."

"Oh yeah?"

He gave my hand a final tap. "Yeah." Then, stifling a

yawn, he picked up a piece of toast and said, "How do you know Biekma's the one who ordered the monkshood?"

"Griffon remembered him. Griffon said Biekma was not someone he'd be likely to forget. Seems Mitch made scenes about the flowers regularly. The blooms weren't large enough. The orange wasn't bright enough. The foliage was too thick."

"Couldn't he have removed some?"

"That's what I asked. Wrong question. Griffon was appalled. Said I obviously had no sense of artistic statement. He said Mitch had tried that once, and they'd had a big row about it. He said he stormed into Paradise and told Mitch if he ever touched another arrangement it would be the end of their business."

"I'd like to have seen that."

"It was probably one of the few scenes Mitch Biekma lost control of. Or at least that's Griffon's story."

"I guess Griffon is doing okay if he can come on like that."

"He told me he was the best." I laughed. "I hadn't asked." I took another bite of the eggs. "Here's the other thing Griffon told me. Mitch Biekma insisted that the monkshood come root and all."

"So that's where he got his roots. And you figure he surreptitiously clipped a few leaves for his customers' salads. So, he really did need the plants fresh."

"Right. Ground aconite for soup, leaves for salad," I said.

"Didn't Griffon find that a little odd?"

"No. According to Griffon, restaurant people are odd, period. Some of them insist their vegetables be delivered not only with roots in tact, but with the dirt still around them—to be sure they're fresh! He said he wouldn't bother questioning any of their requests."

Howard's plate was empty. My own was three-fourths full. Even if I hadn't been so wired, I would never have finished it. I scraped half the eggs onto Howard's plate. He nodded. It was a ritual too well established to merit comment. I couldn't recall the last meal we'd had when Howard hadn't finished enough to feed a normal family and sat vainly trying not to stare at my food.

"This case is like the Myth of Sisyphus," I said. "First there was the poison. Raksen finds out what it is and where it was, and what does that get us? Nothing. Anyone could have filled that jar with aconite. The jar was standing in the pantry all day long. I've got Yankowski, but I can't believe he's the killer. And Howard, I just cannot believe that someone put up a note telling Earth Man to come back at the time Mitch poured the poison into his soup; that someone took down that note before Mitch died; and that all that was just a coincidence."

"So you're back to Earth Man, huh?"

I had hoped Howard would have more of an insight than that. Frequently he did see my cases in ways I might not have. But instead of presenting me with a revelation, he just yawned. He, of course, hadn't had the five-hour nap that I had. How late he had been up the previous night dealing with the aftermath of his drug sting, I didn't know. But no amount of exhaustion numbed his appetite. He picked up his fork and began the final push on the eggs. Out the window the sky had lightened to battleship gray; the suggestion of the city skyline was clearer. Howard finished the eggs and put the plate on the floor. He yawned. "More coffee?" I asked.

"Mmm."

"Or wine? They have a wine cellar of sorts here. No poison, just wine."

"I think I'll stick with the fridge. There were a couple of bottles in there." Howard got up, and after stacking the plates and grabbing both mugs in one hand, he headed into the kitchen. In a minute he returned with two glasses and a bottle.

"I guess I'm not being much of a hostess," I said, accepting one.

"You aren't likely to be featured in *Sunset* magazine."
Swallowing a yawn, he laughed. "At least not till you've
found the killer. I know what you're like when you're close
enough to taste a collar."

I laughed. "Revolting image of the day."

Howard merely smiled. I could tell the hour was catching
up with him. "As I was saying," he went on, "I understand
your professional eccentricities. Even the best of us can be
single-minded."

"By the best you mean—"

He nodded, forefinger to his chest. "But I'm willing to
help you. After all, you're only a woman."

Picking up the discarded newspaper, I smacked him.

"Hey, what's that? You think I'm a dog?"

"Well, you may require some training."

Howard caught my eye. "I'm doing my best to understand, but like Jackson says, you can't know what it's like to
be black if you've never been."

"Maybe so." I smiled and clinked his glass, then leaned
back and drank. "And maybe I didn't need to snap at you."

He tried to suppress a yawn, and failed. Then he smiled.
He caught my feet between his. I hadn't realized mine were
cold. The warmth of his feet made the cold parts colder, but
it also made the warm warmer. I smiled and reached for his
hand, covering it, in part, with my own. Outside, the edges
of the redwoods and the eucalyptus in the yard beneath
were becoming distinct. The first tentative rays of morning
were breaking through the night. In the distance, over the
Golden Gate Bridge, the clouds separated, like a sheet suddenly torn, and the blue of morning peered from behind
and then was gone. It might not reappear all day. No matter. I turned toward Howard, looking at him slouched back
in the armchair. His mop of red curls stood out from his
head. When I first knew him, he had worn one of the uniform hats, the ten-gallon type. It had left a ridge above his
ears. I could remember staring at that ridge night after night
over burgers at Priester's. He had been the friend I had

needed in those bleak times, when I struggled to realize that my marriage had crumbled, that it had, indeed, been rubble for over a year.

How many times had I focused on his wide, sudden grin, and the laugh that burst out in great rippling swells and obliterated all thoughts? Rarely had I let myself meet his eyes; I had been afraid of being drawn in, of drowning. I needed his strong friendship to hold on to.

Getting involved with a man you work with is dangerous. If it fails, the awkwardness is ten times greater than the vanished pleasure. Making a mistake with the man with whom you share an eight-by-ten office . . .

I put down my wine glass. I ran my fingers across his shoulder and looked at those deep blue eyes. Or more accurately at the lids. Howard was asleep.

CHAPTER 27

Six-thirty Saturday morning is not a good time for much of anything, except driving down steep empty streets. I knew I should be relaxed before I tackled the steep drop of Marin Avenue. I was too wired now. But I was too wired to do anything else. I got in my car and drove up to the top. I sat there, car poised at the edge of the intersection. The street looked like a giant slide at an amusement park: steep, slick, and permitting no escape. My face was already clammy with fear. I stepped on the gas.

In the forty-five minutes that followed, I drove down three terror-filled times: the first, staring compulsively at the pavement ahead to distract myself; the second, with the car windows closed, radio blaring; the third, swearing the entire way. In those three drives the only thing that decreased was the altitude, certainly not my fear. Each failure to shake it made it worse. Maybe I needed help, a psychiatrist—hell, a lobotomy.

I stepped on the gas and drove slowly along the gently sloping streets to the Albany pool.

Lack of sleep, and a stomach full of omelet, toast, coffee, wine, all churned in fear, are not the prerequisites of good lap swimming. But I needed the exercise. More than that, I needed some mental distance from the Biekma case, and from myself.

One of the fast lanes in the center of the pool was empty. I slid in, adjusted my goggles, and pushed off, feeling the soft embrace of the cool water. The weight of breakfast hit me in the second lap. My stomach knotted. My arms felt as if they were inside a ski sweater. My legs flopped behind me, refusing to coordinate, as if they were controlled by opposing teams. I gasped for breath, taking a wide-open turn at the end of the lap, keeping my head above water to get my breath. I pulled harder, catching the water at the top of each stroke, pulling it swiftly down to my side. And when that came more easily, I focused on my kick, and then the breathing. By the time I hit the half-mile mark, everything had come together—the pull, the kick, the breathing. The water felt thick and fast beneath, supporting me as I skimmed above it. I was making flip turns, somersaulting to bring my feet to the wall and pushing off to a glide that took me nearly a quarter of the lap before surfacing.

I finished my mile, climbed out virtuously on shaky legs, and stood under the pelting hot shower, feeling the water massage my neck, letting my breath relax, only slowly allowing thoughts about the case to creep back in. There's a focus to every case. Sometimes the focus is the killer. It's his anger or craziness that is the key. But with the Biekma murder, the focus was Mitch himself. What had he done to precipitate his own death? He had poisoned his customers. But why? I couldn't believe Mitch had been willing to destroy Paradise just to discredit Adrienne, as she and Yankowski suspected.

I squeezed some ChloroCleen shampoo—overoptimistically touted to remove chlorine buildup—onto my hair, and let it sit. Mitch had built Paradise from nothing. All his money, as well as Laura's and Laura's father's, was tied up in it. Mitch wasn't a financial innocent. How would he live if Paradise failed? On Laura's salary? That would barely cover the house payment. On the royalties from his upcoming cookbook? I doubted that. One book does not a lifetime support. And without Paradise, there would be no sequel.

I scrubbed my skin with the ChloroCleen soap, which vainly promised to get the chlorine smell out of my pores, then rinsed my hair, and finally added ChloroCleen conditioner, which assured me it would make my hair soft once again. ChloroCleen also made body lotion, and skin toner for swimmers who chose to delude themselves after they got out of the shower. But Mitch had poisoned the customers. Why? Why would he go to such lengths to destroy his own income? He hadn't been promised a TV job; that was still just a possibility. What was he going to use for income in the meantime? The answer had to be where the financial answers were—in the books at Paradise.

As I walked down the steps outside, I glanced at my watch. Still too early to call Pereira. I drove to the station, picked up the last jelly donut from the desk man's box, got a cup of machine coffee and the newspaper. A picture of Paradise's metal garden was on page 3. The headline read, NO PROGRESS IN BIEKMA SLAYING. The subhead added, "Escaped witness found." Found! Like he'd been left in a basket on our doorstep! A glob of red jelly fell on the text. It seemed appropriate. I tossed the paper in the trash.

At ten o'clock I called Pereira.

There was no answer. I slammed down the phone. So much for consideration! I'd waited too long and she'd gone out. Unless, God forbid, she was away for the weekend.

I got another cup of coffee from the machine, came back and tried Pereira again. Still no answer. Irritably, I pulled out my notes from Thursday night's interrogations. It wasn't as if I couldn't fill my time dictating. I'd have to do it soon.

But I didn't move. Pereira had told me about the Paradise books. The only things she had found odd were the payment from Bump and Grind to Mitch, and Mitch's double payment on the kitchen equipment. I picked up the phone book and fingered through to the B's. But there was no listing for a Bump and Grind. I called Information. No help. What was Bump and Grind? It could be an exotic dance studio, but it could as easily be a crowded coffee house.

I dialed Pereira again. Again, no answer.

Okay, the equipment company. I flipped through my notes.

Saturday was not the best time to contact a leasing company, either. Had it been another type of company, I might have been out of luck entirely. But Reli-Quip provided a twenty-four-hour repair service. I called the number, and after one round with the dispatcher, and another with the owner, I got the bookkeeper.

I explained who I was. "I'm investigating a murder."

"Biekma, huh? I saw the newscast. Guess you guys need all the help you can get, huh?"

"We always appreciate the public's cooperation," I announced in a frigid bureaucratic tone. "What you can tell me now is why he made a double payment this month?"

"That all? It's a penalty because he was breaking the contract. He had another six months to go on it. But he decided to return the equipment—the whole kitchen will be back here the tenth of next month."

"Was he dissatisfied?"

"How do I know? I'm just the bookkeeper. As long as they pay their bills, I assume they're satisfied."

I called Pereira. Still no answer. There was nothing I could do till I got her. And suddenly, I realized, I was exhausted. I left a note on Pereira's desk on the off chance she stopped in, and headed for my car.

I swung by her apartment and put another note on her door, telling her to call me. Ten minutes later I was home and in that wonderful king-sized bed.

It was seven-thirty when she called.

"What is it that's so important, Jill?"

"Biekma," I said without introduction. "He canceled the lease on all his kitchen equipment. Was he negotiating with another company?"

"Hey, wait a minute. I just got home. Give me time to put my purse down?"

"I've been trying to get you all day."

"Lucky for me I went out, huh?" When I didn't respond, she said, "Okay, back to Biekma. The answer is no. He hadn't leased new equipment. There was no contract. And I would have noticed an initial payment that size. Believe me, there wasn't any."

"You're sure? He could have stuck a contract anywhere. As for the payment, isn't there some way it could have been entered in the books that you would have glanced over? After all, you weren't looking for that."

"Jill," Connie said, sighing, "I am positive. If there had been a payment to a new company in those books, I would have spotted it. But I am also a realist. I know you. So I might as well go and look through those books again now."

It was less than an hour later when Pereira called to corroborate her conclusion—there was no payment on order for new equipment. In that hour I had had time to make some almond–tahini-butter toast and coffee, and settle back in bed with them. Expecting Pereira's statement, I had considered the consequences of Paradise's closing.

"Mitch couldn't sell Paradise without Adrienne's okay," I said to Pereira when she called. "And Adrienne wasn't about to give it unless she ended up with control."

"No backer would put up that kind of money and not maintain control, Jill. It would be suicide."

"So Mitch sends back the kitchen equipment and doesn't order more."

Pereira laughed. "Guess that'll show Adrienne."

I dragged the other pillow across the bed and bunched both behind my back.

"Well," she said, "there's only one reason he would return the kitchen equipment."

"Because he was planning to close the restaurant." I pushed myself up against the pillows.

"But why would he close? If he wanted the time for his cookbook, or his television appearances, why wouldn't he just bow out? Paradise could get along without him. He wasn't even allowed in the kitchen as it was."

"Connie, how long had Adrienne barred him from the kitchen? About three months. What else had been going on nearly three months?"

"The food poisonings?"

"Right."

"But why?" she asked. "Was he getting even with Adrienne?"

"There was more to it than that. My guess is he would never have done anything so drastic as destroy his own restaurant just for revenge. Think about Mitch Biekma. He spent years preparing to open Paradise. He was obsessed with it. Nothing came before Paradise. He fought with his neighbor, he used his friends—and his wife—he lived crammed in between his desk and file cabinets. When he planned Paradise he figured he would become known as a great chef. But it didn't take him long to see that he would never be in the same league with Adrienne. What he was, was an amusing host. Then he realized that he liked publicity a lot more than he liked cooking. He wasn't satisfied entertaining one small roomful of diners.

"Suddenly, Paradise became an albatross. He'd gotten what he wanted from it: fame. He was ready for the big stage. Then the danger was that people—TV people—would discover he had never been the culinary genius behind Paradise to begin with, and that the recipes in the cookbook were Adrienne's, not his. Talk show researchers had already been to Paradise. They knew he wasn't in the kitchen anymore. So if the word got around that the food at Paradise was improving without him, these researchers would wonder. Soon they'd question whether the recipes in the cookbook were actually his."

"So Mitch couldn't let Adrienne shine, right?"

"Hardly. What Mitch needed was for the kitchen to decline without him. With the poisonings he made sure it did. Adrienne realized the implications of that type of food poisoning; it wasn't serious enough to attract suspicion of anything more than bad food preparation."

"Still, that can't have done Mitch any good. After all, it was his restaurant. If the kitchen wasn't clean, he was responsible."

"But he could have said he did everything possible. He fired everyone but Adrienne, and kept her only because of their contract. He could have come up looking like a martyr, betrayed by his cook, who didn't keep the kitchen toxin-free."

"If anyone could have pulled that off, it would have been Mitch Biekma," Pereira said.

"All he needed was a little time, a little more exposure, to be considered seriously as host of 'San Francisco Mid Day.' So he decided to make Paradise fade away. And, in doing so, Mitch not only planned to protect his budding TV career, but to pay back Adrienne for banning him from his own kitchen. And by getting her he'd get her boyfriend, Yankowski, who had made a fool of him with Earth Man. How's that for a scheme?"

"Sounds like the Mitch Biekma we've all come to recognize. No one on the staff mentioned the closing, though, did they?"

"No. No one mentioned Mitch telling them, but that doesn't mean they didn't find out."

"How, how would they have found out?"

I lowered my feet to the floor. "There had to be hints. Mitch did the books himself. Adrienne never saw them. Even Laura didn't. So he was covered there. But maybe he didn't order some kind of food he normally would for next month, or something like that. Some small omission that would alert a person who was already wary because of the poisonings. Something that happened recently."

"The boxes!" we said in unison.

"It was on the news, in the papers," Pereira said, "those crates of weights, and benches, and Nautilus machine parts."

"The health club equipment that was delivered to Paradise 'by mistake' Wednesday," I said.

"I saw Biekma on the news, Jill. He was laughing, saying it was a great faux pas."

"That must have been one of his better performances."

"It was. No one would have guessed he was hiding anything. The guy was a real pro."

"So," I said, standing up, "Paradise will become a health club."

"The Bump and Grind. That explains that payment. It also explains what Mitch planned to live on. Mitch and Laura own the building. Bump and Grind was making a rent deposit."

"And their equipment just arrived a bit early."

"And you think that was enough to tip off the killer?"

"Oh yeah. Everyone in the kitchen has been in a turmoil over the food poisonings, thinking they were destroying business and reputations. Then this health club equipment arrived. What happens with a dead business? It gets replaced."

"By a health club that will close by ten and not bother Rue Driscoll."

"And Paradise's demise will leave a slot for Ashoka Prem's restaurant to fill."

"Guess Adrienne and Yankowski don't think Laura Biekma's such a nice lady after all."

I sat back on the bed and wriggled a foot into a running shoe. "You know, Connie, at first this seemed like your classic laid-back murder. Like it could have happened any time; the murderer just put the poison in the jar one night and waited. But in fact the plan could only have worked when it did, at a few minutes after twelve the day after those health club boxes were delivered."

I could hear Pereira's impatient breath against her receiver; she was waiting for me to go on.

"The killer needed a day to get some aconite. But to wait more than a day to use it would have been to chance Mitch feeling too well to bother with horseradish. His cold was almost gone."

"And it was in the few minutes after twelve that Mitch added the poison to his soup?"

"And when Earth Man came to the door. His presence was the catalyst that made the scheme work."

CHAPTER 28

Had Inspector Doyle been home, I would have gone over my conclusions with him. Now I would tell him after the killer was in custody. I called Howard and outlined my reasoning. The rest I could tell him when he got to our office.

It was eight-thirty when he met Pereira and me. Pereira was in uniform, but Howard was wearing jeans and a striped rugby shirt.

"I just hope we're in time," I said. "Yankowski's had all

day since I interrogated him. He's had time to tell the friend of his choice that he told me Mitch was the poisoner. And that friend's had the rest of the day to tell everyone else connected with Paradise. They're like a family there, that's what they all say. Any word about this case would be all over the place in no time."

"But what about Earth Man?" Howard demanded. "Why was his being there so important?"

"Because," I said, herding them out the door, "the health club boxes were delivered to Paradise on Wednesday. By the time the killer could buy monkshood tubers, it was Thursday. Mitch's cold was almost gone. His nose would hardly have been stuffed up if he hadn't been in one of his rages. He might have added only a drop or two of the horseradish, and stirred that into his soup—diluted it. He might have dawdled over his soup; he might have taken only a spoonful or two before he tasted something funny, or even felt odd. And he, of all people, would know what that meant."

"But what about Earth Man?" Howard insisted.

"When Mitch saw Earth Man he threw the kind of tantrum Rue Driscoll remembered him having in her class. He screamed, turned purple, and ended with his sinuses completely clogged. Then he upturned the horseradish jar and dumped the aconite in the soup, stomped out of the kitchen, and bolted his food. He didn't dawdle; he didn't taste. He swallowed it too fast to realize what it was."

"And the killer knew that seeing Earth Man there with his hand out, so to speak, would set Mitch off?" Howard asked.

"The killer and everyone else in the kitchen," Pereira added.

"No, not everyone. In fact, no one but the killer."

Together, we checked Paradise. It was empty; Mitch Biekma's old black Triumph was gone. Rue Driscoll's house was dark. She didn't answer the door. No one was at Bhairava.

It was on the sloping street beside Adrienne's flat that I spotted Mitch's car. Next to it was the Bhairava truck.

"So all three of them are in there," Howard said.

"Can't these people do anything alone?" Pereira demanded as she got out of her car.

When McClellan, the beat officer, pulled up, we started. He and Pereira took the street the house fronted on, he at the end of the driveway, Pereira at the corner. Flashlights in hand, Howard and I headed through the hedge, across the shaded backyard. As we started up the six rickety wooden steps to the door, the lights went off.

I pounded on the door. "Police! Open up!"

From inside I could hear breathing but no movement. And no response.

"It's all over! There's no sense in prolonging it!" I yelled. "Open this door! Now!"

Silence.

Exchanging glances, Howard and I moved to either side of the door. I pounded again. "I've got officers all around. There's no place to go."

Feet shuffled against the wooden floor inside. I bent my knees in a half-crouch position. In the dim glow of the streetlights I could see Howard putting down his flashlight.

The door flew open. Before I could step forward, Ashoka Prem hurled past. As he leapt from the top step, Howard lunged for his legs, flying after him to the ground.

"Pereira, McClellan, back here," I yelled, holding my ground. I shot a glance down at the pair rolling across the yard. In the dark I couldn't make out Howard from Prem. As if she'd been watching for that, Adrienne rushed out in front of me, slamming my back against the railing. I grabbed her around the ribs, catching her arms at her sides. Her bushy hair covered my face. It smelled of lemon.

She tried to thrust her elbows back, but I had her too tightly.

In the yard Howard or Prem groaned.

"Let go!" Adrienne yelled.

I shoved her forward across the landing. "Get back inside."

"No!" She slammed her heel down on my instep. I yelped, and squeezed in on her ribs. She let out a grunt. I loosened my arms and squeezed sharply, harder. She groaned. Then I could feel her inhale, brace her feet. "Laura!" It came out a harsh, raspy cry.

Laura raced down the steps.

I shoved Adrienne forward. She looped her foot around my ankle. I stumbled, grabbed the railing, fell to my knees. Adrienne was on my back. I slammed my elbow up into her stomach. She gasped.

A car door slammed.

I pushed myself up, grabbed the stair railing, and jumped to the ground. Adrienne grabbed for my jacket. I hit her arms. She reached for the railing, missed. I jumped to one side as her shoulder hit the ground. She screamed in pain.

The engine started. Loud, rough. The Biekmas' Triumph. Where was Pereira? No time for that. "Stop!" I yelled as I ran across the yard, skirting Howard as he yanked Prem to his feet. "I'm going after her. Get me backup. And get Pereira on Adrienne."

A burst of exhaust fumes hit me as I raced through the break in the hedge to the sidewalk. Across the street, a light came on upstairs.

The sportscar jolted forward, up the hill toward Spruce. I ran for the patrol car. It was facing the wrong way. I hung a U, and when I reached the corner she was two hundred yards ahead of me, going uphill on Spruce. I stepped hard on the accelerator. The car sprang forward, narrowing the gap. Spruce was relatively straight. I turned on the pulser light and floored the accelerator. Her sportscar was no match for the powerful patrol-car engine. It wouldn't take me long to outrun her here.

She must have realized that. At the first corner she veered left, brakes screeching.

I turned on the siren, and pressed the accelerator harder,

SUSAN DUNLAP

pushing for the last ounce of power before I had to brake for the turn. On those narrow hillside streets with their sudden cutbacks, my big engine would be useless. There the sportscar would have all the advantages.

I braked, then hit the gas as I turned down into the dark, that familiar fear leaping in my stomach. A canopy of trees blocked out any lights. Without warning, the street twisted. I pulled hard left, barely missing a truck parked halfway across the narrow lane. The siren rent the dark night air. I pulled the wheel back, braced my feet to brake. My hands were sweaty against the wheel cover. My pulse pounded in my throat. There was nowhere to look away now. I stared ahead at the road.

In the distance, I spotted the two red dots of Laura's tail-lights. They disappeared; she had turned. I stepped harder on the gas. These hillside lanes snaked into each other unexpectedly. Laura knew them from visiting Adrienne. This had never been my beat; to me it was a maze.

At the corner I turned sharply, the screech of the wheels louder than the siren. No sight of her. But nowhere else to go. I yanked the wheel left at the next corner, looping back. In the distance her brake lights flickered; she turned right. A drop of sweat fell in my eye. I shook my head sharply. Hitting the gas, I took the corner, barely missing a van parked too near. I caught a flash of lights as she made another right. She was almost out of sight. At the corner I yanked the wheel right.

The block ahead was divided, our lane ten feet above the downhill one. I could see the red lights way ahead. I hit the gas, surging forward, steering the car next to the center divider, away from the eccentrically parked cars along the curb. The car bounced over the bumps and jolted into potholes.

She slowed at the corner. I was closing the gap. She turned right onto the Arlington, another divided road, another straight one. I could catch her there. I would be able to free a hand to call the dispatcher. He could call the Kensington P.D. to assist.

I pulled hard right and hit the gas. The siren strained for its high note. Laura was a hundred and fifty yards ahead now, heading for the block of shops and restaurants. At this rate, I would catch her on the far side of them.

Laura was no fool. She'd see me closing the gap. There were two breaks in the divider at either end of the shopping block. On the far side of the street, halfway between those breaks, was a half-circle parking lot. Two winding hillside roads converged there. Once she got on either road, Laura would be gone.

She passed the first divider break. Was I wrong? Would she keep on straight, up the Arlington? If I followed her and she hung a U at the second divider break, I'd lose her in the hillside cutbacks. To have any chance at stopping her, I'd have to cut through the first divider. If she went straight, I'd lose her. I had to make my choice before she committed herself.

She was a hundred yards ahead now, halfway between the divider breaks. I slowed. I couldn't signal her by turning too soon.

Between the dividers the other lane dipped. Our lane was twelve feet above it, supported by a cement wall.

She was almost at the second cut. Her taillights held steady; she wasn't braking for a turn. I had to choose now. I pulled the wheel hard to the left, speeding across the downhill lane. Just before the parking lot, I slammed on the brakes and screeched to a stop two feet away from a light pole.

And watched as Laura's Triumph spun out in the narrow divider break. Tires screeching, the little car skidded onto the lawn of the building beside it, seemed to stop momentarily, then jerked back into the street. She'd overcompensated. The car hit the cement divider wall, bounced, jumped the curb, spun sharply, and died. The driver's door sprang open.

I grabbed the mike and called for an ambulance. Then, gun in hand, I ran for the wreckage.

She could have been dead. She could have been covered with blood. She could have had broken bones and enough soft-tissue injuries to leave her black and blue. But by the time I got to the Triumph, she was shaking her head slowly, and reaching for her seat belt.

She'd fastened her seat belt! Christ, she could be the centerpiece of the Highway Patrol's buckle-up campaign. "Fasten Your Seat Belt Every Time You Drive, Especially in a High-Speed Chase! Safety Pays!"

She unclasped the belt and moved her feet slowly around to the ground.

"Don't take the chance of moving," I said. "The engine's off, you're okay there."

The Kensington fire department was less than half a mile away. Already their sirens cut through the cackle of my radio. When they got here the medics would check her out. If she could wait, I'd call the dispatcher and we'd roll our own ambulance to a Berkeley hospital. And we'd roll our own tow truck for the Triumph.

Laura looked up. The pulser lights turned her face alternately brick red, then gray. Her fingers rattled against the door handle. She stared at them as if they were an anomaly of the automotive design, then looked away. "They didn't know."

"Who?"

"Adrienne and Ashoka. I want to be sure you realize that. I killed Mitch, just me. They didn't know till tonight. They figured it out then."

"None of them had seen enough to know how Mitch would react, right? Only you knew how to make sure he swallowed all the poison."

She flinched at the word poison. "Yes," she said softly. "They didn't know. They didn't help me. Only just now they tried to protect me, because they're friends. It's like that when you cook together—all or nothing. They didn't plan to attack you; they just reacted. I want to be sure you understand that."

I shook my head. Laura really was Mrs. Nice. From memory I recited her rights.

"You didn't have to bother," she said. "I killed him. Bastard! I gave up my dreams for him, for Paradise. I put everything into Paradise. Mitch never told me he was closing it. I didn't know till I saw the boxes. Goddamn him. I deserve to go to jail. Not for killing him. For being stupid enough to put up with him all those years. He said I was essential to him; I wasn't essential, I was just useful." A tear hovered momentarily at the corner of her eye, then plunged down her cheek. She didn't seem to notice. "I could have been a good chiropractor; I could have healed people. I could have been a decent chef. And what am I? A killer."

The sirens shrieked through the suburban night. In a minute the ambulance would be here. In another, passing cars would stop, neighbors would peer out of windows, or hurry up the street. I had time for one question. I said to Laura, "Why did you use aconite?"

"Because it's like horseradish. Horseradish was the only thing I could be sure Mitch would eat."

CHAPTER 29

I pulled a bottle of white Riesling from my refrigerator. Howard got the glasses.

It was six o'clock Sunday morning. The aftermath had taken us hours. Laura Biekma was in the hospital. We had booked Adrienne Jenks and Ashoka Prem; they were still in holding cells, refusing to say anything. And there were more reporters around the station than there had been at the Reykjavík arms talks. As was too often the case, I felt not elated by a big collar but sad. Just as everyone else had, I liked Laura Biekma. I couldn't bring myself to condone poisoning her husband, but I could understand what drove her to it.

Howard must have been thinking the same thing. "It's hard to picture Laura as a killer."

"Mitch took everything she had, then he tossed it aside. She had put her own ambition to be a chiropractor on hold, and by the time she could have afforded to go back to school, it was too late. So she decided to concentrate on Paradise, to enjoy being a good cook at a great restaurant. And then Mitch destroyed Paradise."

"Real charmer." Howard uncorked the bottle. "Still, everyone at Paradise knew what he was like. Why did she put up with him all that time?"

I shook my head. It was the question I had been asked after my divorce—why did you stay with him so long? The only time you talked was to argue. Everyone knew your marriage was doomed. Why couldn't you see it? To Howard I said, "When you're in a situation long enough, it takes on a sense of normality. It takes a shock to make you recognize what's really going on. For Laura that shock was seeing those health equipment boxes."

Howard nodded slowly. I couldn't tell whether he was recalling a similar experience or just trying to understand. It was a moment before he said, "But Jill, how could you be sure it was Laura who killed him?"

"She was the only one who could have predicted Mitch's reaction to Earth Man. Rue and Ashoka saw him go into a rage at her class when another student made a fool of him. They knew how he hated to be shown up. But they didn't know that Yankowski had used Earth Man to set him up. They might have found it odd that Earth Man was being fed at Paradise, but they had no way of knowing why it was. Even Earth Man didn't know that. Mitch ran into Earth Man in the street once and started screaming at him, but he could only guess why. Even if he'd been told, he would never have comprehended that he was the wrong kind of poor person for Mitch's free meals."

"What about Yankowski?"

"Yankowski had never seen Mitch go into a rage; he might have suspected Mitch would be angry if he saw Earth Man and was reminded of Yankowski's little victory, but he couldn't have guessed Mitch would fly into a rage, turn purple, and end up with his sinuses blocked. No one in the kitchen had seen Mitch react to Earth Man, because Laura made a point of having Earth Man come at eleven, an hour before Adrienne allowed Mitch in the kitchen."

Howard poured the wine, and stood, still holding the bottle. "I wouldn't say this to just anybody, Jill, but from everyone's description of her, it's hard to picture Laura Biekma deciding on a death sentence, much less carrying it out. She was the peacemaker, right? The one they all depended on."

"But they counted on her because she *could* make decisions. They all thought of her making choices in their favor; what they forgot or never bothered to recognize was that those decisions often went against someone else. Rue was sure Laura would agree she needed quiet. If that meant that the owners of Paradise would lose money, she didn't think about it. These people saw in Laura what they wanted to see. They forgot that she was the one who canceled orders, who made the decision to fire people. She handled complaints at the water company. She was used to dealing with bad situations and making decisions."

"Still, it's a shame."

I nodded.

"Laura will get a lot of sympathy. She'll make an appealing defendant. The DA's going to be on your back till her trial's over. I'll tell you, Jill, no matter how clear the evidence is, that's one prosecution I wouldn't touch."

"Me either. But knowing that is kind of a relief." I smiled, not just at relief for Laura, but at my own. Laura had been in the ambulance before it occurred to me that I had driven down the hill. But this time there had been no pavement to contemplate, no music to listen to; there had been only the driving. No way to avoid it.

When I stopped I was covered with sweat, as usual, but I wasn't shaking as I had been when I drove down Marin those three times. And I knew then that the next time I drove downhill I would be sweating, I would be afraid, but it wouldn't be quite so bad. I had faced the fear full on. I wouldn't be afraid of being afraid again. It might be months before I drove downhill calmly, but I would do it.

"You want anything to eat?" I asked.

He hesitated, then shook his head, ordinarily a very un-Howardian response.

I poured the wine and handed him a glass. He let his fingers rest on mine a moment longer than necessary.

"What did Doyle say?" he asked. "Did he redeem himself with you?"

"He didn't think I was too weak to make it in by quarter to eight tomorrow morning."

"Well, Jill, it's tough to be tough." Howard grinned and held his glass up to toast that thought. "That all he said?"

"Oh, no." I put the bottle down.

"Well?"

" 'Smith,' he said, 'a chase like that, you could have been killed.' "

Howard nodded. He was still wearing that striped rugby shirt. It hung loosely off his sinewy shoulders. He had a slender, well-defined chest.

"Doyle?" he prompted.

"Oh." I took a sip of wine. "Well. He said I could have been killed. And if I had been, we'd have no case because I haven't done the paperwork."

Howard laughed.

I drank some of the wine.

He leaned back against the counter.

Suddenly, I was aware of the silence, a silence unlike any of those in the four years we had been friends. The Tibetan Buddhists talk about pockets in time. I doubted this was exactly what they meant. Maybe this wasn't a pocket, but time was moving so slowly it was as if I could hear each second tick off. I put down my glass. Howard reached behind him, fumbled for the edge of the counter, and slid his glass on the counter. Our hands met, and for what seemed a very long time I felt the warmth of his flesh, the thick mounds at the base of his fingers, the hollow of his palm, the tension throbbing right below the skin. I reached out between those long thin fingers, and felt the pressure and the restraint as they clasped in around my hand.

Together we leaned forward, letting the touch of our bodies come slowly, savoring each new sensation. It was Sunday; we had the whole day.